SOREHEAD

by

Zack Kopp

ISBN 13: 978-0615777528

Published by Magic Trash Press

PRINTED IN THE UNITED STATES OF AMERICA

for

Phillip Lee Duncan

Even the greatest of whales is
helpless in the middle of a desert.

—the author's fortune cookie 1/09

HOWARD PLUMBER RECOGNIZED A GIRL WITH BLACK hair combed apart into two long braids playing her dark red violin in the ever-changing lineup of his friend Ty Cropper's band PorchCore at Café Post-Normal one night. He went up to her after the show and said, "I've noticed that sometimes you walk with a cane. What's that all about?"

The girl retained her composure while relating the history of her family, all of them troubled by oversized feet. She was going back in for more reduction surgery soon. "That must've been right after the last operation. That's why you saw me with the cane."

"Yeah, hospitals always bug me with this . . . bad mortality vibe," said the diffident Howard. "Ha ha, but I shouldn't say that, you still have to go back!" He gave her a pat on the arm and her brown eyes looked at him strangely.

"Anyway I have to go." She floated away from him with her violin case and dark braids, symbolizing something.

Howard figured his talking problem since the second skull fracture had to be at least partly psychosomatic, but he'd heard it could take up to thirteen years for all the damaged nerves to reconnect. His policy was plunging ahead blindly, hoping to find the right words, which worked about half of the time.

He'd been writing novel after novel for as long as he remembered, most recently a wild-goose-chase after God exposing the likeness of market research and religion entitled *Kiabonga!*, still unpublished, but so far none of these brave attempts had resulted in anything near self-sufficiency. Howard was working one day per week for his aged mom, filling out deposit slips for the Consciousness Arts church she was sole minister of since Howard Sr.'s death, and picking up whatever freelance writing gigs as he was able, the surest of which so far was writing emerging author profiles and book reviews for a Denver online journal called the Scrutinizer.

Most of his friends had moved away to New York City or Los Angeles by now, and all the friends he'd made at college and grad school already lived in those places, or others equally distant, but Howard had chosen to remain in Denver since his father's death in 2005 out of some instinctive feeling of loyalty to his widowed mom.

After saying goodnight to Ty and a few others and paying his check, Howard caught the bus down Broadway to the small red apartment building he lived in at the end of a long straight block smack against Cherry Creek, with the constant traffic of Speer Blvd. slicing past diagonally in both directions, silver letters reading K ZIP just above its front door, and went back down to his apartment in the basement to compose another chapter of *Strange Tales of Dim Jim*, the psycho-spiritual self-help manual for young adults he was working on currently.

Kiabonga! had been serialized online at coming journalist Johnny Coccaluccio's Metro-Hive the previous summer, and Howard was looking forward to his adventures as a citizen journalist. His next article would be about the rumors of legendary Maker and the Marvins comedienne Roberta Bogchar faking her death, her family's alleged secret government connections, AND her possible reemergence as a personal trainer in Costa Rica sometime in the late 1990s. Hadn't heard about that last part yet, had you? Howard smirked mentally, imagining that article's effect on untold thousands. But he had to start small, it took time.

He wrote two articles about used bookstores in Denver and sent each to a different magazine. A few days later, one editor sent him a check with his last name spelled incorrectly, and after a few more days, the other misspelled his first name on its cover when the magazine came out. Howard sent both offenders the same email, opening gently with two fluffy clouds of marshmallowy niceness like this: "Happy holidays, thanks for letting me write for your magazine," before stating his grievance and dropping a single vulgarity deftly posing as a question in closing, per: "please don't ever do that shit again, okay?"

Howard was overly concerned with the way he looked to other people because of a post-operative irregularity in the shape of his forehead, but he was barely conscious of the tracheotomy scar on his throat until a few influential others mentioned it months after his release from hospital, including friend and fellow Power Mountain student Maria Reynolds, who exclaimed, "It's right on your _____ chakra!" (he forgot which one) one evening in the writing group they co-hosted. Lately he saw that throat scar first when checking his appearance in the mirror, just before the valley and bump of his forehead.

The new pills seemed to be working; he'd only had one seizure since getting out of the hospital. He hadn't felt it coming on, just come back to himself on the green and white couch in his K ZIP living room, increasingly conscious of a wound at the base of his tongue. He never noticed any blood, but let a couple of dental check-up reminders pass unanswered until it healed.

He wanted to be sure the dentist didn't find the injury while probing his mouth because he didn't want his mom to know he'd had another seizure. When she worried about him, it worried him.

"Are they comfortable?" she'd asked, the last time he'd been over there to write down more names and amounts for the church bookkeeping, after noticing the shiny black shoes he'd chosen on impulse at the thrift store.

"Sure."

Howard's new shoes were harrow and stiff. He experienced a thin red line of pain along the first joints of his toes at each step, causing him to walk more steadily.

Instead of going back to the thrift store where he'd purchased them and requesting a refund, anyway a more comfortable pair in exchange, Howard had chosen to think of his uncommonly rigid footwear as but one more among many unpleasant conditions he'd summoned to hammer the needed humility into himself, in the same brave tradition as his friend from Power Mountain, Wilson Bishop, who advocated "harnessing doubt and sharpening it to a state of TAOUBT."

Stabbing pain at every step would sharpen Howard's perception, make his writing more alert. He dared to believe the key to happiness was having absolute faith in the impossible. To beat death, maybe you had to disbelieve it just as strongly as everyone else had faith in its inevitability. Maybe that was TAOUBT. "I'll find out," Howard vowed.

AFTER DROPPING IN AND OUT OF METRO State for several years, Howard got wind of Power Mountain College in Culchack Corners, Vermont, which granted academic credit for students' natural intellectual pursuits, provided they could demonstrate effort expended considering those. People came from all over the world for ten days each semester, then went home and sent in their coursework via monthly packets to their assigned advisors. Howard talked his parents, both PhDs and former college English professors who'd always wanted him to shine in that armor himself, into paying his way to this miraculous institution, and caught the Greyhound bus cross country, arriving one day early for his first Power Mountain residency just after that great big number eleven came down in New York City. Even though Power Mountain had been a "low residency" program, which meant he'd only spent eleven days in Culchack Corners per semester, the magic private city of buildings and fields and surrounding greensward atop that hill in Vermont still loomed large in Howard's mental landscape. The long white rectangle of Greystoke dorms, where most people stayed during residencies, the crenellated structure of University Hall, and the locked and supposedly haunted chapel on that building's top floor.

He checked into a hotel on Main Street in the town of gray cobbles and clapboard architecture. A mountain of trees towered over the movie marquee and voices carried from kingdoms of friendly young people outside. Howard sat down in the blonde wood chair at a table by the window in his room upstairs. He felt glad to be there. He felt worried and sad to be there. *The stars are sobbing,* he wrote. *The moon is wringing its hands. Been a long time since my emotions changed so much and back again so soon then back again so fast. Maybe never before.*

Staring down into the mountain of trees outside his hotel window, he told himself, "That's where it's at. That's church." Terrible grammar, but just as he said it, six chimes struck on the town clock outside. *The night has its dark reasons*, wrote Howard. In the morning he carried his suitcase up a tall hill from the center of town to the Power Mountain campus and got the key to his room from a uniformed old man with a frozen, wrinkled face, white hair and a hard, r-less accent who told Howard to call him Security Offica Bob.

Howard started making friends among the other misfits. It felt like being one of the X-Men, which had once been his favorite comic book, every character with a personal expertise in a different incredible power. Wilson Bishop was a multitalented creative type from Rhode Island with tight brown curls, a leather hat and a soul

4

patch. He played guitar and sang spontaneous lyrics and wanted to learn how to write. He and Howard co-founded an "irregular journal of quantum thought" called the Stomach after meeting, publishing prose, verse and art over the next few years, even interviewing counterclockwise icons like Z. Zippo, founder of punk zine Slash and Burn, publisher and editor of both *Cranks!* Anthologies, and keeping readers/up to date/on who's in charge/of what's unknown™.

A middle-aged woman named Marvel Kelly had escaped from Prxxscorpismics, a pseudo-religious organization accused of being a cult, after years of life-threatening mind games, and was doing a study on its creepadelic precursor in John Humphrey Noyes' Oneida Community, founded in 1848. "Good or bad, who can say?" Marvel repeated at significant points in her lecture, emphasizing the seductive public relations of cults, and drawing a parallel to her own experience with Prxxscorpismics.

When P. Rathbone Hermanson declared that all the murder, rape, and war in life resulted from the infection of human society by the alien god Balkbuuz, and Prxxscorpismics was the last bastion of goodness, this isolationist gimmick had explained everything to Marvel as a confused teenager in search of salvation. "Good or bad, who can say?" she repeated, and Howard realized the no-man's-land truth was.

A curly haired woman named Velvet Canna, from Zurich, Switzerland, was doing a study on the use of marijuana by politicians throughout history. Velvet was a Pixies fan and kept talking about her boyfriend Danny from Jersey City, New Jersey, who she'd met on a Pixies fan-site. In time, they married and formed a surf-punk band called Dork Pop.

A skinny Jewish kid from outside Kennebunkport, Maine named Judson Winkler had been drawn to LA by a love of the urban dance style "popping" to learn from the masters in Compton. He seemed possessed of a certain calm wisdom, and had a habit of standing in one place, then reappearing in another as soon as you stopped keeping track of where he was. He didn't know it at the time, but Judson's mutation over the next few years into Funk-Burn Willoughby was to serve as the chief living metaphor in Howard's own appreciation of the galactic dimensional shift afflicting humankind.

Emma Browne from Tennessee with long hair and a voice full of cobwebs wrote just like Flannery O'Connor. Howard was especially struck by her talent and she liked his writing too. They promised each other whichever one of them became successful first

5

would help the other aboard. Emma wore a sparkly fairy suit with plastic wings to her graduation ceremony. She was the first of Howard's friends to achieve literary superstardom with her debut, *Mountain Flower*.

One day Howard and a handful of these new mutants were smoking pot near the side of a dirt road a few blocks from campus when a group of unmet fellow Power Mountain students started walking down it. "Quick, clap your hands," hissed Wilson Bishop, showing great resourcefulness. "Pretend it's a clapping circle." After a minute or so of joyful spontaneous clapping and chanting, the gaggle of potential interlopers was handily diverted.

"Nice going, Claypoole," said bellbottomed, bespectacled Velvet, addressing Howard's latest alter-ego (that was the day they started their long-running gag about the gang of affected English pot smokers who think of themselves as hardcore urban thugs).

Students' days were spent walking back and forth to lectures and study group meetings all over the campus, interspersed with meals cooked and served in the basement of Greystoke by the students of a local culinary institute, or standing around the picnic table outside that building smoking cigarettes. Howard quit smoking halfway through his time at Power Mountain, but always indulged the bad habit at the residencies themselves.

He was standing out there very late one night after everyone else had gone inside, smoking a cigarette, when Security Officer Bob happened by in the course of making his rounds and told him Powa Mountain was the very most powaful spot on earth, baa none. "Once you come heah, you know ya gonna make it."

"Okay, Bob, uh . . . are you reading my mind, by the way? 'Cause I can tell you're very uh broad minded."

"Write the novel!" roared Bob, poking Howard in the heart with his finger. "I can see you got at least one good novel in ya. All you have to do is put it togetha! You've awready written paats of it!" Howard was halfway through writing *Kiabonga!* in an attempt to fulfill that magical old man's prophecy when he had the biggest seizure of his life so far, fracturing his skull a second time and landing himself in the hospital for a six month stretch of slow, deliberate recuperation. By the time he made it back to Power Mountain, Security Officer Bob had been dismissed for unknown reasons and the graduate assistant, Vicky, said she'd been trying to find him for months with no success. Howard wasn't sure if he'd missed out on something incredible or merely experienced a refreshing of his personal database.

Vicky gave Howard some pages from a phone book—"Bob's

6

last name is Baxter. I haven't called all of these yet"—but he never ended up making the calls.

One day during his last undergrad residency, Howard, Wilson Bishop, and the eight foot tall 300 pound Jonah Pelsbottom, an excellent writer who kept a blog called Weekday Sundown, set out driving around and around along curving mountain roads, past lakes, up and down hills in Pelsbottom's car, smoking pot and talking about "the eternal return," reminding Howard of the belly dancer's hips they'd all seen revolving in University Hall that afternoon at the presentation of Velvet's final thesis. The apparently blind circle Pelsbottom drove led directly back to the Power Mountain campus like a mystical equation, which further apparent circularity of everything excited Howard still further, though, to be fair, Jonah lived in the area, and probably planned it like that.

Howard's parents sat in the front row when he received his Bachelor of Arts degree inside University Hall from the late Richard Harlingson, who'd been his advisor that quarter, his mom crying, his dad looking proud, cane leaning against his knees with the four traction grips on the bottom.

Wilson graduated one semester later than he with a degree in something he'd invented called "Utter Science", and Howard flew back from Denver to witness this transcendence. He and a few others carried in several dead trees from the woods behind the campus and set those up in buckets spaced throughout the gym surrounded with tiny bottles and scraps of fabric from the Culchack Corners junk shops, taping details on truth, thought, belief and identity culled from Wikipedia to the tips of all their branches.

Before Wilson presented his black book, Howard and Jonah Pelsbottom stood backstage, Howard repeating all the possible pronunciations of the word "prosopopeia" in a voice like Security Officer Bob's, and Pelsbottom reading from the Wikipedia page describing that rhetorical device, while Judson Winkler stood motionless offstage in a powdery fall of white flour.

This temporary autonomous zone of intentional aesthetic and linguistic cacophony continued to a particular zenith of discomfort, joy and incredulity, at which point it leveled off, and Wilson Bishop stood up behind the podium with a gnarled branch strapped to himself under his coat, twisting up around his neck and coming out over the top of his head to hang down in front of his face with more scraps of paper affixed, He reached up, plucked these off, and quoted from them during his speech on creativity as theft and thought as feeling. Among other points raised during his speech, Wilson Bishop proposed that inter-psyche channeling was natural to human development, since it called into question trusty handicaps like selfhood and belief in death, and provided a readymade way past them all. More scraps of paper with notes on rhetoric and selfhood on them drifted down from the balcony as latecomers entered the gym.

HOWARD CAUGHT THE BUS TO MONGO'S NEW house, somewhere doubly-askew from his usual grid, for a bag of pot, which was currently illegal in Denver without a card saying it was for medical reasons. Those were purportedly easily obtained, but Howard didn't have one since the idea of his habits being tabulated rubbed him wrong. First he caught the number 12 to 15th and Stout, where a kid in a white sweatshirt and a baseball hat, with strong black eyebrows and bright tennis shoes shuffled back and forth in front of the bus bench, chanting, "What's your *name*, girl? What's your *name?* Can I grab it one tine, can I grab it one time, what's your *name?"* A woman with yellow hair cutting past in the darkness smiled at the kid dismissively tolerant.

When the bus pulled up, Howard climbed on and asked, "Can you let me off at 26th and Cherokee?" The driver, who resembled a young Desi Arnaz, nodded confidently. "I'll look for it."

After dropping his fare in the slot, Howard sat down on one of the seats facing into the aisle. The bus was crowded. His immediate neighbor, a balding gnome with long brown hair and mustache, smiling eyes and dirty fingers over the yellow plastic walkman on his knee, asked, "26th and what?"

"Cherokee. Am I on the right bus?"

"I think he only goes to Wadsworth. I think you want Sheridan. I have to think for a second." The man closed his eyes. "He only goes to Wadsworth," he said again, then assured Howard he was on the right bus, saying he thought Cherokee was the first or second stop after Sheridan. "But he only goes to Wadsworth. That's why I had to stop and think for a second."

"Okay, thanks."

The street names meant nothing to Howard, but the gnome's assistance helped him feel he was on the right track as the bus made a series of sharp twists and curves up and down small, dark streets. When it reached 26th and Cherokee, he rang the bell, climbed off and walked a few blocks up a sloping black street to Mongo's house as the bus passed out of hearing behind him.

Mongo used to be a bus driver himself. "Howdja like the route?" he asked in his kitchen a few minutes later, and rubbed a hand over his bald head.

"Oh, not bad—it had a lot of twists and turns, which was—disorienting slightly, I mean I didn't really know where I was for a while, but you know, it didn't take very long, it was fine."

Mongo had recently acquired two puppies from the same litter, one gray, one black and white. Howard sat with him and his wife Carlotta on their back porch smoking a pipe and talking as the

9

two dogs tussled and growled at each other in the yard behind them. The black and white dog lapped up the last drink of water from his bowl, then kept licking away at the empty bowl.

"What's going on, pup?" Carlotta asked it rhetorically (the damn thing didn't or wouldn't speak English), "You trying to make some more water appear, heh heh." She was brown-haired and barefoot with black tattoo rings around both arms showing under her black T-shirt sleeves.

"That's possible, you know." Howard chirped brightly. He felt like sticking up for himself, even though he'd never talked about expectation or "belief" as a magnet for occurrence with either of them in the past.

After buying a quarter from Mongo, he walked out the back door past the school bus partially covered by a blue tarp that used to be Carlotta's apartment before they got married, then back down the black slope of street and across a busy road to the bus stop.

It was cold. Howard kept tensing his arms and chest and shoulders inside his gray jacket. More cars and cars kept coming past. At one point, he heard leaves crunching and looked back over his shoulder just as a plump, pale woman stepped out from the parking lot inlet behind him. She stood still for a second, looking back at him or past him down the street. Howard turned away, assuming she was waiting for the bus too, but the next time he checked, she was gone.

He saw a few other people. Someone riding a bike erratically and scraping the pavement with a loose pedal or other dangling part. Another biker. A couple of joggers, or maybe just people running. He practiced relaxing his arms and just letting his torso hang loose in the jacket instead of tensing up his shoulders as he'd been. He reasoned he'd have more luck magnetizing warmth the less energy he wasted on being all tense and constricted.

He kept finding himself standing under a NO PARKING sign beside the street as if that was the actual bus-stop sign even though he knew it wasn't. Some unconscious reflex. Each time he realized he'd done that again, Howard walked back to the bus-stop sign a few feet away. After waiting a short while, he struck out for the next stop, thinking walking would warm him right up, but after less than half a block, realizing he didn't really know where he was and couldn't risk missing the bus, went back to the NO PARKING sign and stood there for a second before realizing and replacing himself.

He kept practicing how glad he'd be when the bus stopped for him, looking away then back up with a gleam in his eye. When it finally came rolling up, Howard felt a rush of happiness. The driver had white hair and a beard. Howard had been planning to fake him out with the expired transfer, but he climbed on, dropped his fare in the slot, then sank into a seat.

☻

Dim Jim Driscoll knew all things Patagonia, all the symbols and slogans surrounding the history. He thought about them all the time.

It was a land of hot sun and big feet. Ferdinand Magellan's perception of the natives, dressed in skins, and eating raw meat, clearly recalled the uncivilized *Patagón* in Francisco Vázquez's book. More than this, it was a lodestone of a never-never-land pursued by all great cultures since before time began. One day it got so hot Dim Jim went to the store and stood in line for what seemed like hours, waiting to buy a small pad of ice cream, staring down at the newspaper rack while cultivating a mental Patagonia of polite disinterest in pop star Neptune Buenos' new 3-headed child as he dangled it over a balcony.

Dim Jim started to sweat. Who is *my* father? he wondered. Is New Mexico my father? California? Or Timbuktu? Wyoming? Or maybe it's Texas. I'm feeling so hot. He felt plagued by uncertainty. How old am I? He knew he had to keep on jumping back. The ice cream pad started to melt. And for that matter, who is my *mother*? Dim Jim complicated matters. What about Terabithia? Or Atlantis? In the good old days, he reminded himself, they didn't even *have* ice cream. Not in Patagonia. Just Super-Lime-Fizz. So refreshing, and sure tasted good when you tilted a can down your throat in the heat.

But who am I? he screamed at himself. "Boo hoo," he uttered, "Boo *hoo*." All the birds outside echoed his sadness, children walking by were seen to sniffle and choke along with his great disenchantment. The ice cream was melting and running down Dim Jim's arm. Suddenly everything screeched to a crashing halt. Time to pay.

He looked at the clerk. "You are not from Patagonia," he diagnosed, with a confident not to say sardonic smile.

"Be that as it may, sir, that ice cream costs 39 cents. We're not in Patagonia. Patagonia's miles away. You're not from around there either, I bet."

There was a pause. Dim Jim bit his lip. "I've been there," he avowed unconvincingly.

He considered himself part of a great search.

"Hah! 39 *cents*!"

11

THE PHONE RANG. AND HOWARD GOT UP from the green and white couch and picked up the receiver. "You rang," he accused.

"Hey, this is Jesse Dilling, I'm just tryna find a Howard Plumber?"

"Speaking."

"How's everything going for ya today?"

"Fine, how are you."

"Oh, I couldn't be better. Listen, I'm calling from Corporate Advantage Industries this morning!"

"Yeah, you know, you've called before and I'm not interested." Howard took special care to emphasize the last two words, as if speaking to a child, remembering all his years of stupid phone-jobs, plus the four at Zylon Research doing market research surveys, the way respondents had to blatantly refuse to avoid being called back. The line beeped as Dilling hung up right away. Howard went back to the green and white couch. On TV, the new president was saying something else about the collapsing economy.

The last two presidential elections had been stolen by someone whose dad was a longtime CIA agent and former director, with family ties to Nazi fans and royal bloodlines, who started an unending war for no reason, suspended habeus corpus, kept making all these bossy propositions like Real ID and the Patriot Act, and seemed embarked on a mission to destroy the environment singlehandedly. What's more, inconsistent official testimony and convincing evidence about the planted explosives required for those buildings to fall straight down as they did had Howard fairly convinced 9/11 was an inside job to plant fear, patriotism and bigotry among all the citizens. So when John McCain said, "Let there be no doubt I will win this election," Howard understood a coup by whatever suicidal shadow-power perpetrated the Bush years was really in effect.

When they announced the winner, he felt numb. Wait a minute, I voted for that guy. Had there been a revolution? Nothing seemed to have changed.

Howard saw politicians as a social subset of gray haired white men in suits always standing at wooden podiums or sitting in long rows of pews and desks, making decisions completely irrelevant to his own reality tunnel.

As a result, he was skeptical of accepting miracles from the political sector, but increasingly conscious of the miraculous potential all around him.

"Trees are inside out seeds," he declared in his mind, reminding himself of the unseen potential of every seemingly tawdry scrap. Coming back to himself from the coma, he'd felt like a blind man learning to see with his hands. Simple things had mattered more. He completed *Kiabonga!* and his final undergrad semesters while adapting to this new take on reality, each lesson learned with the newborn trust of the baby's first attempt.

After graduating and seeing Wilson graduate, Howard hosted one semester of a class on Truth and Fiction in Autobiography at the Free University on Colfax, then decided to go back to Power Mountain for grad school. He kept telling his parents they ought to let him take a train instead, but they were worried he might have a seizure, so Howard Sr. drove him all the way to Culchack Corners and back for those grad school residencies a couple of times even after a hip replacement.

"Sitting in one position all day driving doesn't hurt, it's the walking I don't like." He told Howard he wanted to walk with the help of a staff instead of a cane, since that was an upward pulling motion instead of a downward prodding one, but didn't know where to get one.

The two always stopped in Hannibal, Missouri, boyhood home of Mark Twain, on their way to Power Mountain. That whole town had been recast as a shrine to its most famous son, stocked with T-shirts and flags and coffee mugs embossed with Twain's droopy mustache or paddleboats going down the Big Muddy, There was even a vacant square of gravel with a sign reading "Huck Finn's Home" behind the Mark Twain Dinette where Howard and his dad ate breakfast before leaving town. All the staff there wore dark red work shirts with the restaurant's name across the left pocket in white cursive script. "Do you sell those?"

The waitress gave Howard a puzzled stare. "I'm sure we *could*. Let me ask the manager." She came back
in a minute and let him have one for ten bucks. It seemed like the perfect souvenir.

Walking past a blue car on his way back from the
toilet at a rest stop in upstate New York, a voice butted into Howard's thoughts: "Say, I notice your license plate says Colorado! how do you get to Boulder from Denver?" The old man had a cartoon map in his hand with the big words BOULDER AND DENVER surrounded by cartoon parks and skylines and ski-lifts. It looked like it came from the back of a cereal box.

"Well, Boulder's west of Denver," said Howard. "I never go there much."

"But which highway do you take to *get* to it? And how *long* does it take to *get* there?"

13

"I don't drive actually, whichever one goes west. About half an hour?"

"Would that be I-25 or I-70?"

"I don't know, I don't drive."

As he got back into the car, a man wearing a T-shirt and shorts with a badge on a string around his neck walked up to the driver's side window. Howard's father rolled it down. "Can I help you?"

"I see your license plate's from Colorado," the cop began. Apparently he thought the Howards were part of an operation to import illegal immigrants from Mexico, ten or fifteen of whom were standing around a maroon van, also with a Colorado license, at the other end of the rest stop parking lot, attended by another plainclothes cop. It was hard to imagine them all fitting inside that van.

Howard Sr. explained he was taking his son to school in Culchack Corners, and the cop let them go. As they drove away, Howard told his dad about the strange old man with the cartoon map who'd asked him which highway led to Boulder. "You think that was some kind of diversion?"

"Sounds fishy."

Later the same day, his dad fell down walking into a gas-station somewhere in Indiana as Howard stood smoking a cigarette around the corner and watching a nice-looking woman approach the station. As it turned out, this woman was the one who'd helped Howard Sr. stand after falling. The next morning, his dad told Howard about a dream he'd had the night before about a field of white flowers and a poet's voice narrating: "all these useless white flags."

Something went wrong with his dad's calves when they got back from that trip. Acupuncture helped a little. He went back into the hospital with sudden, unexpected boils and bruises all over his body, and the quacks said something was wrong with his platelets. The last few days of his life, Howard Sr. kept moving his lips and trying again and again to say something to Howard when he visited him at the hospice, far too weak to make a sound.

Howard told him, "I'm listening to you, and I'll hear you later." Whatever that meant, as hard as he could. His dad nodded. They made a deal.

HOWARD WANDERED AROUND THE THREE OR FOUR jumbled racks of shoes on the showroom floor at Pay Mart, scanning the black and white tabs sticking out of each box and trying to find the right size. A saleslady bobbed up, short and fat with her dark brown hair in a bun and an earnest, worried face. "Can I help you find anything?"

"I'm looking for a pair of black dress shoes, size 12, with treads, and these aren't organized by size, so I'm just—"

"They're organized by *style*, sir."

"Well—just—black dress shoes, then, size 12, that's what I'm looking for. Like these here. But so far, none of these have any treads, so I'm just—"

"For a little boy?" she said, training her earnest eyes on Howard.

"No—" He pointed at his chest.

"For you? Well, then, these are the *children's* shoes here."

She followed him back around the rack and said, "You know, they pretty much cleaned me out of all my Thom McBann's, you know, the Christmas rush and everything."

She tried showing him a couple of pairs of black shoes, but neither pair had any traction.

"Yeah, I really don't care about Thom McBann or anything, I just want a pair of shoes that fit, size 12, black shoes, with treads."

"Well, I think your best bet for that kind of a shoe would be a Thom McBann Tread-Well. But like I say, they've pretty much cleaned me out of all my Thom McBann's."

She bobbed around a little more and finally went away. Howard found a pair of size 12 steel-toed black Thom McBanns, carried them to the front of the store and bought them, sharing a fake laugh with the cashier, Serena, a friendly girl with light brown skin and blonde hair, when he almost dropped his bag as she handed it to him. Howard walked out of the store, threw away the receipt and walked to a bench made of woven red metal beside the lot, where he took off the hard stiff shoes with the curling black panels and tried on the new ones. They felt almost as tight as the old ones. His feet had grown? Fucking Pay Mart.

He laced them up and walked away into the sunshine, thinking, Well, maybe they'll size to my feet as I walk around in them. Halfway across the supermarket parking lot, passing the automatic doors of a grocery store, he decided to go back to Pay Mart and face the mad music of by God trying to get himself a pair of shoes that fit . . . he knew they'd want a receipt, and he'd have to reach into the trash to get his back, but thought he could probably find it pretty easily, so he turned around and headed back the way he'd come. He couldn't remember for sure in which of two or three trashcans he'd thrown the receipt. They all had these cone-shaped metal tops. He lifted one off and reached in. He found lots of receipts but none seemed to match his purchase. It had only been five minutes, Serena was sure to remember him.

Howard went back in and told her he'd lost his receipt. "Yeah, that's something you'll have to take up with the returns desk."

The girl behind the returns desk was dark and shapely and small. Her nametag read LUCINDA. "Well, you need a receipt," she told him.

"I tried digging in the trash once already, couldn't find it. I just bought these, like, five minutes ago—from Serena, over there."

Howard pointed back over his shoulder.

"Well, do you have a driver's license, or ID?"

"I have an ID."

Lucinda told Howard something else about the receipt and prospective sales prices which didn't compute, then instructed him to find another pair of the "exact same shoes" in the size he wanted. He walked back over to the jumbled racks of shoes, searching in vain for identical shoes in his size, but surprised himself by finding a better-looking pair in size 13, even cheaper, made by Shoe Street, not Thom McBann. Howard knew he was really a size 12, but what the hell, maybe all these Pay Mart shoes were mis-sized one way or another.

He went back to the return desk and told Lucinda, "I couldn't find the exact same kind, but these are even cheaper, and I'll eat the loss." This seemed like the perfect solution to Howard, despite the six or seven extra dollars, but at least one of them didn't understand. "You need a receipt to do that," said Lucinda.

Howard went back outside two or three more times, searching all the different trashcans unsuccessfully, coming back in, haggling about this and getting nowhere until at last he blew his top: "I just want a pair of shoes that FIT, lady!"

Lucinda's eyes were shiny and dark. "I know that, but you said you wanted the difference back, and to do that, you need a *receipt.*"

"No I DIDN'T, I told you I'd *EAT THE LOSS!* That means YOU make a *PROFIT!* Didn't you say something about an ID? Here. I HAVE an ID." He flung it at her.

She sold Howard the new pair of shoes and he went back to the red metal bench at the edge of the lot and put them on. He

16

walked away across the parking lot, feeling the oversize rims digging into the backs of his heels with each step.

That evening he saw footage on YouTube of a small hot sphere floating over the sun like an angry boil. According to the sidebar, this was Planet "X", called Nibiru by the ancient Sumerians, the extremely rare orbital intersection of which body with Earth is allegedly responsible for every major shift in this planet's topography on and off record. The crust-cracking effect as it passes by most closely, the sidebar continued, will obliterate two thirds of Earth's human population and is already expected by every major world power, who have collectively decided not to reveal it to everyone else, for fear of global pandemonium.

☻

Dim Jim Driscoll thought Mother Nature was incredibly beautiful—everything folded up into itself and giving birth to itself over and over again. He thought nature was very significant. But nothing new was growing there. Just the same old bushes and flowers and trees. The sun was still on fire, and civilization was still sticking out of the ground all over the place, so you could still go grocery shopping if you wanted puffy treats. But there was so much trash all over the joint, smeared bits and tin cans piling up. Something new was yet to be. Dim Jim was a complicated man. He approved of veganism in an ethical sense but his diet consisted of meat, milk and cheese. The contrast kept him happy. Look at all this farmland being wasted! he fumed. Civilization sure sucks.

It got dark. Someone is coming! dogs barked as Dim Jim came walking down the street. Look out! We are alarmed! Look out! A man is walking down the street! There he is! Look out! Good dog, thought Dim Jim as he came along, always the gentleman. No one emerged to confront him. The animals' owners were all in their houses watching the Patriot Box and eating puffy treats. Everyone else is so stupid, he thought.

Almost before he knew it, Dim Jim was overcome by noxious heaps of green slime and fish guts. Some kind of dump in right there in the middle of the street, stinking up the whole neighborhood. All this fertilizer being wasted! he fumed. It seemed the perfect time to stop and celebrate Happy Fiesta Day, so he got out his blanket and sat down cross-legged atop a small mountain of crud for a minute. A man with two black eyes came walking over when he was deep in meditation. "It's a big responsibility," the man said, "legislating happenstance the way we do . . . Every thought . . . is as real as a rock. What monsters are we . . . that we PRAY, when we're the only ones in charge? . . . ahhhh haw haw haw HAWwaaawwwaaww!"

Dim Jim blinked back into normal consciousness as this unbidden philosopher swatted at the air around his body. "You been fightin' someone recently?" he inquired.

The man walked away briskly when questioned, still batting at the air, apparently troubled by imaginary figures. Dim Jim stood up and folded the blanket and put it back into his pack and kept walking along the road. There was a feeling of great urgency. He had to make it by SUNSET, no matter the cost.

At the same time he knew he was still in the 21st century, and figured what the hell. He just kept going. When he got to the next town, Dim Jim ate lunch and rested his sun-blistered feet in a small café then started walking down the main drag. When he came to an auto dealership with a blue sign that said Better Than O-Kay Corral and a giant light blue advertising cowboy stood beside it smiling ambiguously, extending one friendly white glove in a wave or a shake, Dim Jim threw his butt down in the street and started up the drive.

As he neared the showroom, a man with a leathery prune for a face jogged out waving his arms. "What the hell," this man demanded, "here you are dropping your cigarette butts in the street, you dirty dog, don't you care about nature?" The skin of his face was purple and taut.

Dim Jim smiled at the strange-looking man. He wasn't about to let this one get away. "Listen, is this an auto dealership?"

"The very best!"

Dim Jim wanted to learn how to drive. The man with the leathery prune face led him into a cool brown office and assured him the Better Than O-Kay Corral was prepared to offer him fifteen free lessons if he promised to buy his first car there as soon as they gave him his license. "We want you to know we're on your side!" Dim Jim signed up right away, and soon he was racing around the training area in louder and louder cars supplied by the Better Than O-Kay Corral, even screeching his tires like the reckless teenagers in bad bygone movies all wearing their hair in DAs with their upper lips curled—till they finally gave him a license.

"You signed the form," the dealer reminded him. "Now you'll have to buy one of our cars."

Dim Jim's own pompadour had come undone in the press of speed, and a waxy blob dangled across his forehead. "Hey, I didn't know that was part of the deal!" he protested (he was having a very good time).

"Sir, you signed the form," the man with the pruney face which also resembled a swollen purple boxing glove repeated. The Better Than O-Kay car dealership took back the license they'd given Dim Jim and turned him back into the cold street with nothing to drive.

The giant cowboy seemed to smile especially at him when he looked up. I still have faith in you, it seemed to intimate. You can still make it, Dim Jim! Three blocks away he hotwired a blue Volvo with a tangle of gardening tools and sprinkler-heads in the back and started heading east, where the sun came from. That was just as good as the sunset anyway. I'll show you manners and culture, he thought, you barbarians! He felt glad to be getting away.

IN ALL HIS YEARS OF WALKING AROUND on this earth, Howard Plumber had only recently noticed peace signs blooming in the cracks that come after a snowfall and melt. The first one looked man-made, but as he kept going, he started seeing more and more, less and less perfectly stylized, all over the sunny sidewalks between his house and the bank, undeniably organic. Now he couldn't tell if the first one was man-made or not. Of course, anyone else might see pitchforks, or the skeletons of fish.

I know there's war all over the world, he reminded himself. But maybe things are changing now in some big way. There'd been an item in the news about a hitherto uncontacted tribe in the jungles between Brazil and Peru, three members of which had been photographed, two painted red, all aiming arrows at the giant metal locust aiming its TV eye at them.

A few days after seeing that picture, Howard told the sweet faced, toothy girl named Betty Bolt he was seeing at the time how he took it as a sign of the flashy, modern outside catching up with the hidden, primitive core. Betty told him she'd read or seen or heard somewhere that the photo had been faked, but she didn't remember where. Betty had a way of bringing him down like that. They weren't dating now, but when they'd met downtown for coffee the other day, and Howard had told her about the new book he was working on, her annoyingly imprecise response had been, "The only criticism I have of your writing, and it's not a criticism really—but you're always writing about manifestation, and it seems like you should try a new approach."

She was talking about his last book, *Kiabonga!*, and Howard had to admit that in at least one way, everything he'd written since including what you're reading now was fully and clearly an outgrowth of that project, but "I don't think that's a valid criticism," he fumbled, "because that's the central issue of my consciousness right now, you know, and I have to keep on writing about it until I figure it out."

"What about those Dim Jim stories?"

"Well all that stuff is kind of a joke, you know, it's like a metaphor of some fool living by his wits in search of the best—"

"Some Shang-ri-La," concluded Betty.

"—state of mind that anyone can have, see, but he always falls short of. *Strange Tales of Dim Jim* is a series of allegories for the Y.A. market, you know, but I'm never sure where to draw that line, like what makes something too mature for kids, you know. I wanna use him as the scapegoat for a series of object lessons about—"

20

"I like your shoes."

His new pair of fake Chump Dexter high-top basketball sneakers, just like real ones, but no trademark star. "Oh, yeah, thanks. They're fake, but they have this extra stitching up the side, see, so I think they're more durable, probably." Looking down, Howard noticed what appeared to be some threads coming loose at the heel, but just as he said, "I guess they're falling apart," the wisp of whatever it was blew away to reveal his shoes were perfectly sound.

At the bus stop on the way home, a kid in a black coat with white devotional marks above the bridge of his nose stood outside the shelter quietly chanting "Hare Krishna, Hare Krishna, Hare Krishna, Hare Hare," clouds of steam coming out of his mouth.

A woman was sitting on the bench behind the glass. "You know what time the 12 comes?" Howard asked her. She shook her head.

"It probably says on the schedule right there," the devotee offered, then stepped inside the glass shelter with the woman and checked the schedule behind her to find out when it came.

"So you're saying a mantra," said Howard. "I do that all the time myself silently in my head," he volunteered. He'd developed three or four so far, and had seven or eight specific places in his neighborhood for blessing people from his life who'd parked there once or used to live there.

"Oh, you repeat Sri Krishna's name too?"

"No, just my own, you know, affirmations."

"It's good, isn't it?" the kid asked with smiling desperation as his bus pulled up.

"I think it's fine."

As that kid's bus rolled away, Howard thought about the bumpy part of saying one thing over and over and over again in your mind; sometimes he worried it limited his breadth of thought. Then again, maybe it sharpened his will.

HE'D BEEN BRUSHING HIS TEETH EVERY DAY, even using mouthwash, which he usually didn't, but for all that exertion, the gentle-voiced Asian dental assistant found lots of "deep pockets" in the gums at the back of his mouth when Howard went in for his checkup, reading those off into a computer as she picked at his teeth with a fine spike—"Computer, listen. Tooth number seventeen . . . Bleeding. Tooth number twenty-three . . . Bleeding. Tooth number sixteen . . . Bleeding. Tooth number seventeen . . ." He lay there clenching and relaxing his fists until she'd finished.

"Your father liked to watch *Law And Order,* you know that one?" asked his mom over lunch at a Mexican restaurant near the dentist's office after his appointment. "And he used to like me to watch it with him." She said the images of crime suspects, dead bodies, and handcuffs sometimes came back to her the next day, and she didn't like it. "So I think watching TV all the time like that—it's okay to do, as an experiment—but why would you want to subject yourself to it? You know?" She wore a look of gentle sturdiness. She'd seen something he'd written about an experiment to transform reality through watching TV and was appealing to his sanity.

"It's the ads that get to me," he answered. "All those jingles that ring in your head." Howard don't love television, but he watched it all the time, or left it playing in the background like a sedative while typing or reading a book. Can you picture him sitting around in his stupid apartment watching TV shows he hates all day long till the jingles and theme songs all ring in his head like canned laughter? Was he numbing himself?

"Your father used to mute the ads."

Howard had seen him do that. "Yeah, I usually do too." They finished their meal and she drove him home and dropped him off. Howard went inside and started thinking about making money, earning his keep, paying his way. For all he knew, it was all about tracking down the ideal market for his particular brand of reportage. He'd never been clever with money. He don't even like going to the bank. Standing there in that line. The other customers. All the different tellers and their personalities.

One day Howard made another deposit and withdrew twenty bucks from his last twenty-three before it cleared. The sexy lady teller with long black hair and porcelain skin said, "I see you work at the Denver Post, hmmm."

"What, no, I don't work for the Denver Post."

"You don't?" she wondered, looking up from the computer screen with her bladelike nose and big smooth forehead.

"I'm a freelance writer, but I've never been published in the Denver Post."

"That's probably why, then," she said. He wasn't sure what she meant by that. Next she tried running his slip through the machine on the counter but something went wrong.

"They read it as one dollar," she apologized.

"They?" Howard said peevishly. Was he looking for a fight?

"I'm sorry?"

"Never mind." Oh, the tensions.

A few days later he withdrew two hundred from the latest deposit and the smiling over-friendly male clerk whose giddiness he'd failed to connect with in the past was his teller. "Howdya like that weather today?" Chip leered enthusiastically as Howard stepped up to the counter.

"It's a nice day," said Howard, then remembering global warming, "so that's either cause for alarm, or it's just a nice day."

"I think it's nice," Chip enthused, with his spiky brown hair. "I'm not gonna worry about it."

"Right, it's never a good idea wasting your energy."

"Especially when there's nothing you can do about it, ha ha ha!" Some desperate glee in his round happy eyes.

"Yeah, that's true," said Howard, or coughed up another pat answer, letting Chip win the social contest, thinking of him as mere a social hoop, to be jumped through as quickly and efficiently as possible, instead of one of the innumerate reflections of himself he ought to see everyone else as.

An old man with brown skin and tight gray curls wearing a brown business suit walked past him on the bridge over Speer Boulevard when Howard was walking home. "Well, how are you?" the man said genially.

Howard had seen this man walking or standing in his neighborhood of apartment buildings big and small a few times before, always very well-dressed, with a dignified air, and taken to thinking of him as some kind of neighborhood angel, in line with something Betty Bolt had told him once about how everyone was really gods or goddesses in some alternate reality, which he'd decided might apply to this one too, hey why not. So whenever they crossed paths he'd taken to thinking of it as a sign, but hadn't yet determined what it stood for. He lifted his hand in response. "Nice to see you."

Howard was checking his mailbox when his walrus mustached gray haired neighbor across the hall, Gabe Kotter, came dribbling his basketball up the walk into the lobby. Kotter hailed from

Brooklyn and seemed paralyzed in an attempt at reliving his lost middle age as a basketball playing high school teacher revered by MassAmerican pop culture. "I just ordered a book about all the grants you can get," Kotter informed, stepping forward slightly.

"Yeah, that's something I'd like to know about, too," said Howard, stepping back a little. Kotter had a way of always standing a little too close when you were talking to him, with an eerie blank look on his face and tufts of gray hair sticking out of his oversized head.

"I'm gonna send out a bunch of applications," the apparition continued, "anything that seems doable, since the more applications you send, the more likely it is. Of course, nothing's guaranteed, you're always taking a chance."

"Yeah, I'm a freelance writer, I know all about that."

"Oh yeah, what kind of stuff do you write?" Kotter took another half step forward and Howard backed away a little more.

"I'm working on something right now about Roberta Bogchar's possible reemergence in the 90s as a fitness trainer in Costa Rica. Roberta Bogchar of the Maker and the Marvins."

"Hmm, sounds interesting. Those were sure some crazy times. I ever tell you about my uncle, Maximilian T. Kotter?"

The wily Kotter had a way of turning every comment others made into an ingratiating yarn on one of his seemingly numberless uncles, but Howard wasn't much of a joiner. "I'll give you a link when it's up. See you later, Gabe." He reentered his apartment and closed the door behind him.

Getting all those interviews for the Stomach had been so easy he was beginning to think maybe that was how he could finally dig himself out of dependence on that bookkeeping job for his mom. Simply by choosing the perfect subjects and questions and being brash or brave enough to jump right in and ask the right people for interviews. Could that be all there was to it?

All he knew for sure, that Roberta Bogchar article was hot shit. When the Maker and the Marvins comedy bunch she'd fronted were at the height of their popularity in the mid sixties, the government's secret mind control project was called MK ULTRA, and besides the rumors she'd faked her death, it had been suggested Roberta Bogchar was an unknowing agent of this program, all her gags loaded with subconscious triggers for a trusting populace. So far, no one had joined these rumors in a single article, as Howard Plumber was planning to, and he expected it to win big.

He sent an email about Bogchar's alleged MK ULTRA

connections to Funk-Burn Willoughby in Los Angeles, who replied,

"That's funny, I just spent about 3 days really diving into MK ULTRA for the first time in my life. The rabbit hole went down so deep and I got really scared and then my heart opened wide and I sent love to them and everyone involved. I had a few really intense experiences about darkness and I think it's no coincidence that all of this stuff is coming out onto the table right now. I think in order to create a reality of light, we have to be able to see the darkness, really look at it. It's beautiful, what we're creating!"

●

Dim Jim Driscoll lived beside a busy curving road that connected the business hub of Doggy Park to the suburbs in the south. It was always buzzing with traffic, from early in the morning until late at night. The noise of sirens came into the room all the time through his open window. He just wanted to transform the energy coming out of the set and use it to rewrite reality. Some day maybe he would get to Patagonia this way if he tried hard enough. It was getting to be an obsession with him.

"Maybe I am in the grip of the same inexorable force," Dim Jim cried, "the same compulsion to drowsy bliss that has drowned and defeated all great thinkers of yore. How is it, then, that I of all people, can—"

Dim Jim was interrupted by a knock at the door. He stood up and walked over and opened it. "Hi, there!" said a long-nosed Indian lad standing on his doorstep with a flower. "I am the answer to your question."

"Go away!" Dim Jim slammed the door.

Hours later the knock came again. Dim Jim sighed deeply, stood up and went over. This time it was the little old postman.

"You are not from Patagonia," Dim Jim legislated.

"Nosiree*BOB*," screamed the laughing messenger, "I'm from San Fransisky, son, sure as this here package is special deliv'ry! Look see!"

The postmark was blurry, Dim Jim couldn't see it all. He thought he could make out UCSON, tried to place it on a map, but there was nowhere he could—wait! Of course! Tucs'Q'uxmbaabal! That was one of the cities in Patagonia, a name from the ancient language known only to the most devout of researchers! He was sure of it! He squeezed the package very hard to feel its contents' shape. He really wondered what was in there. "But I can't just—I just can't—"

"What's the matter, son? You're Bob Maxson, ain'tcha?"

"Well. . . in terms of your best target audience for this Pandora's Box type of thing, I suppose I could help you, but—well, no—no, I'm really not."

His shoulders slumped. "I guess what happened is *someone*—well, someone must have misspelled the poor man's name, then for some reason, *you* thought the package was for me, because you knew my love for Patagonia, or—is that what happened? Robert Maxson lives across the hall."

"Okey-dokey, chipper!" The little old man seized the mangled parcel and scuttled across the hall to Maxson's apartment and knocked. A tall, slim youth with a funny crewcut and eyes the color of pennies came to the door and accepted the package. The old man tipped his hat and jogged away up the staircase.

"Sorry, Bob," said Dim Jim, making what he hoped was a streetwise gesture with his pointing finger. "I thought that was for me at first."

"That's cool," said Maxson.

HOWARD NEVER LIKED GOING TO THE BARBER, having all the details of his life inventoried and reviewed by a stranger in exchange for what might be an awful new look, but unless he bought clippers of his own, it seemed a necessary evil. One day he decided to try this new place he'd spotted in a tall blue house on the corner a few blocks from K ZIP.

"So you in school?"

"I have a part-time job right now."

"Oh yeah, where do you work?"

"One day a week I do accounting." Howard never brought up writing at the barber's, as it tended to bring on more questions. He was still trying to sell that Roberta Bogchar article. He heard back from the site Z. Zippo recommended as a good fit, but they didn't pay.

"Okay!" The barber spun the chair, handed back his glasses, then after he'd put them back on, held up a looking glass and asked for thirty dollars, please.

"What the hell?" Howard protested. regarding the whole lumpy bone of his skull sticking out in the mirror. Sometimes all it took was style and confidence to cover up his funny looking forehead, but a bad haircut made it much harder. "At SuperHaircuts it's only eleven!" he protested. "All I have is this twenty, I wasn't expecting it to cost that much, sorry, fuck."

"This'll do."

The barber snatched the twenty from his hand. Howard put his straw porkpie back on and walked out of that barbershop into the cold sunlight. Fucking barbers, he swore silently. Sometimes they even cut Howard's hair as if to highlight the depression in his forehead, as in this case, and he was never sure if this meant they hadn't noticed his slight craniofacial disfigurement at all or simply because of the hang-loose attitude seemingly shared by the whole human race besides himself, so he never brought it up. Usually he just told them to leave a lot of bangs.

He finally found a pot connection in his part of Denver. A girl named Miranda with straight hair parted in the middle who had worked at the head shop where Howard bought his cigarettes before quitting. The first time he'd been to her place a few blocks from K ZIP across the park, he'd been sitting in a ray of sunlight in her living room and she'd asked him, "What's that on your throat?"

"Ah, my throat. Well, my throat." Howard told her all about it, then demurred, "Ha ha, sorry to give you that whole ugly history."

"That's actually the name of my boyfriend Scott's band."

"Ugly History?"

"No, the Skull Fractures." Scott's band had only a cult following stateside but commanded godlike fame in Central and South America, home to a thriving cookie monster rock craze, and worsening drug cartel violence.

Howard and Miranda started talking about the recent swine flu outbreak, how there might be some unfriendly element in the vaccine to cut down the population in advance of 2012, when Planet X swung through and leveled civilization. "Or maybe they'll use the shots to plant tracking chips under the skin for some other weird reason," suggested Miranda.

"I sure wouldn't want that vaccination," he told her, "No way—fuck . . . but then I'd be the guy who refused the vaccine, 'a likely carrier,' they'd probably quarantine me or something. Yikes."

Howard had deliberately left himself open to the equivalent likelihood of everything, so it scared him when apparent reality seemed to go against what he was trying to enact—talk of enforced vaccination with poison made him feel caught in a Mobius strip of fearing the swine flu or ignoring the swine flu when he never even wanted to think about junk like that in the first place.

"You know about aspartame?" Miranda asked him. "My mom is an alcoholic who always mixes her drinks with Diet Soda, and she's been getting stomachaches lately."

"Hmh. Yeah. You know about fluoride? That fluoride's effect on the mind is supposedly to depress the ability to resist commands?"

"And the U.S. is one of a few if not the only country with mandatory fluoride in the tap-water and most of the toothpaste. You know about 'chem-trails'? Mysterious streaks of vapor left in the sky by low-flying planes?"

"I've heard about those."

"Yeah, that freaks me out," said Miranda, the government sneaking things into my bloodstream like that. But there's so much evidence for and against everything."

"Sometimes I think as long as you keep on blowing their cover all the time that way, they can never completely sneak up on you, all those dirty outcomes."

Howard thought about Miranda's comment walking home. Maybe the internet already "had" everyone, not just him. Most celebrities had their own Facebook or MySpace pages these days. Even some serial killers. He'd recently found an YouTube page featuring brand new still photos and near daily tape recorded telephone interviews from prison with gorilla kidnapping Hole in the Hill cult leader Hal Blare, whose minions used to break into zoos after hours, tranquilize gorillas with blowguns, kidnap them and dress them up in clown suits, then lay them down on street corners (needless to say, some people got killed when they came to and tried to break out of their costumes). When the cops nabbed Blare, he'd defiantly shunted the blame, saying, "These are your children, not mine. You're the ones mocking the wildlife, not me," since he saw his whole life as a reflection of the times.

HOWARD'S FRIEND MARIA'S BOYFRIEND, JOHNNY COCCALUCCIO, HAD tapped him for inclusion in a new site he was starting any day, saying, "Hold that Bogchar article." Johnny C was noteworthy in the freelance journalism world for his ongoing interviews with veterans of the war in Iraq diagnosed with PTSD and denied assistance by the institutions designed to care for them. Johnny also played guitar in a punk band called the Bio-Hot-Bunch (of "Sweet Ball of Crud" fame) with whom Howard shared a number of Facebook friends.

Howard interviewed a girl named Peg Smiley he met at Power Mountain for the Scrutinizer. She'd been in the writing workshop he co-hosted with Maria Reynolds, and a story of hers had been published recently in an anthology of pieces by female veterans. At one point, he brought up the swine flu and Peg told him after the Navy had inoculated her brother against anthrax in the wake of 9/11, a projection the size, color and shape of a bowling ball—"not a tennis ball, a *bowling* ball"—had grown out on his arm right next to the hole. "They hadn't finished testing it, I guess," she said.

Peg had just gotten back from Taos, New Mexico, where she'd been on part of a tour to help promote the female vets anthology. While there, she'd become aware of a mysterious humming sensation or sound just above or below the direct noise of life wherever she went, in the street, at the bookstore, back in the motel room, and asked her husband, "Don't you hear that humming?" He couldn't hear it, but after she typed the words, "Taos + hum" into the search engine, that phrase had its own Wikipedia entry. For centuries, Taos residents had been aware of it. There was talk of mighty ancient spirits or underground alien bases. Others thought the government was doing it.

Howard told Miranda that story the next time he went to see her. "I lived in Albuquerque as a little kid, but I never heard of the Taos hum before. Or maybe I did hear about it and just forgot."

"Military installations," she guessed.

"No, 'cause it's in all the Indian legends going back for centuries. I mean, supposedly. So it's older than—our military, whatever it is. Who really knows. I don't know. Someone knows. Maybe we can find out on the internet."

"Yeah, the culture's been changing so fast lately, and the internet helps speed up the change. Maybe you're already too far inside it to notice. The internet's already got you." And then she smiled. But who was kidding who? Since the Possibility brothers and Holger Donovan moved away, the internet had assumed their collective position as Howard's social outlet in the form of networking sites like Facebook and MySpace, especially after making so many connections with people outside Denver at Power Mountain. "I see it more as a symptom of change than a cause," he defended.

Because he'd met so many people from all over the world at Power Mountain, all of whom were his friends on Facebook, Howard's newsfeed provided a panoramic view of mass consciousness, to the degree such a thing could be visible in people's status updates and the things they posted. Despite to the untrained eye seemingly being grounded in Denver, the internet kept Howard everywhere.

One of his classmates in grad school, Dario Zazzarino, a Jesuit scholar and self-styled "Goth" Occultist had married a woman he hated and had nothing in common with, then divorced her after a year and moved to Asheville, NC, where he was teaching a class in medieval mythology or something along those lines, and recently he'd been making oblique references to "the Beloved" in every new update, which had begun as an affectation a la Rumi, but recently seemed to have taken on specific relevance: "28 days till I see the Beloved!" so maybe he had a new girlfriend now. Even though Howard never got to know Zazzarino very well in person, he could tell you what had been happening in Dario's mind in the last year just from his Facebook output.

Another classmate, Elvis Sunshine, was a woman who identified as a male and had revealed herself to be an unflagging womanizer in her pink button-down shirt and Johnny Quest haircut over the course of three or four residencies, once even making a pass at Maria Reynolds (who declined), smacking her lips and pointing, "You know my room number."

Elvis claimed to be an undercover agent for the DEA and seemed constantly on the go to places like Hawaii, Brazil and Vatican City, and periodically posted an ultra-sound pic of a mysterious object lodged in someone's throat, presumably her own, to which she made reference infrequently.

"Selective omniscience," Howard posted one day, while riding a wave of this everywhere-at-once-ness.

"Exactly!" posted Wilson Bishop in response. They hadn't spoken in months, but Facebook enabled preservation of their rapport.

About the recent swine flu outbreak, incarcerated cult leader Hal Blare said this on the YouTube page of California filmmaker Jordan Sections: "That's only the tip of what's coming, it's just the beginning." (which assertion Howard took with a grain no a ton of salt, since for all he knew, his life depended on it). Whereas, until now, Hal Blare had only existed figuratively in Howard's imagination as a storied madman, now Howard had access to his thoughts on modern times, had, in fact, increased access to everyone else, through the internet.

He logged in to his Facebook account and caught wind of an outfit offering Distant Energy Healing Sessions, offering that service free of charge to anyone who added his or her intention, which he did right away, sealing the deal by "liking" the page in question.

His living room was full of light.

A helicopter flew over the building, making all the windows rattle in their sockets.

ABOUT TEN PEOPLE CAME AND WENT OVER the course of the night, having one big conversation composed of a lot of little ones plus patches of silence and different kinds of laughter. At one point, Howard was talking political worry and freelance writing with his bespectacled former roommate, Gordon Callahan, who asked him, "Yeah, where's this investigative journalism kick coming from?"

"Well, that's not it exactly . . ." Howard explained his Roberta Bogchar article and Gordon said he thought it sounded great—"It has everything."

Johnny Coccaluccio showed up in a black leather jacket and a red bow tie, Maria Reynolds on his arm with dark hair and a long pretty face, then Lonnie Culot and his wife Maxine. Lonnie was one of Howard's first friends in Denver, now stepfather to her three kids, ranging in age from seven to sixteen years of age. It seemed like Maxine was in a bad mood, she wasn't saying anything.

Nelson Habercorn was married and had six or seven children by now, none of whom Howard had met. His wife Angie was busy tending the brood that night. Howard met Nelson at one of the Bat Sandwich events way back in the days when those wild jams with no set object or performer that went on all night happened once or twice a year in Denver. They'd played guitars together in a band called the Stowaways once. He knew Holger Donovan too. Nelson brought Howard a book of American Indian stories as a late birthday present, inscribed: "This will likely be the best year so far and then add some extra."

"Thanks, man, that's the best inscription ever."

Tewodros Magness came, a wide-faced black man from Washington DC, who was a popular hip hop MC locally under the name TWA 800. Tewodros used to interview respondents in a fake English accent in the calls he made from Zylon Research, which the supervisors let him get away with since it usually meant a complete.

The most convincing vocal alias Howard had been able to muster had been an old man named "Willy," and he'd never been able to complete a survey so disguised, so It had never achieved the same degree of unofficial tolerance.

"Why is your building called the K ZIP?" he asked.

"I don't know. Maybe it used to be a radio station. Either that or it was founded by a couple, like Kirk and Zinnia or something."

"Zinnia?"

"Ha ha, sure," agreed Howard. He kept drinking all evening, installing and adding to a state of disorderly happiness. Maria had briefly been infatuated with the dashing, bearded Mothman researcher slash Power Mountain advisor Charlton Spatsky, whose

33

eyes looked like coconut almond treats to her, she said, then grown nonplussed for some reason, and imitated him blaming every broken twig on Mothman. Tewodros Magness said he believed there were aliens among us here on Earth, right how, but they were time travelers.

"Or extra-dimensionals," added Space Dave.

The ceiling of Howard's apartment was covered by infinite swirling loops in the white paint, a purely subliminal effect that must have taken hours of concentration whenever someone did it sometime in the 1940s. Howard had never even noticed it himself until several years after moving into the cellar at K ZIP. "You see these infinity symbols all over my ceiling?" "Maybe it means I'm *under infinity*, whatever I do in here is small compared to infinity."

"Unless maybe it means what you're doing will last forever," suggested Maria Reynolds graciously, and he thanked her for it.

The next day Howard placed a call to a woman named Alina Vera who'd taken the class on truth and Fiction he'd taught for the Free University after graduating from Power Mountain for the first time, and they arranged to meet that evening at a coffee joint called Stella's, which operated out of an old white house in a leafy central Denver neighborhood. Alina met him on the porch and they went inside and ordered drinks and took two stools at a table in the first room past the counter.

Alina had sleek black hair, a curvy body, and seemed almost too sincere to relax. Either that or Howard took her too seriously. Once he'd leaned forward to kiss her, "May I?" and she'd said she didn't think they knew each other well enough.

There was a book about Orson Welles in the shelves behind his head, and Alina told Howard a story about a woman she knew who believed Welles killed Elizabeth Short, the Black Dahlia, since, among other things, a set-piece he designed which closely resembled the posed halves of the Dahlia's corpse when discovered was cut from the film he was making after the story broke. Everyone else inside Stella's had laptops and earphones. It took him a while to get comfortable talking there, since he felt like he was interrupting something, but soon Howard was waving his hands telling Alina all about the guy on YouTube who thought the other planets in this solar system were secretly covered with people and primates and horses, but NASA was keeping it dark. "I'm always drawn to people like that, that kind of story."

"But you have to be careful," warned Alina. "My mother was a paranoid schizophrenic. Everything confirmed her paranoia. It taught me to be very careful about omens. Anything can show you something if you choose to see it there." "Everything becomes an oracle." "Right."

"I dated someone like that once."

"And what did it teach you?"

"I learned how powerful and fragile people are. She had a breakdown and my mom and I took her to the hospital. My mom had a friend at one of the hospitals, and she couldn't remember its name, just where it was. Driving up, we all saw the name, St. Luke's, and Luke was the name of the guy she thought was arranging everything in her life against her."

"Who?"

Her former boss in Portland, Luke. Supposedly also a member of the Vietnamese mafia. So she knew she was in enemy territory. Then the doctor my mom knew wasn't even there, so it seemed even more like a setup."

☻

A few hours before Howard's first date with Marlene, the girl in question, a brown bird had flown into Howard's bedroom at K ZIP. That was a sign of impending disaster or death in some cultures, he found out later. He opened the window without a screen occluding it, then stood back from his bed to give the bird room to get its bearings and fly out. It swooped around in giant circles several times before soaring out into the parking lot through the black bars.

After Marlene moved in, the two of them hauled his threadbare brown couch up the stairs and dumped it in the alley behind K ZIP, then carried home another, covered with green and white stripes, and so heavy they had to stop and rest a couple of times on the way, from an alley three blocks north. A block or so before they reached the alley behind K ZIP, a police car drove past and a voice inside chuckled over the mounted loud speaker. "Stop right where you are, heh heh, just kidding."

They moved the couch against the wall behind the coffee table where the old one had been. "It must be strange, seeing the world as a writer. All the metaphors everywhere." Marlene's light brown hair was cut in a straight line low across her forehead, which made her look like she came from the 1920s.

"Sure. Even this couch is a metaphor."

"Of our love," she agreed.

"And I knew this guy once who when he didn't have any place of his own, he'd say, 'Yeah I'm on the couch again now.'"

"Staying on somebody's couch."

"Yeah, like a stowaway."

"I'm on the couch again myself."

"No you're not. I invited you here. What?"

"Sure I am."

"No you aren't."

That night they made love on Howard's futon in the same room where that bird had flown blind circles before their first date, and Marlene said she wanted to make him see stars. When he said he was already seeing them shine, she said, "Then I want to make you see stars changing colors."

One evening on his way to the liquor-store for a pack of smokes, Howard walked right into a low-hanging branch. It was dark and his thoughts were elsewhere, so full of this wild, cool girl, his ladybug, as he'd begun thinking of her. He rubbed his bumped head and kept on walking down the dark sidewalk.

A tall, thin man in a baseball cap emerged from the sports bar he'd just walked past and rushed up behind him. "Hey buddy, you alright?"

"I'm alright."

This man followed Howard inside the liquor store and made a show of squinting at his forehead under the lights hanging over the counter. "I don't see any blood," he announced. The clerk looked at them. "Yeah, he just walked right into a tree-branch out there," explained the meddler.

"You okay, buddy?" asked the clerk.

Howard shrugged. *Buddy*, he thought.

One morning after telling him the night before she knew he was working for "the puppet master" in some way, Marlene sat facing the wall in a corner of the bedroom drawing a picture captioned, "No More Game Or Monkey!"

"As soon as my tax money comes," she pronounced, without turning her face from the corner, "I'm gonna get out of here. It's over."

"But why are you drawing that picture? I'm not playing any game with you."

"I never said you were. Don't be so presumptuous."

". . . but I'm the only one here . . ."

"I know."

"So can't you explain why you're drawing that?"

"Please leave me alone."

Howard walked back into the living room, sat down on the green and white couch and switched on the TV. She came out of the bedroom a few minutes later and asked him for the phone number of her former employer in Portland, which, as one of the "minions", she presumed he already knew by heart.

"What was the name of the store again?"

She told him. He looked up their number on the internet, then logged off and gave it to her. She left a message for her old boss, who she said was a member of "the Vietnamese mafia," letting him know she was ready for him to market her art. He could put it on useful objects like coffee mugs, so she wouldn't feel like she was selling out to abstraction. So the "Game" was about art too somehow. After hanging up, she looked at him accusingly. "So I guess you got what you wanted now."

"Listen, I'm not playing any game with you, " he told Marlene. "But I'm sorry if it feels that way. I mean I'm sorry if you can't believe I'm—"

"I'm not in the mood right now." She twisted her lips at him in a way she had.

"Wait, what mood, no, I'm not trying to trick you—"

"I'm not in the mood for the game right now, OK?"

"Well, what are you talking about, the game? I'm just trying to—"

"Everything you do is staged. This tennis ball you gave me, there are puppy dog tracks all over it. You didn't think I'd *notice*?" She flung away the offending toy to ricochet around their cluttered living room, a tennis ball the author had found in the neighborhood somewhere with cutesy puppy-tracks embossed. "You're trying to train me to FETCH?!""

"No, wait, I never meant anything like—"

"And these SHORTS!"

She ran back into the bedroom, grabbed a pair of his shorts, then ran back out, pointing at the manufacturer's name: *LEI*, right there on a pair of his own shorts—a pair of his own shorts testifyng against him. "Very clever," she added, twisting her lips again.

"No, listen, I never knew they were called—"

"SHUT UP, I SAID!"

Marlene was making a lot of noise and the boys in black showed up at Howard's apartment. The graying lead man scanned the bookshelves and the coffee table for weapons or drug paraphernalia as he pushed his way in,
smiling like a walrus. "What's the problem here?"

Howard tried to explain it. ". . . it's really a kind of psychological, emotional problem, and I know you guys really don't handle that . . ."

"Heh heh, we handle that sort of thing all the time."

The cops took their IDs and ran a check. Marlene said, "I'm gonna have a donut. You guys want one?"

"Oh no, we eat bagels these days," smiled the head cop.

"Want a bagel?" Marlene asked brightly, holding one up.

"Ya ha ha, no thanks."

Neither one of them had any warrants, so after a while the cops left with a warning to "Settle down!" All Howard's interactions with the cops while he was with Marlene shared a similar incongruous slapstick quality, as if it was all a sweet, dangerous joke. Their time together sure had left some marks.

Howard got up and went into the kitchen when the cops left. "Aaah, we're outta coffee," he snarled. "You wanna go to the store with me?"

Marlene looked up through the bangs of her 1920s hairdo. "Yeah, alright." They put on their coats and went out.

☻

There were ladybugs all over the ceiling in Howard's motel room in Oswego, New York on his way to the next Power Mountain residency with his dad. Marlene had wandered off following clues from *The Art of War,* an ancient Japanese handbook on troop placement and combat strategy and suspicion, a few weeks earlier. That's the name of. "These rules apply on every level of society," she told him, "the way people interact." And he believed her when she said that. She'd been gone for days and maybe she was even dead. Howard killed at least ten ladybugs with a rolled-up TV Guide as they advanced across the ceiling from the bright sunset window, six or seven hundred miles away from Marlene and her troubles, his father sleeping in a neighboring motel room. Eventually he deduced the ladybugs were attracted to light, and left the bathroom light on. He fell asleep beneath a slowly crawling trail of them that night, hoping they'd stick to the ceiling.

Howard had been studying "personal symbolism" that semester at Power Mountain, which was apt, and ironic at once. He cried reading his final paper to the group, sitting outside on the lawn in the sunlight. Back in Denver, he started blessing Marlene's name each time he ducked under that branch, and wishing her all the luck there was. There was a "NO WAR" stencil on the sidewalk just past that sports bar, and whenever Howard came to that slogan by daylight, he'd step on the word "WAR" while blessing everyone with peace before ducking under the branch.

ALINA VERA PICKED HIM UP OUTSIDE K ZIP and they drove to this light museum with round black windows on the outskirts of town in a parking lot full of warehouses Howard had heard about on Facebook and was planning an article about for the Scrutinizer. When they got there, the gallery owner, Connie Trask, a tiny woman with white hair, 80 or 90 years old, was dancing around ethereally among all the glowing idols and film strips. She took Howard into a room and asked, "Now what would you like to know?"

"Well, I guess just something about your art . . ."

"I'd rather not *explain* the art," she said, making an emphatic gesture with her fist. "I'd rather have *you* write about what it says to *you*. You have to understand, my purpose with all the art I make is to get people high."

"High?"

"*High*. Stoned."

Connie pointed at a painting on the wall. "That's a chakra piece there," she diagnosed.

He pulled down his collar. "You know which one this is?"

"I'm sorry, my eyes—"

"I have a scar right here on my throat," he pointed at it. "I'm just wondering what that chakra's called."

"Well, it's the *throat* chakra."

"Oh—"

"But you have to understand, most of my relationship to the chakras has been based on colors—as an artist."

"Aesthetic effect."

"Right."

Then the fractal filmstrip segment started in the next room and they both went in there. Howard chose a seat beside Alina Vera on a couch-shaped flat cushions very low to the floor. She turned her head to him after a few minutes of sliding shifting purple shapes and said, "I feel like we should be on acid."

"Yeah, I wish I'd brought my bag," said Howard, but felt conflicted. Was this escapism, or was this kind of beauty overdose necessary and healthy from time to time? How did that old woman feel, living with art like this every day? Did light- magic-amazement wear off, or was it endlessly regenerate? Lots of questions like this. "After all, I'm a citizen journalist now," he thought.

Alina's friend Sadie arrived, tall and blonde in a white dress-shirt, with a chummy, easygoing manner, and told Howard she thought he was cute when they were introduced. "Oh, uh, thanks, you're very nice looking, too."

"Yeah, that's about all you can say, huh?"

"Hum uh, what?"

Sadie spotted Alina and started talking to her. Howard stood there expectantly for a couple of seconds then wandered into another room feigning interest in a statue of a giant blue head. Before he left the gallery, Connie Trask apologized for not having been more forthcoming in their previous conversation, and he told her not to worry, that it had been a pleasure to talk to her. He only hoped he could do her story justice in the article he wrote. He went to the bar next door with Alina and Sadie and several of their friends, where Sadie asked him, "So what's wrong with your eyes, you got some kind of milky eye to not know how cute you are? What did this to you?"

"I don't know—public school? Maybe you're the one with the milky eye thinking I'm cute, haha."

"What, I have nothing to gain from you, why would I lie, I'm *gay*, I have no ulterior motive here."

"That explains
it." "What?"

"Oh, nothing."

Howard still liked Alina and wasn't quite sure how she felt, but had been ready to sail away into a guaranteed fling with Sadie if so prompted, which absurd dilemma had been a subtext of his night until that moment.

He'd been making the most of that Scrutinizer gig, posting at least two new pieces a day—and almost every new post had in-text links to other stuff by him, to maximize the hits, each of which earned a penny—(the more hits, the more bits). He got a comment from F. P. Deringer's widow, Roulana, taking issue with his profile of her late husband on the Scrutinizer. "F.P. may have been schizophrenic, but someone was definitely harassing us, we just don't know who!" Roulana had been Deringer's roommate in 1974, during which time their house was burglarized, a mysterious explosion occurred, and suspicious characters were spotted in their neighborhood, possibly government agents. Deringer's books about their time together were written from a dislocated, omniscient position, at a time when he felt he had seen through the veil, and led to F.P.'s reputation as some kind of postnormal prophet.

"I agree with you completely," Howard responded. "and I sincerely apologize if that didn't come across in the article."

He and his mom met for dinner before she left to chair a Consciousness Arts seminar in Vermont, after which she was attending a big family reunion for her side of the family in New England. Howard suggested a sushi place in his neighborhood he'd spotted on his way back from the bank but never been to. His mom proposed to get there by driving in the opposite direction up Speer and Howard began the latest round of would-be diplomatic redirections, a role made even harder by his talking problem since the brain injury. When they got there, the kewpie waitress asked them, "Sushi or hibachi?"

"Well, I'm having sushi, she might not be having sushi . . ."

The waitress led them into the hibachi section, where every table had a built-in hot plate for the chef to chop up vegetables in front of you. This, of course, was the last thing Howard wanted. "It's just some people's idea of fine dining," apologized his mom.

They ended up sitting in the sushi section after all, where one seating change failed to entirely eliminate the setting sun's glare before Howard gave up with a snarl. "Ah, this fucking place. I was in a good mood. I wanted to take you somewhere nice to eat. It always blows up in my face. My whole life. Never mind. Never mind. It's okay. Do you know what the throat chakra stands for, by the way?"

"Well, why do you ask?" said his mom, in a voice both timid and brave.

"Well, I've got this tracheotomy scar."

"I don't know much about the chakras, but in my opinion, it's sort of your comfort in expression or not, amounting to the choice between being the servant or the master of your life."

The food was good, spicy salmon and vegetable rolls with wasabi. Howard told his mom a long list of all his recent journalism accomplishments and experiences very quickly, feeling like he was making a report to his employer and had to pass muster, sick and uptight and sorry, since he knew she was about to leave town and he wanted to give her a good send-off, but felt full of evident tension and a real uncomfortable pitch in his manner.

"Ignoring my problem talking to people since the accident feels like denial," he told her at one point, and she cautioned him against affirming negativity. On the way home, he asked what she might do if any trouble about his cousin's gayness arose with the reunion's hosts, who she'd said were "old school conservatives," and likely to cause a scene if they found out.

"I can't do anything about it, I'm not going to do anything."

"Well, you'll have to do something. I'm just trying to help you figure out what's, you know, the best way."

"Do what?"

"I don't know, whatever you're gonna do. However you're going to react."

His mom said she was resolved to keep the whole thing a secret if possible and honestly didn't know what she would do if it came up. "I can't just ask them to change their whole worldview." She seemed exasperated with the conversation, as if she felt he was picking a fight. He wasn't trying to. "You're the one who brought it up!" he reminded her.

Hugging her goodbye when she dropped him off, Howard finally ran down the words he was after: "You're better than 'I can't,' you're a very capable person. That's all I'm trying to say." What a funny game the mind is.

When he went back inside it felt like all the sound had been sucked into a hole on his left side. For about five minutes he sat there on the green and white couch, feeling exactly the kind of gradually mounting silent painless irritation guaranteed to snap your mind if it lasted too long. He drank a glass of water and it passed.

HOWARD REALIZED IT WASN'T JUST HIM BUT the whole world changing at one of the grad school residencies when a bearded freshman with a reddish face from Santa Fe, New Mexico named Lamar Cobson who taught high school math and wrote excellent poems on relativity, distance and reflection brought it up how there was no such thing as consensus reality, even unto politics and history, that you could choose what happened to yourself-the-world, a heretical notion Howard himself had become convinced of recently but had been keeping under his hat. "You believe that? Me too!"

Lamar was doing a study on poetry as a vehicle to transcendence. They both liked reggae and agreed that Rasta slang like "I and I" meaning all are one and "isms are schisms" effectively predicted the personless human collective both felt about to take form. Lamar made the excellent point that the largest and smallest objects were only this size in relation to man's measurement. "I am not above, and you are not below. We are equal and we live with love. Yes I." Lamar taught Howard the handshake he'd perfected to accompany this mantra, and the two of them greeted and parted this way all week long. Maria Reynolds was getting over an ugly relationship, doing her culminating study on diving into the new reality. Howard's was on writing against the grain of convention.

They all felt clued in to a knowledge beyond that prescribed for the masses, and there came a moment in a Greystoke stairwell, very late at night or very early in the morning, after all the faculty and staff had gone home for the day, the three of them comparing slogans about this Great Divide:

"Nothing is true, everything is permitted," said Howard.

"I like that one," said Maria.

"Me too, have you heard that before? Or those who know don't tell. That one makes sense."

"Those who know it don't show it," said Lamar.

"Yeah, but those are both too hierarchical, I think," said Howard. "It's not about being superior."

"Well, but maybe they had to make it sound like a law that way, to enforce secrecy."

"Who?"

"Yeah."

"And it is about being superior in a way, having that knowledge," said Maria.

"Well—but it's not about bragging."

"No."

"And they shouldn't keep it secret anyway," said Howard, "what the hell."

A woman named Marybell Lucas had a long ponytail and a beauty mark above her mouth, and had waitressed years ago in a comedy club frequented by late great outlaw comic Bill Hicks. "Bill was a nice guy."

"My friend King Baker knew him," Howard told her. Denver's one armed former junkie comic King Baker had been a kind of mentor to Sad Comic. They'd grown apart in the months since Baker's last brief relapse.

Marybell was married and had recently moved from Houston, Texas to St. Louis, Missouri, where Howard's family spent two unhappy years before moving to Denver in 1983. "It was all suburbs where I lived," he told her. "and I was a kid so I never got into the city. I bet it's much nicer."

"My husband and I are having a good time so far." Her beauty mark danced when she spoke.

A bunch of them were walking down the hill into town one evening towards the end of Howard's final residency and Marybell's cell phone rang. He still didn't have a cell phone or see the need for one, but more and more, everyone around him had them. It had started to take on the appearance of some corporate or government plot he'd unknowingly avoided. Before leaving Denver, he'd seen a clip on CNN that said all cell phones were equipped with listening devices. Not just GPS tracking capability, but actual listening devices potentially in use at any time. The feature hadn't specified who or what might be paying attention on the other end.

Howard started wailing about all that when Marybell got off the phone with her husband: "And they don't even *say who's listening.*"

"I think they need to hear it!" she cried joyfully.

"What are you talking about? Who, no, what!" But his blurt got lost in the gang of laughing voices as the bunch of students continued down the long hill into town, and Howard dropped the subject.

The next evening he helped a woman with impressive poise, brown hair and glasses named Heidi Luger with her presentation on Andre Breton. Heidi was closely attended by an outgoing poet named Don Constantinople who kept cracking wise about everything, which had an effect on Howard's confidence.

The following morning his only pants split right at the crotch, and after walking around all day trying to hide it, he confessed to a beautiful tall pale curly haired girl wearing glasses named Kendall and the two of them went down the hill into town to find a new pair, then back up it again. Kendall was married and ran a dog rescue service in Amish country while writing a true crime book about a con game she had inside information about. She had lupus and was addicted to painkillers. Called him "hon" a couple of times.

Howard knew some of these women had to be available, but not which ones or how to approach them. He wasn't alone in this dilemma. Lamar Cobson threw a folding chair into a tall hill of snow off the front porch of Greystoke very late one night or early the following morning to relieve his bundled nerves about all these beautiful women from all over the world who were writers surrounding them suddenly as if by magic.

One evening a few students were standing around the picnic table in front of Greystoke. After receiving the news from that semester's grad ass that her X-boyfriend had hacked into her Power Mountain email account and sent incriminating letters in her name to the headmaster, Maria started crying and drifted off across the quad in a long white dress to her dorm room on the other side of campus.

"Is she alright?" asked the new security guard, whose name was also Bob, though he was several years younger and never wore a uniform as had his predecessor, just inside the heavy white doors of Greystoke when Howard went in to get his winter coat. "Ah well, you know, relationships are hard," said Howard, grudgingly coming to terms with that lesson as the two of them entered the lobby. Perhaps his personal hologram required manifestation of absolute lack before manifesting total satiation, for purposes of equal balance. Could it be that simple?

"The last woman I was with, Howard," Bob told him, "she was mentally sick in a way. No matter how hard I tried, I just couldn't seem to be what she needed me to."

"I know how that feels."

Just then, a woman with frizzy blonde hair showed up on the front steps in search of her missing teenage daughter, last spotted near University Hall—"She's not answering her cell phone." Bob Two left with her, concluding a signature example of the synchronous chains of occurrence Power Mountain is known for.

Howard went back outside and Heidi Luger bummed one of his cigarettes. They talked about Andre Breton, something he said once about poets never mentioning the stars with anything earthly. "They should say something about the stars and the *roof*, they never marry heaven to the earth. That's what poets are supposed to do."

"'The stars are chunks of ice in God's black drink'," Howard quoted a poem he'd written years ago on acid, channeling some postnormal force. "I wrote that years ago, on acid," he apologized. "I think it's pretty good."

"Yeah, that is," Heidi agreed.

She told him she was just getting over a divorce and had a five year old daughter named Kestra. Howard tried relating a conversation he'd had with his mom before leaving for the residency. "Ever since my dad died, I keep asking my mom to clean the basement, and offering to help clean her basement, and the other day she said one reason she hadn't done it yet was she was saving all the records of her side of the family down there for my kids to look at in the future."

"Do you have any kids?"

"I don't have any kids! And I was like, 'Well, Mom, you know, I'm not even dating anyone at the moment, and with the world as it is, I'm really not sure if I want to bring any kids in,' and–whoo— that was the wrong thing to say."

"Did she cry?"

"I don't know, I think so. Maybe so."

Everyone gathered in a white room behind the stage in the chapel before the graduation ceremony. A bell rang and they all went out on stage and graduated.

BACK IN DENVER, MARIA REYNOLDS WAS ABOUT TO start a hypnotherapy practice, so Howard told her about his talking problem and she agreed to hypnotize him in case that might help. He lay down on the green and white couch and Maria sat in a blue chair behind him, reading from a list of positive cues he'd written down before she came. Right away he knew he couldn't breathe deeply enough to relax all the way, since the couch was too short, and the voice she was using to assure him "interpersonal interaction is skillful and smooth," seemed way too affected. Part of his mind stayed thinking about all that stuff so he never went under, but he still thought it was a step in the right direction (since you always look better from outside yourself, and holding your problems at arm's length like that can work wonders).

On the way to Safeway after Maria dropped him off, Howard ran into his gray haired neighbor Gabe Kotter dribbling his basketball up the uneven sidewalk. "Hey Howard, I never did ask what kind of articles you wrote." Howard synopsized his Roberta Bogchar article for him again. "Yeah, that's gonna be published on a new webzine in about a month."

"That's rich. You ever hear the one about my uncle Seymour Kotter."

"Yeah, you told me about him. Thanks, Gabe." Howard went back downstairs to his apartment.

A writer named Santiago Valdez was planning to serialize his uncle's autobiography, *Vato Peligro* or *Johnny Goo Goo Eyes,* which he described as "a Denver crime gem," on the new site. Yago spent several years in Hawaii as part of a punk band called the Hell Hounds, and had self-published a book all about his adventures. A great writer and old friend of Howard's, Sam Dent, formerly Sam Kane (both pseudonyms), originator of a bygone Denver zine called Hypodermic Jawbone, would be joining Yago's meeting with Howard at Café Golgotha. Sam was black and Howard was white. Yago Valdez was Mexican-American. Writing about it later, Howard decided it said something about this society that capitalizing the words black and white seemed phony or pompous, but not capitalizing Mexican or American seemed stupid or rude.

He stepped over a board laid across the path to their meeting and it reminded him of his third semester Power Mountain grad school advisor Charlton Spatzky, who said he felt obligated to prove the existence of Mothman, that laws might be enacted against the killing or capture of these creatures. Whenever he discovered sticks laid across trails while tracking Mothman in the wild, he regarded them as "no trespassing signs" placed by those uncanny batlike apparitions to dissuade pursuit. His dedication was inspiring or pathetic, since in Howard's opinion, those oversized beings were good enough at getting away, one would have been found by now if that was possible. "Leave Mothman alone," Howard wanted to tell him. But denying the amazing out of fear was even worse, so Howard was proud of Spatzky's faith.

When he reached Café Golgotha, he ordered a lime flavored Italian soda, and chose a table out of the sunlight. Yago showed up first on his bike, wearing a blue T-shirt and jeans, with a shaved head and a sharp gray beard coming out of his chin. He'd been working long hours "flagging," or standing in traffic holding up metal paddles reading SLOW.

"I don't think I could do that," said Howard.

"It pays well, but all that hard work is sucking my free time."

Sam Dent was full of intelligent practical worries and all the right questions for the absent Johnny Coccaluccio about advertising and possible changes to the site when he arrived wearing a sharp black suit: "I've noticed on Dlineator that they don't even explain what it is, this new site, they just provide a link." Dlineator was the name of Johnny C's newest citizen journalism site, currently very popular among that crowd, partner site to the webzine Howard would be editing.

"They don't explain what it is—what?"

"No. There's just a link and it calls it the partner site, but that's all it says."

Howard mentioned It felt like his eyelids were turning to paper and Yago said, "Yeah, I get that sometimes, like a little flutter?"

"They're not fluttering, though. It just feels like they're drying up or something. I've never felt anything like it before. This morning I washed them off with soap after taking a shower, then rubbed in some lotion. They feel tingly and sensitive now."

Yago Valdez sat there looking at him shrewdly with his sunglasses pushed back on his head. He didn't seem very impressed by Howard's half-assed business meeting. Before he got back on his bike and rode away, Howard told him he'd fill him in after talking to Johnny C on Wednesday. On the way back to his place, Howard showed Sam the first peace symbol he'd seen in the sidewalk cracks between K ZIP and the bank and assumed was man-made—"See that?"—and started telling him the story. "But I've seen a few anarchy symbols and lightning bolts too."

Sam laughed politely when he said that, then his cell phone rang, and as Sam talked to his girlfriend, Howard realized what kind of story he'd been starting to tell right before she called, about all the strange symbols he'd seen in the cracks, and decided not to bring it up again.

"Nice place," said Sam when they got to K ZIP.

"Yeah, it's not bad. Five hundred a month."

"When I first came to Denver from Chicago, I always stayed in cheap hotels, renting a room by the week. Fifty bucks a week."

"That's a good idea," Howard agreed. "Instead of renting an apartment."

"Yeah, and paying a deposit, that whole hassle."

Sam and Howard smoked some pot, then Sam headed back to his apartment in the desolate commercial strip of Colorado Boulevard and I-25, which he said reminded him of a J.G. Ballard novel. Howard's eyelids felt normal again. The skin lotion method had worked nicely. He changed a few things in the Bogchar article, took out that part about trying to call fitness freak Peirson

Pierson, who claimed he had proof the woman in Ontario was really Bogchar, since he never answered either time Howard called, and changed the wording here and there—like instead of saying Roberta's third cousin was "intimately involved" with MK ULTRA, Howard said he "would have had access to it."

He arrived first to the next meeting with Johnny and Sam, which took place one afternoon a few weeks later at the Greasy Spoon Cafe.

"Where is the girl?" cooed the matronly pigeon-voiced waitress when she brought the menu.

Howard hadn't been to the Greasy Spoon since breaking up with Betty Bolt. "We're still friends."

"Good, good."

Sam Dent showed up next, then Johnny C., who said that Bogchar article wasn't ready yet, but almost. He said Howard needed to send it to the C.I.A. on the off chance they respond with actual data. He said he would put Howard in touch with "the right guy" to talk to. He appeared to be totally serious, and to see it as another noble part of the journalistic process.

"Are you kidding?" You might say Howard's feelings were mixed about that, but supposedly it was a free press, so he never exactly refused.

They talked things over for three or four hours till the Greasy Spoon closed, then kept talking a few more minutes walking up the hot sidewalk to Jack Jorkensen's Anarchy Now! bookstore–gallery hybrid a few doors down. Johnny C went in and said hello to Jack while Sam and Howard stood outside smoking cigarettes in the sunlight and looking across Broadway at the bar and diner there. Then Johnny C took off and Sam and Howard went in to talk to Jack, an old guy with oversized gogs and a carefully upswept pompadour, wearing a Hawaiian shirt, who said he hated the internet but might let them host a launch party at his store. Sam went across the street to meet his girlfriend at the bar and Howard started walking back home.

That afternoon Lonnie Culot called inquiring about sources of pot besides Mongo and Howard introduced him to Miranda. The issue of Westword on her coffee table when they arrived had six or seven pages of ads for medical marijuana dispensaries. "I'd like to know how to get certified as a caregiver," she told them. Her boyfriend Scott sat silently on the couch wearing headphones during Howard and Lonnie's visit, going over guitar parts on his laptop for the next big Skull Fractures tour.

"I'm not sure I want my name on anybody's weird list like that," Howard told Miranda. The latest Facebook posts by a songwriter in Austin, Texas named Eddie Flavius, very talented but darkly cynical in effect, who he'd just interviewed for Johnny Coccaluccio's new website, had been links to a statement by former C.I.A. mastermind, J. Peabody Somebody, at the birth of the computer age, saying how "advantageous" it would be to have a database with information about all American citizens, including race, sex, and political orientation.

"The good thing, though," Lonnie pointed out, "is you always have a connection if you need one." He had a point there. Mongo had been a reliable source for some years, but the quality was always low. This would never be an issue at a medical dispensary funded by its patients' satisfaction.

"I'd just like to know how to *legally obtain* it," said Miranda.

"That would be quite a loophole," fumbled Howard, "legality." Despite having been a habitual smoker for years, he'd never taken to stoner paraphernalia, and was still having trouble getting used to all the medical marijuana dispensaries on all the major streets sporting green crosses and declarative names leaving nothing to the imagination like "Papa's Fat Sack" or "Bud Suckers". Miranda brought Lonnie his bag and he and Howard headed back to K ZIP to smoke a little.

"Her boyfriend's in that crazy band, but he seems so gentle," Lonnie told Howard on the way. "He hardly ever talks."

"Seems like a nice guy, though."

"She's really cool, though, I've talked to her." "I agree. She seems really intelligent."

50

"Did you know she's into Yoga?'

"Right, and music. I guess she's really into Nirvana. She has this pillow on her couch addressed to Kurt Cobain."

"And David Lynch."

After Lonnie left, Howard went home and tried three or four times to send mass-mailings about the new webzine on Facebook, but it wouldn't let him send to more than 20 people at a time, so he went through narrowing it down to only contributors three or four times, but every time he tried editing the list it didn't take. At last he gave up and went to Yahoo, now he had the skeleton of a mass-mailing ready to go out tomorrow after sprucing up the prose and adding another ten or twenty emails. Ah, publishing. He reviewed Ken Braddock's book *F.P. Deringer is dead, dammit* for the Scrutinizer that afternoon, and F.P. 's widow, Roulana, left another comment saying she liked that one, too, adding, "But I do wish that you would look at my fictional biography of my husband, *Daylight Owl*." Howard made a mental note to order a copy as soon as he had cash to spend, then sent out a mass e mail announcing the new webzine, called Doggerel, yet still in honor of Johnny C's commitment to the journalistic torch of truth, and inviting submissions of poetry, prose, art and pics from several writers, artists, and photographers he knew. First to respond was Roulana Deringer: "Cool!" Next, with perfect seriocomic timing, Johnny Coccaluccio sent this:

Howard, I spoke to Cuco yesterday. He's reluctant... I'm not sure why other than he fears we won't bring in the ad revenues. So I've got to sit down with him. Sorry about this. I thought Cuco was on board. He gave me indications that he was, including suggestions to change the name and everything. I don't know what happened.

Johnny C

Johnny's younger brother Cuco was a budding web design genius whose participation in the webzine was critical to its launch. Howard wrote back expressing alarm and dismay and Johnny C encouraged discretion and patience: "There will be a site." The power went out with a loud, lingering hum a few minutes before he went to bed that night and Howard had to feel his way through blackness to the mattress and lie down. After about ten minutes, the power came back on and he was able to turn on the fan that spinning at the foot of his mattress blowing air up toward his face through the hot, thick feeling that had landed on Denver with the summer.

ON HOWARD'S LAST VISIT, DOCTOR MARK HAD asked about his MFA in Writing, which Howard supposed he knew about from consulting his records or talking to his mom, and seemed bent on building an ongoing conversational relationship with him as a fellow booklover. "So you mentioned John Fante the last time you were here," the dentist opened after tilting Howard backward in the chair and shining his lit cyclopean headgear down on him.

"Right."

"So what are you reading now?"

"Well, I just read a book by Roulana Deringer that was great. F. P. Deringer's X-wife. Do you know who F. P. Deringer is? He's a well-respected science fiction writer. *Tghuibnk!* "

Doctor Mark reared back slightly when Howard made that noise. "Bless you, here's a tissue. So this is a book by his wife?"

"His widow."

Howard lifted his head and wiped off his nose with the tissue, before resuming the humiliating backward angle.

"Hmm . . . well-respected science fiction writer, widow," ticked off Doctor Mark. "And this book is not science fiction?"

"Not exactly. It's a long story. I shouldn't have started telling it." What Howard meant by that was he wanted his trip to the dentist over as quickly as possible, and the more he talked, the longer it would take.

"I've been reading Dante's Divine Comedy," said Doctor Mark.

"Oh yeah, the *Inferno*?"

"Huh, no, the *Paradiso*. It really says something about our society," the dentist continued, as he and his beautiful blonde assistant Micki used a metal spreading device called a retractor to pull apart Howard's lips and take a picture of his teeth, "that people only think of the *Inferno* when Dante's name is mentioned, and never the *Purgatorio* or the *Paradiso*."

Howard had figured the dentist was probably reading the *Inferno* since it seemed to be the most popular one in that series and most people go for the popular stuff. In a way they were agreeing, but Howard hadn't read any Dante himself, and he couldn't talk at length just then, so he didn't clarify. "Well, I know some writers named Fante," he offered. "John and Dan."

"Hm, Fante. What kind of stuff do they write?"

"Ah, fiction, big influence on Charles Bukowski."

"Hm, Bukowski, eh?"

"Right."

After shooting him up with numbing medicine, Doctor Mark

started telling Howard about the many translations of *Don Quixote* over the years, and which ones were considered more or less valid by various groups, and why.

"What would you consider a good translation?" asked beautiful Micki at one point. "From German to English, or English to German?"

Howard wasn't sure what she meant by that. "Well, I don't know, the whole concept of a good translation is sort of alien to me," he ventured. Then one or another instrument was back in, depressing his tongue and picking or grinding away at his teeth. When the two of them weren't leaning over Howard, he could see a bright blue sky and treetops full of rippling leaves visible through the window.

"Okay, I need a B-2," said Doctor Mark.

Micki handed him one of those and he did something to one of Howard's teeth with it. Micki was wearing a white shirt covered with purple designs and a pair of matching purple pants. Howard's eyes kept going over there. She was on his left, chewing gum. The bottom of her throat was beautiful and smooth. Dr. Mark was on his right, with a bright light hitched to his visor. They both wore goggles, his with inset circular lenses. "Just turn a little bit to the right again, if you would," the dentist kept saying. Hours later, Howard's whole head still felt pulled out of shape.

He was on his way to the grocery store when he realized he'd forgotten his bag and would have to use a plastic one instead. "Oh well," he decided, and kept walking. Just then, a bird digging for worms in the grass beside the sidewalk jumped in front of him, its back turned, and hopped backwards toward him slightly. Howard stepped around it and kept walking before realizing that for all he knew, that bird hopping backward toward him like that for no reason was a prompt from mother nature to turn back and go get his bag instead of wasting plastic as he'd almost done. Howard turned around and when he got home, found he hadn't taken that morning's seizure medication yet and swallowed the tablet.

☺

Dim Jim Driscoll woke up and walked into the kitchen scratching his belly. He picked up a pen from the counter and walked through the house into his front yard holding the pen and thinking about it, thinking hard. I found this pen in a motel room, he thought. This very pen, beside a notepad embossed with the motel logo. The last person to use this pen might have been writing a suicide note right there in the motel room where I found it, or a love song straight from the heart, or just doing their taxes, or filling out a resume, or doing a crossword puzzle, or describing brain surgery, or something else totally different from whatever it is I write with this pen, and I'll never know what it was that last person was writing—whatever it is the hell they fucking do—and it might have been really important! Then he went back inside and sat down on his green and white couch, full of despair, remembering way too much and trying to forget it all at once. He brewed some coffee, poured himself a cup, and sat down at the table to drink it. Without warning, he went into another dream.

HOWARD AND SAM DENT MET WITH JOHNNY Coccaluccio and his brother Cuco the web design tech at a bar on 13th full of signed photographs of Golden Age movie stars like Clark Gable and Greta Garbo and agreed the new site name would be Doggerel.com after all, following a tense couple of days when it looked like "Dlinear" was gonna be the tag, since Johnny wanted it to share the same silver D icon as partner site Dlineator, for reasons of brand familiarization. In Howard's opinion, the better the site, the less that sort of thing mattered, but Johnny C had a better grasp of marketing. He published a shortened version of his Roberta Bogchar article on Scrutinizer instead of pursuing Johnny's offer of a C.I.A. connection, staying close to the book review aspect, and not delving into the Costa Rican trainer sidebar very deeply. The transcendently grateful Rebecca Benavidez, author of two books on the Bogchar case, who'd sent him a PDF of her latest free of charge, reposted it so it would get more hits.

"Go ahead and make a page for it on Facebook too," said Johnny. "You can post links to all the new articles there, and just anything you happen to be thinking about."

Little did Johnny C know what he was unleashing, giving Howard that kind of free reign. In no time at all, the Doggerel page on Facebook was a crooked reflection of all the twists and turns and contradictory signposts provided by the modern zeitgeist with which Howard's mind had the fortune to interact. Even prior to the webzine's launch, he began by posting links to the articles he wrote for the Scrutinizer there to maximize the readership at that fail-safe gig. It was starting to get results.

Frequency of posts made a big difference in getting more hits at Scrutinizer, as did catchier headlines. Casting about for an article subject, Howard did a search for Roberta Bogchar's X-husband, Rodrigo Pallas, who was supposed to have introduced Roberta to aerobics, on MySpace. When he found the right profile and sent Pallas an invitation to the upcoming longer article about that Roberta-as-Dentist possibility, he replied immediately, communicating his lack of interest in a rather sour tone, and Howard was troubled briefly by the sense he'd fouled the privacy of Rodrigo's memories. Ah well, no matter. He tracked down email and snail mail addresses for Joline Larue, who muscle freak Peirson Pierson said was really Roberta Bogchar under an assumed name, and sent her an interview request.

Tewodros Magness came over and they sat down in the kitchen and smoked some pot with the fan on, blowing their clouds out the window. Howard started talking about Planet X and

Tewodros said he believed there were aliens among us who were time travelers but not necessarily extraterrestrials. He said he was planning to stay in Denver until after 2012 since it was so high above sea level. He spent most of the visit at Howard's computer sending messages from his Facebook page and using the chat feature while giving Howard a running commentary on all his friends as he chatted with them and read their comments and surfed their profiles. It was kind of annoying, but also a reflection of how much time Howard spend doing that kind of thing himself these days

"Seen Selina Kyle lately?" he asked Howard. Various characters from books and magazines Howard had read over the years had recently begun appearing in his life or revealed themselves as always having been there, and Tewodros had a longstanding crush on Selina Kyle, a pop culture character from fictional Gotham City who'd infiltrated Howard's scene of friends in Denver after he'd tried and failed to pick her up one night at Cafe Post-Normal just before his super-seizure. Selina had a quality of ageless sexiness. She purred when she spoke. In her "Catwoman" guise she was not an adversary of Batman, as such, but known for having a love-hate relationship with him. In her first appearance, she was a whip-carrying burglar with a taste for risky capers.

"I haven't really talked to her since getting out of the hospital," said Howard. "We had an argument a long time ago about Israel's occupation of Palestine being like the new apartheid. That was my end of the argument. I remember she was pro-Israel."

"Well, she's Jewish."

"Yeah, well—some part of my mind always associates her with exactly the kind of unquestioning family loyalty that keeps the wrong people on top, you know? I read this thing where supposedly they just fired poisonous chemical gas into a crowd full of citizens just to make a point."

"What, you don't like Jews?"

"What? No, the Jews did this, I mean the Israelis. Don't you think that's wrong? 'Cause there were babies and old people in the crowd supposedly."

"You like Selina too, huh?" inferred Tewodros,
eyes gleaming slyly.

"No, not at all, I mean I don't dis-like her, she just reminds me of—power imbalance or something."

"*Power imbalance*, what? I think you like her."

At one point Tewodros asked Howard what he wanted from life and Howard told him he wanted to go on affecting people with words and communicating with them, and get paid for doing that, and keep on feeling good about that, like he was just beginning to, "so I think I'm on the right track."

At first Tewodros congratulated him, "Well, that's good. A lot of people never even do that much," then he came with the golden left hook: "But do you wanna be one of the people who can't help but stand out on *their* radar? 'Cause those are the people who honestly don't stick around very long."

"I don't know, man, I'm struggling with that in my soul right now. Do you hear that? You hear what I said?"

"You're struggling with that in your soul."

"Yeah."

"Well, big deal."

It was almost an argument, but nothing was really at stake. They just kept opposing each other. Everything seemed to be cool by the time Tewodros left.

He'd told Alina Vera about his session with Maria Reynolds, and the following afternoon Alina left a comment on Facebook saying she liked his profile pic, then asked if he'd been back to the hypnotist. Thanks, Alina, Howard dodged, you wanna hypnotize me? He told her he hoped she'd let him take it out in trade.

Eddie Flavius started posting videos from YouTube about constitutional abuse at border checkpoints right in the middle of their exchange, making Howard feel like a complacent ass, busy flirting with Alina, unlike Flavius, who'd just posted a link exposing the truth about mailboxes being marked with red, blue or pink dots designating their owners "slaves", "protected", or "expendable" for easy identification after martial law was declared, also something about compulsory swine flu vaccination for American citizens and being tased if you refused. Eddie sure was committed to unmasking that kind of stuff. The way Howard saw it, there would be a big clash between the extremes changing everything sooner than later, and without taking sides, he was looking forward to the aftermath where both became irrelevant. After his conversation with Alina tapered off in the wake of all this self-reflection, Howard sent Wilson Bishop an instant message on yahoo—"Hey Wilson! WIIILSOON!! WIIIIIIILSSOOONAA! Sure hope you're not ignoring me." They hadn't spoken in some time, and Howard was beginning to feel neglected.

●

Dim Jim Driscoll woke up and another thought came to him. Maybe this pen is a magical pen, and whatever it writes comes true. He

57

decided to write only nonsense. That way, whether or not it came true, nothing awful would ever happen. He would write down a world with its own kind of logic and sooner or later he'd get there.

He got up and went into the kitchen, then went back outside. Then he came back inside and went into the kitchen again. He kept going in and out. He was restless.

After a while, Dim Jim found himself in the living room again. Then he went back outside and got into his car and started racing down the street.

Soon he reached the highway and zoomed past a speed-trap a couple of times, even screeching his tires for effect. At last the cop got wind and sirened Dim Jim over. "I'm writing you a ticket!"

"Hey, thanks, officer! Couldja do me a favor and make that out for Patagonia?"

THE PREVIOUS WINTER, BETTY AND HOWARD HAD taken a road trip from Denver, Colorado to the East Coast and back by Greyhound bus so she could attend her second Power Mountain residency and he could see his old friends Wilson and Judson again. He didn't spend much time on campus during her session, though he used the computer lab a few times, where he encountered one of his former advisors, Bertice Maclanahan, who Judson Winkler had recommended for his third semester, when reeling from yet another breakup. Her inability to radiate anything other than love and compassion toward advisees had been very helpful in that instance.

"Is that Howard?"

"Bertice, how are you. Yes, my girlfriend, Betty Bolt, just started here . . ." and he told her the story.

The morning they left Culchack Corners, Howard and Betty had lunch at a place called Koffee Klatch at the bottom of the long hill, where he encountered another of his former advisors, Rudy Diamond Darrell, famous for her novel about super-literate female bear hunter Dorian Dixon, whose mastery of bear hunting paralleled her groundbreaking discernment of Ernest Hemingway's failed masculinity. "Howard Plumber?"

"Hey, Rudy, nice to see you."

She asked him what had ever happened with *Kiabonga!*, the first version of which she'd seen.

"Oh, nothing much yet."

"Well, you let me know."

Encounters like this one gave Howard a sense of Power Mountain as a mystical point of purpose, as if what Security Offica Bob had told him outside Greystoke Dorms that night—that he was guaranteed to make it—was true, and it was nothing but his own need to feel stuck that was keeping him stuck. Could that be it?

That afternoon when they arrived in New York, Howard stood beside their luggage downstairs in Port-Authority's brownish-yellow arrival bay while Betty went to look for Wilson upstairs. She was sick with a cold, and after she'd been gone a few minutes, Howard wondered if he should have been the one to go upstairs but it was too late. A tall black man appeared in a doorway at the other end of the room and gestured to him, shouting, "Hey! Come on!" Howard kept looking over his shoulder to see if there was anyone else the man might be talking to, but no. "Are you talking to me? I don't know what you mean!"

"Hey! Come on!" the man shouted again in response, waving his arms, but he stayed in the doorway across the room and eventually disappeared into it. Judson Winkler appeared in the same doorway a few minutes later, walked up slowly and gave Howard a hug. He was really all there in the face, eyes clear and sharp, with a dark black beard on his cheeks. He told Howard this month's experiment was mandatory daily street performance, which meant total confrontation of all his shyness and self-esteem hangups.

"Well, it's working. You seem a lot more confident."

"Thanks, man."

Wilson didn't say much when he showed up just after Judson. He'd grown muscles all over his body and shaved off the soul patch, but still carried the same tight brown curls on his head. Betty returned and the four of them went outside and stood in front of the terminal, directly across the street from the ostentatious, silver New York Times castle or building. A short, muscular, middle-aged black man with a shrewd mustache sidled up to Betty Bolt with a quarter tucked behind the inner flap of one ear. "Hey man, you have a quarter in your ear!" exclaimed Wilson Bishop as Howard put his arm around Betty and pulled her back slightly.

"What, you never put a quarter in your ear?" the man responded.

"Not since childhood, no," laughed Wilson.

When they went back inside with their bags about ten minutes later to catch the subway, the same shrewd, coiled man appeared in a black stocking cap with 2008 across its base in white. "I like your hat," he told Howard, who was wearing a gray fedora. "You wanna trade?"

Howard realized this man was a full-time hustler who spent all his time in Port Authority or Grand Central Station or any of the multi-zillion other hotspots in New York City to ply his multi-zillion smoothly ingratiating cons—cunningly sticking quarters in his ear or whipping out kitschy hats and offering them in trade, whatever the situation required, which gave him the impression such totally freelance lives were possible in that City of the Whole World, but he still loved his own hat too much. "No thanks, man. "

The four rushed through teeming crowds and turnstiles, through subways, up and down stairs and across streets toward the Staten Island Ferry. Two cop cars screamed past and Judson remarked what an annoying inherently alarmist sound frequency those made. "Just listen to that." The jarring klaxon blare hung in their wake like an ugly sonic fart.

Betty and Howard were a spectacle on the crowded subway car with all their luggage and Howard in his funny gray hat, looking around at all the other weary travelers and thinking about their dreary lives as inhabitants of this metaphorical subway car in fate.

"It's like the country bumpkins come to the big city," commented Judson.

"What time is it?" asked Howard.

"11:30," said Wilson.

"Whoo, that's late. Our bus leaves in the morning at 8;35, I think."

"11:30's not that late," said Judson. "I've always been an extremely nocturnal person, though."

After boarding the ferry, Howard stepped out on the deck with Judson and Wilson while sweet, long-suffering, fever-sick Betty lay down with their baggage inside. Wilson, Judson and Howard stood at the bow and watched the gray wake churning as the boat chugged steadily through the dark water from island to island, the Statue of Liberty towering brightly blue green over it all. You weren't supposed to smoke cigarettes out there, but a girl with pale hair asked for a light and Howard gave her one before they went back inside.

Betty Bolt was lying on one of the benches beside all the luggage. Howard sat down beside her and put an arm around her. Parts of her were all sweetness, others grated on his dumb self-conscious comfort zone, but she was the partner he'd given himself in this adventure of buses and stations and subways and ferries, which had to count for something.

Before leaving Denver, Howard had seen credible footage of what was purportedly a gnome sliding eerily across a basketball court somewhere in Sweden on the Yahoo news alerts. But was real? He brought that up and Judson Winkler replied, "Anything can be proven on video now. All possibilities coexist. That's AND Thinking, as opposed to or-based logic, where there's only ever one right answer. I try not to think OUTSIDE the box so much as live like there IS no box."

"Yeah, alright, I like that."

Whether or not Judson had coined the term himself or simply picked it up somewhere, Howard recognized AND Thinking as yet another perfect catch phrase for this world-about-to-change, addressing itself to the breakdown of standardized logic far better than any he, Maria, and Lamar had come to in their magical Greystoke stairwell moment.

After getting off the ferry, Howard and Betty carried their luggage up two steep slopes, with Judson and Wilson 's generous help, to Wilson and Hannah's apartment, where they were made welcome with Echinacia Tea for Betty's fever and glasses of water for everyone else. Wilson, Judson and Howard adjourned into a narrow room full of boxes and paintings and a desk which ran alongside the kitchen and the dining room to smoke some pot and talk to each other before going to sleep. Howard kept his mouth shut throughout most of this, feeling frazzled and spent from the day's bus trip.

"I'm a master of self-sabotage," declared Wilson at one point. "When I started out in the theater as a little kid, I was on the right track. Then I became a chef, it was just more acting—then playing guitar—then writing—all these things I've done have been distractions from my true calling."

Judson spread his hands. "Which is—"

"Acting."

"You feel drawn to that.'

"I know full-well that I'm being observed at every moment by something beyond myself."

"That really resonates," said Judson. "But I'm on the other end of that—I'm just starting, taking voice lessons, playing folk music along with my dancing, branching out like that—I'm just *beginning.*" He talked about his money worries and Wilson told him he looked rich.

"Thanks, man."

They went outside so Judson and Howard could smoke a couple of cigarettes. Wilson Bishop had recently quit, but graciously stood there with them, shivering in the sharp winter air.

"So you got married?" Howard asked Judson, having understood this from something he'd just said to Wilson.

"I did." He told Howard his wife's name was BB and he had danced right up to her at Burning Man in an instance of perfect synchronicity where she mirrored every move he made exactly, despite not having spent many years learning to "pop" with precision, as he had.

"Sounds like you were made for each other."

"That's just how it felt."

After they went back inside, Hannah showed Howard and Betty to a mattress in a small room with a blue floor and a desk against one wall and they said goodnight to everyone and closed the door. It felt great having sex again after so many hours and days crowded together on the bus, and they did it again in the morning. Betty said she felt like they deserved it in a way, after such an uncomfortable time on the bus. It crossed Howard's mind he might catch her cold, but he wanted to defeat that possibility.

In the morning Howard got into an argument about the Stomach with Wilson, who, it seemed, felt left behind or neglected in some way by Howard's recent preoccupation with interviews. "We're co-creators," he reminded him gravely, but seemed unwilling to clarify precisely what was at issue.

"Well, I know that!" insisted Howard. "Of course I know that. What are you talking about?"

"Let it go," Judson Winkler kept saying from the sidelines.

"Well, but what am I holding?'

A few minutes later, Howard, Judson, and Betty walked from Wilson's house together and caught the ferry back from Staten Island. "See you later, man," said Judson, as a line of homeland security cops with German Shepherds on leashes advanced to sniff their luggage.

The first bus back had five TV monitors spaced intermittently along the ceiling, all continually broadcasting B-grade comedy fluff to lull the passengers if they put on the headphones stuffed into the seat backs in front of them. Howard's nose started running right after they got on the bus, and he had to keep getting up from his seat for more toilet paper from the bathroom.

In Des Moines, Iowa, there was an unexpected four hour layover because of some obscure failure with the bus's wheelchair-loading apparatus. "There are these little sensors that notice the back when there's a wheelchair," averred the mousy gray-haired bus-driver when Howard tried to find out what was happening.

"Is there some way we can get a refund, then?"

"You'll have to ask them inside. I'm just the driver." She shrugged. "But you can't get off until we're finished testing the door."

The bus driver and another Greyhound official, a tall old man with white hair who looked like a giant, worried baby, kept turning the overhead lights on and off and closing the door of the bus to try to finish their obscure exercise satisfactorily, and whenever they turned off the lights and closed the door it got very hot and stuffy aboard the bus. "Why can't you fix it?" another passenger shouted. Eventually they were made to board another bus with a different pattern on the seats, which left Des Moines immediately.

Howard's nose kept running until they were almost back to Denver. He kept getting up and tearing off long strips of tissue from the roll in bathroom in the back of the bus. Each time one of the strips ran out, he gave another self-pitying sigh before getting up for another. He felt he had defeated his sickness entirely, was really beaming about it, no more runny nose here, before the dripping came back with a fury all night overnight.

Wilson reminded him by phone a few days after he got back from his road trip with Betty that Howard had promised him half the proceeds from selling a few Stomach subscriptions at his last Power Mountain residency. What Howard had taken as his mysterious silence in Staten Island had been Wilson being the better man, so to speak, waiting for Howard to bring it up. "I've never felt so imposed on in my life. You said you'd give me a hundred dollars, so I bought that bag of pot specially for your visit, which I couldn't really afford. And Hannah doesn't like me smoking anyway."

Howard mailed him a hundred dollars a few days later, but something still felt unresolved, like they'd failed to fully connect.

Judson Winkler started sending monthly emails to all his connections about his progress with the experiments. One month he decided to test the Law of Attraction, and bought a one way airplane ticket to Bali without any cash in his pocket or contacts there. Using luck, spit and a band aid, he made new friends, ran into old ones from his childhood, became popular locally as a dancer and pseudo-mystical figure, recorded an album, and stayed in a mansion for free. Upon returning to Los Angeles, Judson changed his name to Funk-Burn Willouhghby, and BB changed hers to Divine Circumstance.

"EVERYthing is true if you believe it," he reported in the first of several mass mailings to all his friends. "That's free will. These days seem dark from the perspective of the crumbling systems but the future beckons us forth, into the unknown, into a symbiosis with creation itself. Live the dream! Jump off the cliff! Destiny awaits! The future beckons! And you are it!"

JOLINE LARUE STILL HADN'T ANSWERED HIS EMAIL, but Howard went ahead and posted the second half of his Bogchar article, where he really got into the Bogchar family's connections to MK ULTRA, on a nonpaying site called TalkityTalk, using a pic from Peirson Pierson's website of a slumped, drunk-looking Joline Larue wearing shades and holding up a card that read, "Roberta Bogchar."

In the sampling of voices Howard had seen so far, most other TalkityTalkers seemed to be teens or adolescents with terrible grammar, and when you became another user's fan, or they became yours, a heart-shaped icon lit up, but apparently the site had a presence in numerous countries. Howard's Roberta Bogchar article claimed the "most viewed" spot in the TalkityTalk Arts & Entertainment category the day he posted it, and Rebecca Benavidez was very impressed to see it clean up like that. She reposted the link on her own site, calling him a "respected and well-known journalist and book reviewer," and sent him an email saying no one else had understood the story so well.

Wilson Bishop responded to Howard's email: "Of course I'm not ignoring you, Cap'n. Why?" and he don't feel so guilty about not having finished Stomach number 12 yet. He kept joining those Distant Energy sessions so all the odds would be in his favor, despite their assertion that chills, fever, even pain might be detected immediately before and afterward, as in a "healing crisis."

He got the news on MySpace, from a mutual friend named Lala, that the Sad Comic's spoken word mentor King Baker had died, after years painting Denver with personal shadows in comedy, poems and plays. One more father gone down. Howard didn't have much social presence in Denver these days. The last time he'd seen Baker had been at a bus stop and they'd barely spoken. In a sense, Howard had thought of King Baker as his connection to the previous generation of wise old outlaws. Besides having met Hal Blare in the Mojave Desert once before his arrest and once touring with Bill Hicks, King Baker had been in an early lineup of the Maker and the Marvins before the arrival of Roberta Bogchar, at which point he was ousted because of his infrequent heroin use.

Betty Bolt came from Michigan, hadn't known King at all, and was working that night in any case, so Howard went alone to his wake. Everyone got a yellow card at the door for "Two drinks on King" from the bar at the room's other end. Howard got his first and joined Lala at a table near the top of the stairs in the room where they usually held the dance classes these days, full of tables and chairs and ringed with billboards posted with pictures and stories from King's life. There was a rack on the stage at one end of the big room hung with all his sport coats for loved ones to assume. Howard tried on three or four but none fit. People spoke and read from King's poems and plays and jokes and took turns remembering him on the stage. "King Baker was the first one to make me think poetry readings were cool," eulogized a tall woman with short brown hair named Caterpillar Mullinax who once had a crush on Howard's punky spoken word persona, Sad Comic, "It wasn't until I was, like, twenty that I realized poetry readings weren't really that cool—it was just King."

After the wake broke up, Howard went with a few other people to Lala's house in Five Points and sat with them drinking cans of beer and talking around a bonfire in her backyard.

Standing on the raised porch, where he'd gone to throw away an empty can, watching everyone else around the fire below him, with the shadow of his head and shoulders magnified on the white garage wall behind them, Howard was overcome with the awareness of how much influence his shadow was having on everyone else. Perhaps it was a message from King, all of whose poems and jokes had been founded on the same disproportion. He lost one of his arms to a train in a psychotic break attempting to offer himself up to prevent the apocalypse, and dragged the tear ducts out of one of his eyes after something he saw offended him. Howard started swinging back and forth from side to side, making light of his shadow-show towering over all the people sitting around that bonfire, his tribute to the late great King Baker.

"You're tripping, huh?" guessed Caterpillar Mullinax, who stood behind him munching an apple.

"Nah, just sensitive."

Howard Plumber left soon after this deceptively shallow exchange for the long walk home that made his sneakers hurt.

On the way to his mom's house to handle the bills the next day, the bus rolled past the mortuary where his father's body had been cremated, and just as Howard was making that association, a drowsy fly lit on his hand. He never swatted flies so he shook it away, but it kept coming back to his hand or leg or forearm, legs moving slowly, and Howard realized it might as well have been his dead dad's loving spirit saying hi. After realizing that, he let the fly ride on his hand until the bus came to his stop. Getting off, he noticed this guy across the aisle in a gray baseball cap giving him a puzzled look.

Standing in the portal of Miranda's building later that afternoon, waiting for the rain to stop or move on, a full wind blowing from behind kept any drops from hitting him. Just as he came back in, more lightning cracked overhead, and Miranda said, "I have an uncle who got struck by lightning six times."

"What's he like?"

"A little bit different from everyone else. Like the Flash, you know? He has his own weird way of seeing life, Sometimes you're not sure whether it's dreams or his life he's telling you about when he talks."

"The Flash" was the name adopted by slowpoke police scientist Barry Allen after a lightning bolt shattered a case full of chemicals giving him the powers of superhuman speed and heightened reflexes in the D.C. comic classic of that name. "Sounds like a nice guy."

"He's all right. Sometimes it's hard to connect the things he says."

The Skull Fractures were touring South and Central America, where they were recognized as gods. Scott's black acoustic guitar was on a stand beside Miranda's couch and Howard tried picking out a tune, but it didn't sound right. "Is this in some special tuning?"

"I never know."

"Yeah, me too, got one of those electric tuners now. Still no cell phone, though."

The storm came on hard for the next five minutes before reverting to warmth and sunlight, as can happen in Denver, and Howard walked back to K ZIP. When he got back, he contacted an artist named Tom-Roy Peralca on Facebook to see if he was interested in joining the Doggerel project. They hadn't seen each other since high school, where they'd been fellow pot smokers and shared an art class. "I wish I had something more concrete to tell you. I'm still waiting to hear from the publisher, but that should happen anytime. I sent him a link to your page so he can look at your art."

Tom-Roy came over to Howard's place the next day. "Wow, what happened to you, man?" he demanded. "That scar!"

"Oh—you mean—uh, which one? The tracheotomy scar?"

"All of 'em, man, that big scar on the side of your head!"

"Ha ha, well, a little accident."

Howard tried changing the subject. Tom-Roy's studio, he knew from photos of the space on Facebook, was in the Sufi Center downtown. "So how'd you get mixed up with the Sufis?"

"What do you know about 'em."

"Well—" Howard wasn't sure how to answer, "Islamic mysticism—"

"They taught Gurdjieff for years, man."

"Right. I like Gurdjieff."

George Ivanovich Gurdjieff had been one of the first sources of metaphysical interpretation of reality for Howard, along with Paramahansa Yogananda, both of whom were introduced to him by his parents' library (though he hadn't read anything by either of them in years). Gurdjieff's theory that everyone was prone to trancelike repitition had inspired Howard's pen name "Sad Comic," since he thought what a horrible joke on us all that would be if it was true, and wanted to be the bittersweet minstrel of that handicap.

"How much do you know about him?" challenged Tom-Roy.

"Well, that thing he said about how people are robots. I don't have anything against the Sufis, I just don't want to join any groups."

Tom-Roy lowered his eyes. "Aw, man, you can't not join anyone."

Howard wasn't sure if he'd been misunderstood or not, but he didn't feel like arguing about anything so he didn't respond.

"So what's been happening with you?" pursued Tom-Roy Peralca.

"Well, my dad died in 2005," Howard told him. His voice got very low as he said this, and Tom-Roy nodded slightly, closing his eyes.

"Don't worry," Howard cleared his throat, "I'm not overcome with emotion or anything—I just think I might be about to cough." He coughed. "There. But I saw an episode of Taxi last night on YouTube, where Jim Ignatowski's rich father dies and leaves him a trunk. They never got along because Jim never wanted to be a lawyer or whatever the family tradition was. All the cabbies think it might be full of money, but Jim doesn't care about that, so he never opens it, but they keep trying to get him to do that. In the very last scene, Jim opens the trunk, and his father's left him a tape: 'You are the Sunshine of My Life'. That ending made me cry."

Tom-Roy kept his eyes closed through that story, slowly nodding and seeming to listen with all of himself. "There's two kinds of people in the world, man." he said gravely when Howard had finished, "Those who are parents, and those who aren't. You know, man, I think it's coming soon, in the next few years, that human beings will enter into a very positive destiny, a kind they've never known before."

"Well uh—what do you think about the Mayan calendar?"

"I don't like that shit, man."

"No, I'm not saying it means the end of the world necessarily, just a new—"

"Think about this: maybe your dad is up there in the sky right now, working away on his radio show."

"What?"

"Your dad used to have that radio show."

"No he didn't."

"I came over there once and I remember there was this old radio."

Howard pictured an old radio he'd seen somewhere in his childhood, perhaps at his grandmother's house. "I don't know what you're thinking of man. They may have had an old radio once, but my dad never had any radio show."

"Hey, I wonder why I'm thinking of that!" Tom-Roy enthused. Then he picked up Howard's harmonica and
started playing it. His harmonica! Then he picked up his guitar and started playing it. Howard wanted Tom-Roy to stop doing all that but tried to stay polite: "Will you tune it for me?"

Tom-Roy began tuning Howard's guitar. "We were made from gorillas, man," he went on, "we're like chimpanzees trying to drive a sports car." Howard guessed he was referring to the differently-enabled mental landscape inhabited by humans as distinct from all other earthly life forms because of being extraterrestrial hybrids, and how disconnected they were from all their inborn powers and talents because of how money mad their society had become. "Yeah. I've seen all that evidence, too, years ago," said Howard. "And I believe it. I just don't feel that lost exactly."

"Sure you do, you feel like a wanderer just like everyone else."

"A wanderer?"

Tom-Roy brought up Howard's profile pic of the uncontacted Indian tribe in the Amazon jungle aiming bows at the helicopter watching them. "That's not human, man," he pointed out, "that's invasion by aliens there."

"You mean the helicopter, right."

"We're the aliens, man."

Howard told Tom-Roy he was writing a book about his adventures as a freelance journalist, and lately he'd noticed all his friends were turning into parents. "And you're another example of that," he enthused. "I'll write about seeing you again. "

"Well, just don't write anything about 'Tom-Roy's languidity of manner.' That's been done."

"Sure, I can see how that would happen," bluffed Howard.

CATWOMAN SELINA KYLE CALLED AND OFFERED TO BUY

Howard dinner in Cherry Creek somewhere. On his way through the rich people's neighborhood between the student housing one he lived in to meet Selina at the restaurant she'd suggested, he passed a stop-sign with the word "it" right under the "stop" in large white letters of the same font. The word "sometimes" was drawn into the patch of sidewalk surrounding a telephone pole he walked past. Walking through the same broad, gated streets roofed over by great, leafy trees years ago, Howard had seen another stop-sign with the word "this" added, by the same artist probably. He tried finding that one again, but no luck.

Feared and hated since the 1940s, Catwoman had been featured in an eponymous series since the 1990s that cast her as an antihero rather than a supervillain. She had long soft legs, very wide at the top and very narrow at the tips. Over a greasy fish taco at a French Mexican fusion joint called Casa Louis, Howard filled her in on the latest wrinkle in his investigation of the Roberta Bogchar case: "There's a ventriloquist named Trent Bogchar in L.A. whose dummy sounds just like the young Roberta Bogchar, who he claims is his mother. I sent him an email with links to his previous Bogcharean pieces on the Scrutinizer and TalkityTalk asking his opinion on the investigative work I've done so far, no response yet."

"I neverrr rrreally liked the Makerrr and the Marrrvins," Selina purred languorously, in her patented catlike burr. "but I rrrealize it's considerrred cool to be into them anymorrre, since Rrroberta died so young."

"Or maybe she faked her death," Howard suggested with feeling, lifting one finger, but Selina ignored the bait. "You should rrreally go to an estate sale with me sometime, Howarrrd Plumberrr" she said. "It's kind of fun. I've been going to lots of thrrrift stores lately."

Selina had visited K ZIP and brought Howard a cake right after he got out of the hospital, which was sweet, but he hadn't been as welcoming of her solicitousness at the time as he ought to have been. He still had the plate it came on. In her Catwoman guise, she was considered an international jewel thief with an ambiguous moral code. "Have you been to the new Goodwill yet?" he asked her. "The one that just opened on Broadway? That's a good place, I like that place." They talked about nothing like this for about half an hour in the dim crowded diner with a view of shoppers passing, after which they paid their check, walked from Chez Pedro toward University Boulevard and parted there.

On his way back through the rich neighborhood of mansion-like condos and long private driveways alone, Howard thought he saw a tiny green helicopter floating down through the air in front of him and slightly to the left, maybe some kind of bug, or a leaf, but it made him think of the guy on YouTube who thought all the planets in our solar system were covered with tiny humans. An old man and his wife were walking up the road toward him just as it happened. "Hello," said the old man, in the manner of a warden, passing Howard.

"Hey," he answered, as a spider web broke on his face, which some people say is a sign of good luck.

Heidi Luger came to Denver for an educational conference, daughter Kestra in tow, and they met briefly for dinner at the Indian restaurant on 6th. "The Power Mountain diaspora gets me through life," she told Howard, bright eyes blinking behind her glasses. "It's like having family members everywhere."

"That's true. I got an advance reader's copy of Emma Browne's first novel, *Mountain Flower*, in today's mail. I met her in the undergrad track. I guess it's all about connections."

For half a second, Howard felt like part of a prearranged computer algorithm, then that feeling disappeared. That unfortunate encounter with Tom-Roy Peralca had been Howard's first attempt at journalistic outreach, resulting in nothing besides personal discomfort, since Peralca showed no signs of sharing any art with the webzine. What he needed was another interview.

☻

Dim Jim Driscoll became convinced he had an appointment at the most important building downtown, tall and gray and bullet-shaped, which resembled the stylized beak of an eagle jutting out of the city's pit, since that would explain the briefcase handcuffed to his arm, and the portfolio jutting from his inner pocket. "That must be who I am," he thought, prancing down the pocked sidewalk, elbowing innocent bystanders out of the way. "it's in my blood." So these citizens wanted to live in total comfort all the time? "Not on my watch," he vowed.

The phone rang, shaking him out of his dream state, and Dim Jim's shoulders twitched—he didn't like being interrupted.

"Who is it?" he asked himself, setting down the bag of earplugs. The noise came again and he answered the phone: "Yes, hello."

"Hi, this is your bond kinsman, Sonny Sarbo-Socket!"

Dim Jim squared his shoulders. "I don't know any Sarbo-

Socket," he snarled bitterly into the receiver, taking another slug of black coffee to show his stung pride. Then he changed his tune. "What was your name again? Yes, Sonny, how are you?"

"There's a big show tonight!"

"Hey, okay, well." Dim Jim flexed his padded shoulders. "There gonna be a cover charge?"

Dim Jim's whole foundation was built on rock'n'roll and other unreal things. He knew It was time for a change. His main problem was he kept thinking of time as an unfolding sequence of eventualities like dying someday or the ozone layer running out, not eternally present and already finished beyond the narrow, linear human mind as, in fact, time really was. "Hey, hello? Hello! Hello!!"

THE FIRST FOUR STORIES WERE UP, INCLUDING Howard's interview with Roulana Deringer. His parents were both former English professors and Consciousness Arts ministers, so his childhood investigations of the family library had given him a broad foundation in quality lit and metaphysics. Sometimes he figured time was running out for him to make it as a writer, or else it was really just a foolish dream and never gonna happen anyway, but that couldn't be true for one so steeped in words and culture, could it? Right?

He'd chosen to stay in Denver after his dad died as a service to his widowed mom, not that this had ended up doing either of them any good, and now he felt stuck there. Their weekly interactions were often tense and strained despite the heightened urge to sonship on Howard's part since the death of Howard Sr. Both felt trapped by roles long outlived, hers of the instructive protective mother, and his of the reckless precocious son, respective treadmills going nowhere. A few minutes after he got there one week to write down all the names and amounts of the church's take, the poor thing asked how his book was coming along and there erupted from Howard a really anguished outburst indirectly concerning the distorted monster he made of himself sometimes. "You see my forehead?" he demanded, tearing off his hat. He'd shaved his head again, all the way bald this time. "I have to go through life handsome and ugly like this, deformed and good-looking at once, every day!"

They'd already had their way with Howard's skull, frankly speaking, just like the oil wells and the earth, but he'd been putting off getting it reshaped for nearly thirty years now because of how invasive that procedure seemed. "And now I have this tracheotomy scar!" He pulled down the collar of his shirt and pointed out the other disfigurement.

"I was told you'd have trouble controlling your temper after the head injury," said his mom. "Does it happen with anyone else but me?"

"Oh God, that's not what I'm talking about!" Howard screamed, and the whole thing slid further downhill.

That evening he went to a party with Alina Vera at the home of a couple of friends of hers from the Denver art scene located in the RiNo district northwest of lower downtown. On the way there, the car in front of them clunked over a curb as it turned a corner, which made Howard prick up his ears, since maybe that meant something else was misaligned.

It was a birthday party for Leos, and one of the hosts, a

French woman named Ozanne, offered him a slice of the cake she'd made with a big lion in yellow icing on top. "No thanks," he told her. "but thanks. I really like the frames of your glasses."

Howard didn't know anyone, and felt awkward. He kept wanting to go outside and smoke a cigarette, but nobody had one, and he'd long since stopped buying his own. Sadie showed up in an Argyle sweater, it was nice to see her again.

"Thanks, my husband made these."

"You don't like sweet things?" Alina asked when she heard him refuse the offered cake.

"No, I just saw something in the Yahoo alerts where all high fructose corn syrup has mercury in it, I mean hopefully I wouldn't come in contact with it much, but I hear it's pretty common."

"There's no HFCS in there," Ozanne assured him, looking up from below through the round black frames. "I grow all my own food. What you need is to start growing yours, too."

Alina started crying driving back down Broadway. She said she felt abandoned by her friends and it made her sad. "I'm sorry, I don't usually act so vulnerable."

Howard invited her into the cellar, where she sat down on the green and white couch and he gave her a cold glass of water. He couldn't think of what to say and kept saying things. He tore off his hat and flaunted his warped forehead. "Now this is me being vulnerable. You see my head?!!"

Alina looked at him with soft brown eyes. "Why did you shave your head?"

"Oh—well," Howard had expected to astound her with his fantastic deformity, but she didn't seem to notice. Either that, or he was the only one surprised. "I don't like barbers, so I have these clippers, and for the last several years I just give myself haircuts."

☻

Dim Jim took three or four more of the tablets and found himself somewhere else suddenly. There he was at his desk moving his blueprints into the circle of light from his gooseneck lamp, tiny insects racing off in the corners of his vision. He was a nature boy, deep down, so whenever he saw those bugs running away, it triggered his natural hunting instinct and made him want to run off through the fields, barking like a dog. Yeah, those were his wild years, back then. Soon his nagging wife Sylvie appeared, then little Perry, now teenage, armed to the teeth with a metal detector and his baseball hat always worn backwards, the little scum. Perry had made an ass of himself again and again at the big family picnic last week, bumping into relatives and friends of the family, circumnavigating the park with his metal detector in search of buried treasure from the big bank heist he figured there must have been in that park once a long time ago. "I know those crooks stuck it around here somewhere," he'd screamed. "I KNOW they did!" The little fuck-ball.

Dim Jim blundered out of the room into hallways and hallways of silence that echoed and amplified his footsteps as they clattered down the stairs and back out into the parking lot. There was more. He knew there had to be more.

He sure needed some new boots to walk around in. With a new pair of boots he could walk tall again. He remembered a store near the highway that sold boots of all kinds and thought about that as he plodded back home through the pitted fields of mud, jingling the mixture in his pocket. Most of it was coins, but there was also lint and a couple of scraps of paper, including a pact he'd been keeping with himself for years now, written down with a number 2 pencil and signed in his own blood, age thirteen. He pulled that pact with himself right out of his back pocket and tore it up in tiny pieces, then tossed all the torn scraps of paper up over his head and did a little dance under them as if snowflakes were falling. "What'll they think about THAT move on Main Street?" he wondered, flashing his star spangled grin at the whole enchilada.

THE FIRST THING HOWARD ASKED CHIEF TOBASCO Sound during their tape-recorded interview call was whether or not he believed Roberta Bogchar was really Trent's mother. Sound paused and took a deep breath before answering, in an apologetic tone, as if he wasn't quite certain, "To be honest, no."

"His dummy, 'Punchy,' sounds just like her in the videos I've seen."

"It's a good falsetto," Chief Sound conceded. "I'll give him that. But I want you to know I bankrolled Trent and his dad, Jocko Cheever, for a couple of years to the tune of hundreds of thousands a year, believing every word. That's the important part."

"Okay. So—"

"He said he was the living product of a secret ceremony in Mexico during an eleven month lull between the two halves of the Maker and the Marvins' South American Boogie Box Joke-in Job of '72. That's what he told me, 'I'm the living product!' And there seemed no reason to doubt him. Even Roberta's cousin, circus jester "Wrinkled" Pete Plucnakern, part of the Bogchar family's inner circle, believed Trent's line at first."

"I see." Howard assumed a professional tone.

"Everything hit the fan when I arranged a reality show with Super Exciting Entertainment provided Trent would consent to a DNA test proving he was Roberta's offspring, and Trent refused. Well, I'd just started a Thinking Lobster franchise named after Trent's band, I felt betrayed. Man, I worked so hard to put that deal together with the SEErs. What happened is 'Wrinkled' Pete Plucnakern felt so betrayed after learning Trent had tricked him, he tried setting up the Trip Ship two days before a scheduled performance by the Thinking Lobster. To get busted for counterfeit money!"

L.A.'s Trip Ship was the comedy troupe's home base, notorious for its seventies disco cokehead status. "What? Okay . . ." "But it didn't work! 'Wrinkled' Pete has been known for passing shady deals from the past, and several people turned up dead around him, lots of celebrities, including Deborah Hondo. You know, 'Wrinkled' Pete even has connections to the Cult of Cold Hands!"

"Who, what?"

"The Cult of Cold Hands!"

"You mean Hal Blare's—"

"Gorilla Kidnapping Cult! And that's not all! 'Wrinkled' Pete Plucnakern was Barry Hondo's personal fool for years, you know, the star of Mister Hoopley's Funny Crunchy Happy Family Hour?"

"I've seen that," Howard acknowledged, coming to his own conclusions between the lines. Maybe "Wrinkled" Pete Plucnakern was an undercover agent making sure Roberta Bogchar's double identity as an "experimental individual" of MK ULTRA stayed quiet. The Cult of Cold Hands link was a whole new wrinkle, but it hardly seemed implausible. "So you're saying he killed all these people?"

"You tell me, Howard. He was in the next room when Debbie Hondo overdosed on pills. He was there when the boxer Doug Zuthoff supposedly choked on his own vomit. But in time we became good friends. To begin with, I resisted 'Wrinkled' Pete, but so many red flags came up about Trent!"

Chief Tobasco spoke in a relaxed warble and struck Howard as a nice guy. According to him, "Wrinkled" Pete Plucnakern had told him Jocko Cheever was really a deep cover agent whose only past involvement with Roberta was in the attempt to sabotage the punch lines of all her jokes, which were encoded with messages to a group he called "the Gypsy underground," in Amsterdam just before her presumed death in 1974. A hard copy of Trent's comedy album *Plastic Ass Face* currently sells for roughly $100 on Damazon, but free downloads appear to be available. He and his Thinking Lobster troupe had an engaging jokey parlance, even the spurned Chief Tobasco Sound agreed.

Trent Bogchar sent an email requesting Howard's phone number when he saw that article. Chief Tobasco Sound was a good start, but an interview with Roberta Bogchar's erstwhile son might make his career. The MK ULTRA program had supposedly been discontinued in the seventies, and even if that wasn't true, Howard hoped his investigation of this fringe notable might seem sufficiently antique as to escape notice by the programmers, thus perpetuating the eternal balance between yang and yin, as he'd come to see it, in American culture and politics.

HOWARD WAS WATCHING A MOVIE ON YOUTUBE when Betty Bolt showed up unexpectedly in the middle of an elaborate scene of multiple former television stars fucking in somebody's flashback or dreamscape. He hadn't seen her since that day at the café.

"What's that you're watching? Seems pretty free wheeling."

"Oh, some movie." He rattled off the actors' names.

"So what's up with your walls?"

"Hmm, oh yeah, the walls."

In his latest experiment with redecoration, Howard had removed a lot of artwork, leaving lighter colored patches on the white walls which clashed with the brown tinge from years of pot smoke. "I tore down some posters. It felt like my life was following me around." He looked around the messy, crowded room, the coffee table stacked with books, clothes strewn on the floor. "Yeah, I haven't done any housekeeping in about a month. Hopefully you don't mind."

"It's no messier than my current living space," said Betty Bolt, taking a seat on the red square piece of furniture and crossing her legs. Howard had heard Betty had been staying in a mutual friend's closet. "I feel I should tell you," she continued, "I've been diagnosed with post traumatic stress disorder and agoraphobia. I have a great new friend named Plam who also suffers from PTSD. I actually had a panic attack in the middle of the street the other day and ran right up to her apartment. Plam knew exactly what was happening. She understands me."

Howard wasn't sure how to respond. He'd been her boyfriend for almost a year and never noticed any signs. Was he really that thick? "Well, that sucks. I'm glad you have a new friend." The strange movie kept chattering on as they sat there. Howard had completely lost track of the plot. He wanted to fuck Betty Bolt but he didn't want to be her boyfriend again because that would feel like going backwards. He didn't know if she wanted to fuck him or not, he was just preoccupied with fucking.

Their conversation was stilted, Howard bummed a few of her cigarettes and she left. He heated dinner in the Microwave and, when he took his first bite, was immediately conscious of a strange hard object in his mouthful not intended for consumption.

He extracted the same before swallowing to find it was some kind of mechanical component, golden in color, made either of plastic or metal. He decided not to tear it apart, just in case it was integral to holding the whole world together some way he didn't see. That was his thought at the time for some reason. He didn't know if it had come from the salsa or the taco shells or the ground beef or the cheese, all produced by different companies, but it might have been phase one of a clumsy attempt to enforce nanotechnology on unsuspecting consumers (either that, or it was integral to holding the whole world together some way Howard couldn't yet discern).

He decided to preserve it somewhere secret in his house, as a kind of assurance apparent reality wouldn't deconstruct till he was ready. Then again, maybe it's some kind of tracking device, which means I should destroy it. Yeah, that's what I'll do.

His mom said something about "shared control" the next time Howard went over there and he tried to explain AND Thinking as an option independent of that dynamic. "Maybe shared control is just another illusion, like the concept of linear time and everything else apparent. Multiple realities per person are a proven fact in quantum logic now, maybe we choose among infinite possibilities every split-second. It's the opposite of or-based logic, see?"

Which meant all that stuff about a Planet X flyby causing the poles to shift, and whatever the Mayans predicted for 2012 might be entirely mutable by an individual's willpower, he realized. But everything was another expression of the way things deeply were.

Howard's parents had spent years studying the mechanics of meditation, contemplation and mental healing, at a time in history when these pursuits were explicitly condemned as being fantastical or frivolous, far more so than today, when they've become trivialized out of importance in the public eye. He remembered his mom trying to give him "flying lessons" as a child, and he'd grown up with her talk of "doing treatments," keeping silent and away from certain rooms while she was silently meditating. He often failed to show his mother the appropriate degree of respect for setting this precedent, possibly because of an unwillingness on his part to be regulated. A few days later, she called and told him she wanted to make dinner and talk to him about shared control, and what he'd read on the matter, the next time he went over there to help her keep the books. Of course, he hadn't read anything on it, and whatever he thought was only a guess he was living out. "Okay," he said into the mouthpiece.

"OKAY, SHARED CONTROL," HIS MOM BEGAN, SETTING down the plates. She'd made green chili enchiladas, a favorite of Howard's since childhood. She asked if he thought one person's belief or expectation might effect change on the issue of Obama's giant effort at health care reform. Howard chewed his first mouthful, thinking how to respond. He got the feeling his mom thought it was her against everyone else, when really everyone had equal chances, as he wanted to manifest. Or did they? "Well, it's hard to explain in the context of a political issue like that, you might not understand—it isn't like you're doing it for everyone else—but of course I think that's true, sure, okay. You know how people sometimes affirm the inevitability of death, like a kind of custom? I always used to join in when they did that—'Yeah, death'—but I haven't been lately since I don't have any conscious concern about that." He was trying to tell how he felt it was up to every *ndividual* how all such political endeavors played out, and every individual would manifest a *different* result, that the possibilities were, in fact, unlimited, since this was the explanation best suited to his current understanding of reality. His thoughts drifted back to Funk-Burn Willoughby's latest mass mailing, wherein he'd rhapsodized, "This is the age of the Last Minute Miracle! We've only let things get this bad to bask in the inconceivable bliss when it works out to everyone's benefit just as it seems all hope is gone! Because we're *connossieurs* like that!"

"I guess I've never really thought about this in terms of politics," he faltered. "I think those issues are really all sort of distractions from a root misunderstanding or—misapplication—in everyone, um—or most people—that ah—but I don't know."

"So does it seem like things like that, your separateness from political issues, that you actually enjoy that detachment in a way, to bring it into being?" Howard's mom asked him.

"Well, I see what you're saying, but maybe I wouldn't use the word 'enjoy', maybe 'require' is better."

He tried explaining he thought anything was possible for any individual since no one was in the same reality, something he still believed and doubted with every fiber. The next morning, he threw away an old blue chair he'd been dragging around for several years and replaced it with a new square piece he found in the alley behind K ZIP that seemed hopelessly disjoint to the arrangement of furniture in his living room.

"Well, you could move that over here," suggested Alina Vera when she saw how things looked, "and move these over here, to give the room a better flow, then put this here." Howard reconfigured

80

all the furniture in his living room exactly as she'd advised, emptying all the bookshelves and switching them around, saving out unwanted books for the next thrift store pickup, which he saw as a continuance of the same overhaul. This is the room I'll finish my second book in, he thought. The room I'll call home the next part of my life. Now all he needed was a plant for the corner behind him, where a photograph of Huck Finn's house was taped to the wall, its big leaves making shadows around his shoulders as he typed more *Strange Tales of Dim Jim.*

He had dinner with Alina and she treated him to an ice cream cone at Dairy Queen. They parked on a side-street off Broadway and Howard related his failed attempt to freelance for the Turnip, sharing his impression that the editor wasn't being fair, but it was understandable since he'd probably given her the wrong impression of himself at their meeting at the Turnip's upstairs office on Colfax and Franklin. "Genre is illusionary," he'd offered on that occasion, expressing interest in the "more creative type stories." (Insane monster or benevolent genius?).

"Well, it doesn't sound very professional of her not to respond to your email," said Alina.

"But at the same time, I recognize I'm a special case, so she may be completely within her rights, you know, 'That guy was weird, let's not call him back.' Everything seemed to be fine when I left, but I've proposed a few stories since then with no reply at all, which is a shame, but I don't wanna grind any axes, you know. Could just be my destiny or something."

"Well," said Alina. "Sometimes when you feel weird or different, it's something you enjoy, your distinction from everyone else."

"Oh, I'm not saying that—"

Approximately the same conversation he'd had with his mom about enjoying or requiring detachment from the mainstream for the sake of individuality. Another reminder. It made him feel like an unruly kid. And embarrassed to be that. The comfortable failure of that. Alina drove him back to the K ZIP and came inside to see his rearranged apartment. Howard thanked her for inspiring the change. "Sometimes a practical suggestion really helps. It's like seeing yourself from outside."

The last few days he'd been posting bulletins on the Doggerel Facebook page with links to different articles on the site— his piece on the light museum, and interviews with Roulana Deringer and Jordan Sections; Funk-Burn Willoughby's piece about extraterrestrials, "Contact looms as space-time compresses"; and

Johnny Coccaluccio's memorial of his inspirer, late Denver junk-shop owner Sonny Bosley.

A lengthy comment had been posted in response to his article on the light museum, elucidating several points he'd neglected to mention in his own lazy scrim. That interview with Chief Tobasco Sound was next in the rotation. Tom-Roy Peralca had been posting bulletins the last few days advertising his love of freedom, and willingness to fight for it, alongside photos of bikini clad models posing at a shooting range and possibly at the Sufi center with an AK-47.

He got a sales call from this cable provider reminding him about the digital upgrade in a couple of weeks, and prompting him to sign up, and Howard told the sales agent he thought the coming upgrade gave him a good shot at giving up TV altogether, but he'd call her back if he changed his mind. She seemed surprised by his response.

He sent the draft of *Kiabonga!* to a free self publishing service online. For the author pic, he used one of himself sitting on the picnic table outside Greystoke playing guitar, with Ron Selvak, self-appointed host and patron of every residency since he joined the program, smiling approvingly. The cover pic he chose was of a man's worried, staring eyes, the only one of all the built-in images available that seemed to suit the novel's theme, and balanced with the beaming Selvak and the off-the-cuff invented encomiums on the back from imaginary fans with strange names. Howard thought it looked nice. He still hadn't purchased a copy, as he couldn't seem to make the website work, but it was published now. In a couple of scenes the would-be-writer protag, conceived as a cartoon of Howard's "worst side," sneers knowingly about the qualitative inferiority of "self-published" books in perfect self-reflective irony.

HOWARD FLUSHED THE TOILET BEFORE STARTING TO do the accounting at his mom's and the handle fell off, which he thought might be a signal that something was wrong with the flow between them in some way, considering the interconnectedness of all things. When the great tsunami struck, his parents' water heater had broken down and his own toilet across town in the K ZIP had overflowed.

He tried reaffixing the handle, but it wouldn't go back on correctly, sticking out at an angle. He removed the houseplant from the back of the toilet and lifted off the lid, which was already cracked in half and covered with a blue towel, and tried reconnecting it through the tank, but couldn't make it any truer. It gave him the feeling that he was a disrespectful bum and his poor Mom's life was falling apart because of him and it sucked.

"Uh, mom?"

She couldn't fix it either.

"Yeah, I'm not sure what happened, it just fell off when I flushed it."

Alina Vera called that night when he was very high and unexpectedly asked him, "I forget, why did you break up with your last girlfriend?"

"Well, she saw the Stomach MySpace page and at first she thought it was the official Power Mountain litmag. I told her she was wrong, but she'd already formed this whole thing in her mind anyway, then she—ah, have mercy, Alina! What are you gonna ask about next, my relationship with my mother?"

Alina told Howard he sounded bitter and Howard told her he didn't feel bitter and apologized for sounding that way, but yeah, it was weird fucking times.

"All your jokes are hard." she said.

"They're not supposed to be." Howard tried to explain AND Thinking, and not believing in absolutes. "Anything can be proven, and nothing is meant to be. There is no consensus reality. Circumstances don't matter. Only state of being matters," he concluded, quoting a channeled extraterrestrial being called Bashar. He probably didn't explain it as well as he could have

"That kind of deep thinking might keep you from enjoying life."

Their conversation had the same quality of ultimacy as the one he'd had with Tewodros Magness, like an argument with himself about his chances of success. She kept asking him all the worst possible questions, making him face the dismal way he saw his life, and he said things about "not enjoying this existence much," then tried to reassure her he wasn't talking about suicide, and no, he wasn't mad at her, there was just this big shell between him and the outside world, and she was in that unfortunate role at the moment.

"Of the outside world?"

"Yeah, you are, but motivated by sweetness, I mean I know you're trying to help me, and thanks. I just don't believe in absolutes, that's all. You can come up with evidence to prove science, religion, politics or whatever you like, and what happens to you depends on where you invest your faith."

He kept telling her forms of that. Then he mentioned he'd been referring to his apartment in the basement of K ZIP as a "cellar" in the book he was writing about his life since the sidewalk outside the K ZIP was stamped KELLER-LOUP, which translated to "cellar" in German plus "wolf" in French, and maybe that was another gag on Howard by God, since Sad Comic had been wolfish, and Howard felt like a starving wolf.

"A cellar is where you put things for storage," Alina told him. "People hardly ever visit."

"Yeah, that sounds just like my place." One more hard joke.

Whether or not she knew that's what she was doing, when Alina said that bit about enjoying your life, Howard realized he'd begun to slip back into a very deliberate self-perpetuating track of definitions again himself, reminding him of the incredibly liberating nature of the big new philosophy he was really after.

So far he couldn't figure out how to purchase a copy of *Kiabonga!* from the publisher's site. There was no button to press to place your order after you filled out all your information on the checkout page, just one that said "back," and of course, when you pressed that, you were taken to the previous screen, and all the information you'd just entered, including your credit card number, disappeared.

He'd tried three or four times to buy copies, and attempted five or six times already to state his remarkable case, which must have had a simple solution, in the clearest possible terms, with their online customer service department, but the site kept responding with these automated FAQ sheets that never mentioned anything like what Howard was after, and it was driving him blistering fucking nuts. There was no phone number to call.

Fortunately, Lonnie Culot stopped by that afternoon, showed him what to do and Howard ordered a couple of copies. It turned out he had to "zoom out" to make the button needed to place the order appear on his screen, which simple function he'd completely overlooked.

"So Venus Fly Traps are the only meat eating plants," he told Lonnie. "And they only grow in an area where a big meteor struck." He'd read that in a book by John Keel.

"There's more than one kind of meat-eating plant, man," replied Lonnie. "And they grow all over the world, not just in one biome."

"Biome." Howard had completely forgotten the years Lonnie had spent studying botany. "Oh, sorry. Well, thanks for telling me."

While Howard had been getting his degree in deadly jokes at Power Mountain, Lonnie had been tending a turbulent family of someone else's children, and now had a son of his own just learning to walk. "If Chester comes over here, he'll probably be taking a lot of things off shelves," he warned.

"Yeah, I do have a lot of precarious stacks in here."

"But don't worry, I'll shadow him pretty closely. He won't have too much range of movement. Ever since he was born, every room I come into, I think about how he'd react to it, a kind of early warning radar I've developed."

"So what's his sign?"

"Well, he's supposed to be a Capricorn. But all those categories are so general, they could apply to anyone. How is a planet millions of miles away gonna have any effect on you?"

"Well, it does—menstruation, the tides . . ."

"If you read those things in the paper, they could apply to anyone."

"Well, sure, but that's just the sun sign. There are rising signs and moon signs, too. You need all three to get a real horoscope for anyone. And you can't trust the ones in the paper, they just put the sun signs in there and—"

"Since Chester was born," Lonnie said, "I'm a lot more careful about what I trust. Having kids changes the way you think. Scientists disproved astrology years ago."

"Well, scientists, I hate scientists—I don't like any groups who think they have the one true answer about anything. But I believe in astrology. I'm a ram with a lion inside, means I go very fast and I'm sure of myself. I don't wanna argue about it, though. I mean I can't prove anything about this, I'm—"

Lonnie stiffened as if struck. "I won't accept anything else in my life," he avowed. "You can't just discount someone who's spent his whole life depending on science. You can't just disregard people like that. "

"I'm so sorry. I never meant to discount anyone. What I'm

trying to say, you can put your faith anywhere. Everything's true."

"That's not what it sounded like, man. You said you hate scientists." His bad feeling came at Howard in chilling waves.

"No, what I'm saying is nothing is absolutely true. there's no sole truth, since *we imagine everything into existence.* AND Thinking is supposed to be all-inclusive! We have *every chance.* And science just seems so—boring and mechanical compared to that. Do you know what I'm talking about now?"

"Not really, man. It sounds like you're putting down scientists. Makes me worry about you. What about getting a driver's license?"

"Well, uh—"

"Just think how nice it would be to be able to go to the mountains whenever you wanted to do that."

"I'd rather wait until they come out with a totally non-polluting car."

"You'll be waiting a long time, then."

"Yeah, by the time they come out with a non-polluting car, they'll probably have a hovercraft developed, and I'll wait for THAT to come out."

"You got a tissue?"

"And by the time that comes out, they'll develop the personal jet pack, it'll give me something else to wait on, at this rate, I'll be waiting forever – uh, sure, hold on."

Try as he might to laugh it off, Howard was afraid of cold facts, and deeply in love with fantasy. He didn't have any paper towels left so he went to the bathroom, tore some paper off the roll and brought it to Lonnie, who carried a whole other system of laws on his shoulders.

There was a big lit fest coming to town in the next few months, where Howard hoped to find a publisher for the book he'd been writing all year, or at least make some juicy connections. "Make it count," Lonnie warned him.

"Yes, that's occurred to me," Howard assured, with an eye to blunder into something fortunate at the big lit fest upcoming. They each apologized a second time, and Howard patted Lonnie on the shoulder as he walked out of his apartment, hopefully not for the last time. but something felt severed.

There was a car show at East High that afternoon. Howard saw a couple of vintage hotrods on the way to City Park to see Justin Martinez and his wife, Lakshmi, who'd recently moved to New York and were back for a visit. When he got there, he stood beside the playground with everyone else drinking cans of beer from a cooler and talking to the people he knew. Selina Kyle was there, and Kaz and Bosley from Concepciones Gallery, where Howard sacrificed a television with an axe as part of the last Bat Sandwich event on the eve of the 21st century. Kaz had a seven or eight year old son named Benson who kept riding his bicycle around the picnic table where they were sitting with Justin Martinez.

"After being there a while," Justin told Howard, "I realized I've always been a New Yorker." The first event he'd produced in that city had featured Lakshmi in the role of a character in transit from Sri Lanka by ocean vessel, and the songs she sang to keep herself company at sea and narrate the voyage. "She's Indian, but she's totally Americanized, so she used the songs her mother used to sing to her as a kid for inspiration." Justin smiled for the first time telling this part of the story, so Howard could tell it was a tender kind of venture, the most personal part of the show.

"I didn't bring any food to share," he apologized. "but I've got some pot we could smoke."

They walked away from the playground and sat down in the center of the hot grassy field with Justin's brother and cousin and a couple other friends of his and passed a pipe around for a few minutes. Howard spotted Ty Cropper talking to Lakshmi beside the swing set, and walked over to them. "So Lakshmi, Justin was telling me you've been singing."

"I hadn't heard about that," said Ty, smiling graciously. Lakshmi had been In PorchCore before moving to New York. "I'd like to hear it sometime."

It was a hot, bright day. Pits of gravel and green fields around them, garish hot rods from the car show at East High sailing around the park, lots of laughter and shouting and raw emotion from all the kids running around the playground. Howard walked away from Ty and Lakshmi to the porto potty beside an elaborate wooden jungle gym and took a leak inside.

"Not mine," he told the mother and child waiting outside when he emerged, lest they think it was his shit smeared all over the place in there. Then he bowed around saying his goodbyes and walked home through Capitol Hill while the sun set.

THE NEXT MORNING, HOWARD WAS IN HIS bathroom looking at himself in the mirror, getting ready to go over to his mom's house and help her keep the books, when a moth flew out of the sink and the black plastic frame of his glasses came apart in his hands, splitting right at the bridge. He tried sticking the halves back together with some super glue from the drawer in his kitchen, which didn't work, and flecks of super glue dried on both lenses before he could clean them. He went back into the bathroom and looked around for that moth but couldn't find it. Bad eyesight was hard to beat. One of Judson Winkler's monthly fasts, before leaping with faith to Bali and returning as Funk-Burn Willoughby, had evolved into two or three months without glasses, attempting natural healing of his eyesight. Some progress was made over the course of several months, but even he'd given that one up eventually.

Howard still had a pair with an expired prescription on the top shelf of a kitchen cabinet. He put those on and headed for the bus stop, standing there with the broken pair in his pocket as he waited for the bus to come. A police car turned onto his street, symbolizing ordinance, and when Howard saw it he heard himself utter a groan so defeatedly hollow of tone it inspired him to start singing to himself about how the bus was coming, here comes the bus, here it comes, the way Lonnie Culot and he had done as teenagers on acid on their way back and forth through the same honeycomb of a city. He got out of the world in that way for a second.

When the bus came, Howard got on, took a transfer, then sat down behind the back door, picking away at the crust of dried glue on his fingers. He rang the bell right before his stop and the bus rolled past it. "Sir, you passed my stop," he called to the driver.

"*Sir*, you waited too long to ring the bell."

Is he being sarcastic? Does he think I'm being sarcastic? Howard was back in the world. "Okay, how far out of my way do I have to go . . ." The driver let him out before crossing the intersection and Howard ran across one lane of traffic to the stop.

The upstairs bathroom at his mom's house seemed very bright when he arrived, brighter than he'd ever seen it. The broken blue toilet had been replaced by a white one, and the blue tiles around the sink with white ones. After he filled out the deposit slips and stamped all the checks, his mom drove him to an optician located on the ground floor of a building on Cherry Creek Drive, right across from the bus stop where Howard caught the second bus to her house each Monday. "They might be able to make a new pair faster than Caesar Forever," she told him. That was the name of his insurance provider.

Howard waited with his mother in a room full of spectacles on mirrored shelves as the friendly white-haired bear of an optician took his own broken pair into the back of the shop. While they waited, Howard mentioned the idea of moving to Boston and his mom reminded him Caesar Forever didn't offer coverage anywhere in the East Coast, and told him without the deal they were getting from them, his anti-seizure meds would cost four hundred dollars a month.

"Do you know how handcuffed that makes me feel?" Howard flew into a tirade, his constant sensation of psychic and emotional impediment, always there but usually suppressed, suddenly blooming to the surface. "Now here I am in this room full of glass, and ah—"

He threw up his hands and stormed outside for a second to stare at nothing in the parking lot, triggering the cheerful electronic doorbell chime as he stormed back in. The big friendly white-haired bear of an optician shuffled forth from the rear of the store, where he'd been setting Howard's glue-flecked lenses into a new set of frames for him to wear until the new pair was ready. "Did somebody happen to come in just now?"

"No," Howard spilled the beans. "We had an argument and I went outside and came back in. That's why the bell rang."

"Oh, okay!" the bear rumbled in a mellow, jovial voice before returning to the back of the store and emerging with a couple of boards with mounted thicknesses of glass or plastic, explaining how Howard's prescription was twice as thick as the thickest of those if he went with polycarbon lenses, but if he went with trivex ah blah blah blabbity-blah blab like that. It seemed he wanted Howard to choose among the mounted lenses somehow, and was recommending one of them implicitly.

"How am I supposed to choose among these, man? I'm not an optician. Use the one that works best, I don't know!"

His mom must have been having a terrible time, but she wasn't complaining about anything. Howard was grateful for that. Walking back to the car after telling the optometrist to go with whatever he thought was appropriate, he told her, "Thanks for sharing this terrible relationship with me."

Howard's mom laughed slightly. "It's good we can fight with each other and still know everything is all right instead of burning our bridges completely, as people often do. I've counseled people who haven't spoken to their parents in years."

That evening on YouTube Howard saw a video of a young

woman in ambiguous military-looking attire warning earnestly of a plan to covertly implant citizens with nanotechnology disguised as swine flu vaccinations beginning this October, reposted by the same guy who believed in tiny humans and giants all over the planets in our solar system. "They *will* do this. They *will* do this," she repeated, as if giving instructions. "They have projected this thought, this is what they're planning to do." At the end of the clip was a blow-up of a memo purportedly concerning the micro-devices in question, official-looking but also ambiguous.

☻

Outside was a whole neighborhood full of kids and over the years they all ate at this diner, one point in a giant graph of invisible personality and history. That's the kind of thing Dim Jim was always thinking about in those years when he considered himself a philosopher. Deadeye Dick from the Herald Chronicle wandered in looking in for the next big story. "So . . . you're Dim Jim . . ." he ventured.

"Dim Jim Driscoll, none other!"

It's really him! thought Deadeye Dick. He'd heard of the famous Dim Jim. "So . . . you live in these parts?"

"Born and bred!"

"Well, well."

Dim Jim regarded all people and things as examples of the limitless potential inherent in Being. Parts
had been stylized and refined in Deadeye Dick's personality which he'd had chosen to sublimate and suppress in his own. He did not completely approve of all the directions Dick's sample had taken. Even so, everyone was his relative

Suddenly Sheila, raven-haired girl reporter from the Tribune, slipped into a booth with a gaggle of male counterparts, already totally cool with the hardcore diner set of social drop-outs, making the small goatee crouching spiderlike below Deadeye Dick's bottom lip appear totally Insincere and hokey.

"Howdy, ma'am," said Dim Jim as she bustled past, tipping his hat, a magical rainbow of glittering dust spilling forth. There was a lot on his mind.

90

THE CLOCK RANG AND HOWARD WIPED THE sleep out of his eyes before walking out into the living room. There was a knock on the door. He opened it just in time to find a package lying on the doormat. "Thanks," he called after the postman's legs running away up the stairs to more speedy deliveries. "No problem," floated back the voice, just before the sound of K ZIP's front door swinging to. Inside the parcel were two copies of *Kiabonga!*, complete with the two mad staring eyes Howard had chosen for the front, and those quotes he'd made up on the back. A nice looking book, sure to sell like hotcakes. But there was no copyright page. It opened right to chapter one. On the left hand side, which was recognized in the publishing industry as a sign of ill luck. I filled out the form on their site, what happened? Did someone else make a mistake? Did I make one? And the whole thing's already been published online at Metro-Hive, Johnny C's first webzine, doesn't that count? He needed to talk to someone, get some answers, but guessed he would have to "submit a ticket".

Still, he wasn't discouraged. More characters from literature and pop culture were beginning to appear in his real world experience. Howard tracked down one of his favorite figures from Carson McCullers' work, Frankie Addams, on Facebook. Frankie was a tall, thin woman with long brown hair and an open, friendly face who'd been a former coworker of his years ago in the deli of an organic grocery called Health Store. As he was leaving to meet her at her house a few blocks from K ZIP, Howard caught sight of a beautiful fat blue mattress covered by a pattern of silver leaves leaning against the wall of the neighbors' garage, and spent the next ten or fifteen minutes wrestling it down into his apartment, then extracting the previous mattress, a futon covered with anonymous brownish spots, and returning it to the alley where he'd found it a few years earlier. But when he tried to put his sheet on the new mattress it wouldn't fit, kept slipping away from the corners.

"So you're some kind of journalist now?" Frankie asked him when he got to her apartment.

"I just wrote a review of my friend Marvel Kelly's book about escaping from Prxxscorpismics."

"That's cool. But if you think about it, there's not that much difference between falling for Prxxscorpismics propaganda or Catholic propaganda."

"Well, that's true. There's more to it than that with Prxxscorpismics, though. Did you know the founder began as a Satanist? Yeah, he was Lucifer Stokely's acolyte. And Hal Blare began as a Prxxsciorpismicist. Don't get the idea I'm into weird shit, though, I'm not. Except for the Hal Blare gorilla kidnapping cult, I've always been fascinated with that story."

"Yeah, that is what society does in a way. Make nature into a sideshow instead of respecting it."

"It's a metaphor, yeah. See, people need to know this stuff. That's the kind of journalist I wanna be."

"But why did he call it the Cult of Cold Hands?"

"He won't say. No one knows. And it might not even really have been called that anyway. That might just be the media's mistake."

"That's cruel, putting suits on gorillas like that."

"In a way I think Hal Blare sees himself as living out an object lesson about people's sickness."

That evening Howard and Frankie went to a spoken word reading with jazz at a bar called Sparkle on 9th and Lincoln and sat together at a tall table in the center of the crowded room full of dark brown shadows and loud horns. A friend of Frankie's named Serena showed up and said she'd just finished smoking a joint in her car. "Do you have any more?" Howard asked her.

"Man, pot is the worst drug ever!" she responded unexpectedly, with fire in her voice.

"Oh. Well, I think it's different case by case, you know, it has a different effect on everyone."

"I know some people think that. But that's why! 'Cause it seems so harmless!"

Howard admitted too much pot sometimes made interaction with others difficult by driving him too far into himself, but told her he'd always attributed that to his own immoderate use.

"It steaks your thunder!" Serena
insisted. "Well—"

In that moment Howard recognized her as one of the cashiers from Kay Mart on the day He'd gone to buy shoes there. "Hey, do you remember—"

"Alright, *the Sad Comic! A round of applause!*"

Frankie Addams had signed Howard up as the Sad Comic since she remembered him using that pen name. When he reached the stage, the MC leaned down and asked me. "Are you the Sad Comic?"

"I used to be the Sad Comic."

"Well, you just signed up on here as the Sad Comic a few minutes ago."

"No, Frankie signed me up that way. My friend signed me up a few minutes ago. I'm just Howard."

"His name is *Howard!*"

Howard's printer was out of paper so he hadn't brought anything recent. "All right," he began, "here's a little underground Denver history . . ." before bumbling through a piece he'd written sixteen or seventeen years ago concerning their French houseguest Gilbert's comedy of errors with a transsexual prostitute named Doomie Sue Goodman Morgan one night in the living room of the shotgun shack on 18th and Clarkson Howard had shared with Garza Garza. He didn't realize it until the host squinted up from the audience halfway through the piece and gestured for Howard to bend forward, but hardly anyone could hear him because he was too tall for the mic.

"Some underground history," sneered someone in the audience.

Well, he'd know better next time. Serena left during his reading, so Howard never got the chance to recognize her to her face.

Billy Possibility's X-girlfriend Kat Works came over the next day and she and Howard ended up going in on a bag of Miranda's pot, far superior in quality to the strain he'd purchased recently from Lonnie Culot, another batch of which Kat had picked up herself from another source. Before she and Howard left, Kat and Miranda took out their i-phones and demonstrated the features to each other. "Wow, you guys are from the future," Howard observed. "I mean the present."

"We're i-friends now," joked Miranda. "You don't even have a cell phone, do you? Well, at least the man can't track you."

"I was hoping."

Kat Works was a computer whiz, and after they came back from Miranda's apartment she showed him how to include copyright information in the *Kiabonga!* template on the self-publisher without fucking up the pagination, so he could try making that change.

"Thanks, Kat. A lot of simple things I still don't understand, even though I spend most of my time on this computer."

"See, you're from the future, too."

After doing some research on the internet, Howard decided the kind of sheets he needed were called "deep pockets," Swallowing the irony, he decided a trip to Pay Mart was in order.

☻

All the trees were showing off, eagerly flaunting their thousands of beautiful bladelike leaves. Hell yeah, you dirty, pretty braggarts!

Dim Jim told himself as he bumbled along the sidewalk. You living sticks. A drumming, clattering, clearing rain came down making love to the seeds underground, giving life to the blooming things, so many drops it felt like drowning.

Good shot, Rain! he mocked it. You hit another seed! All these joggers, don't they have parks for you people?

All this silently in his own head as he kept on stepping aside to make room for legions of more and more joggers, then one of his legs went right into a rain puddle—*ploosh!*

It's OK I forgive you, but sometimes you're hard on me, Rain, and that's why I respect you.

I'm afraid of you sometimes too.

Whenever your drops come down on me these days I think maybe it might be another new government plague.

For instance right now I don't think it's really raining. Or else why would there be all these joggers? Even the joggers have cell phones now. Everybody has them now but me. Even a kid I saw this afternoon in cowboy boots and purple flares, pacing around outside 7-11 with a cell phone up to his ear, saying into it "Hello! Hello? Charlie?"

Dim Jim didn't like cell phones, no he hated them. No, he didn't understand them. Lately it seemed like there was a person with a cell phone on every corner, making him feel like everyone was tracking him. Why would anyone want a cell phone, he kept asking himself, except in cases of extreme emergency where it makes perfect sense like keeping track of your kids or your parents or something. Just answer me that! He saw something on TV exposing cell phones as potential listening devices, even when turned off. The report didn't specify who might be listening. Dim Jim was glad he didn't have a cell phone, then he realized everyone else had one lately and whatever he said was just as audible on all their devices. Was he one of them too, if he liked it or not?

"God damn it."

Dim Jim didn't like dogs. But he lived in Doggy Park, full of joggers and cell phones and dogs. Not to say I don't like dogs, he kidded himself, but I see a lot of dogs on my postal route, and they have a killer instinct. Sometimes they go mad and tear people to shreds. It's called bloodlust. I give thanks to what there is for all we've got, but I'm more of a cat person, really. Meyow.

HOWARD'S OTHER NEIGHBOR ACROSS THE CELLAR HALL
besides Kotter didn't have a nametag on his mailbox, and Howard
had never seen him. The apartment directly across from Howard's
served as a way station for connections from the Episcopalian mafia
who owned K ZIP. Last night while Howard had been typing, a man
started knocking on that door across the hall and shouting through it
at his unknown neighbor: "I've been here about ten minutes and I
can hear you moving around in there, if you don't let me in soon, I'm
leaving." His neighbor wouldn't let him in. Howard kept typing. About
half an hour passed and there came more knocking on the door
across the hall. This time his neighbor answered. "I'm sorry you're
the second delivery person who's come tonight . . ."

"Oh, did you get the wrong delivery or something?"

"No, actually . . ." began his neighbor in a strangled voice,
but the rest was too muffled to hear.

"Well, thanks for your business!"

Howard heard feet run away up the stairs, then the sound of
his neighbor's door closing. He kept typing. It was Friday night.
Some other new arrivals at K ZIP were having a party in one of the
apartments upstairs, lots of laughter and chattering.

Suddenly a voice outside Howard's window: "Oh, you *are* as
stupid as I think you are!" Then the loud, chilling noise of a walkie-
talkie bleeping on the walkway between this building and the next
one. "Yeah, I see you." Then the walkie-talkie noise moved inside
the building and up the staircase away from his window, and all that
laughter and chatter upstairs fell suddenly silent.

Howard got up, stashed his water pipe and stood near the
door to eavesdrop. He heard old Rosie's murmuring voice out there
talking to the cops, who told someone, "You're going to jail," a few
times.

"You say *I'm* going to jail," came a man's voice in response,
but the rest was too muffled to hear.

Apparently someone had jumped out of one the windows
upstairs and tried to escape from the cops. "I'm not gonna be able to
sleep tonight," Howard heard Rosie say, and a would be mollifying
voice saying: "I really didn't mean for it to be this bad."

After ten or fifteen minutes, the whole thing had settled itself
in some way, and Howard went back to composing the tales of Dim
Jim. In a way, they told him something about his life, and perhaps
they mirrored his life. He wondered about it.

As he was heading for Café Golgotha to meet Frankie
Addams the next afternoon, the character "Ray" from Jonathan
Demme's 1986 film Something Wild confronted him with clenched

fists in the parking lot behind K ZIP: "Hey, do I live above you? Have I been bothering you?"

Ray was wearing a white T shirt and blue jeans with rolled cuffs over a pair of silver toed cowboy boots, black hair slicked straight back, making a sharp widow's peak on his brow. Howard recognized his voice as the one he'd heard negotiating outside his shy neighbor's door before last night's raid. "Well, I don't like the cops, don't bring the cops here. Having parties is fine, just keep it cool."

Howard continued past his unruly neighbor to Café Golgotha, where he and Frankie had a conversation about the Health Store deli where they'd met. "Yeah, I've never been good at, like, personal interaction—I mean with customers—customer service like that," he told her. "That's my biggest flaw. What's yours?"

"My flaw is drinking, actually. I love dancing, but not the bar setting."

"I barely drink, but I like smoking pot."

"I see that as a form of running away from myself."

"I think it's different for everyone." Howard kept looking at Frankie's beautiful hands on the table. "You know, you're one of my favorite characters from all literature. I picture you in a light blue summer dress, with barrettes in your hair, playing jacks on the sidewalk." He had a hard time not worshipping her. "That book starring you was a million times better than *The Heart is a Lonely Hunter* or *Ballad of the Sad Café*, I think. I mean, those are great books, too, but I sure fell in love with your spirit, reading *Member of the Wedding*!"

On their way from the coffee house to a show at the Whammy Room, Frankie told him her father had died on October 11th, and that this time of year she always felt a closer contact with the other side. When she said that, Howard realized the anniversary of his own father's death came the following day, and made a mental note to pay some kind of tribute.

The Whammy Room was a warehouse crowded with people. They stood at the back as the band sang, *Arcadia, where have you gone,* which reminded him of something Frankie had told him that afternoon about indigenous religions outlawed by Christianity masquerading as Christians to survive. "Yeah, like *Santeria*!" he'd exclaimed.

"What's that?"

Howard had explained to Frankie what was to the best of his knowledge some kind of Yoruban blood worship religion that

96

substituted saints for African deities, adherents to which were behind a spate of murders in Matamoros, feeling guilty and stupid the whole time that all he knew about was the psycho stuff, just like before with the Cult of Cold hands. "But maybe that was just some evil offshoot. You know how things get miscast in the media."

Howard's new glasses had thick black frames on top flaring slightly at the sides into black earpieces, and an iron bridge over the nose. The lenses' bottoms had ultra-thin metal frames tending toward invisibility. They were way too tight, but he'd been able to loosen the screw at the base of the right earpiece, which helped somewhat. So far he couldn't figure out how to loosen the left side, which didn't seem to share the "leftie loosie, righty tightie" schematics of its opposite equivalent. Each day wearing them hurt slightly less as Howard's head developed calluses, adapting to the pressure behind his ears. The backs of his ears and the sides of his nose were tender and red. Each day putting on the new glasses felt slightly better than the day before, but by the afternoon, his whole face was killing him.

"I got these new glasses," he told Frankie during intermission, "and they're killing me. They have these little pads for the nose." He took them off and showed her. "I remember having those on my glasses as a little kid, but not on the last several pairs. The earpieces are pressing down hard behind my ears and totally killing me. I hope I'm developing calluses from it somehow. Do you think I will?" he asked her.

"Er—maybe you need to have them adjusted."

After the first set concluded, Howard and Frankie slipped through the crowd to a counter for cups of water. As they waited in line, he told her, "You know, this is very unusual behavior for me, not something I usually do, all these people, so if I seem kind of stiff or startled, I apologize." Like something a mad scientist with three brains might say on venturing forth from his undersea lair for the first time in ten thousand years.

The next band up was electro-matic with a few violins in one corner of the stage and repetitive lyrics asking had they ever wondered what the problem was, or telling them to reach down and grab the gold, my friend, right here underground.

"Hey," said Frankie. A table had come free in front of them. They sat there for another few songs, then Frankie turned her face to Howard and told him, "I'm ready to leave whenever you are." They ducked out through a half-door at the bottom of the curtained wall and she gave him a ride back to K ZIP.

On the way to his mom's to do the bookkeeping the following

morning, Howard went back to see the bearlike optometrist, who was sitting at a small wooden desk in the center of the room full of mirrors and pairs of glasses on glass shelves, just like a spider in the middle of its web. "What can I do for ya?"

"Well, my new glasses are hurting me. I've tried loosening the screws and that didn't seem to help. Can you do anything about that?" Howard took them off and handed them over.

Yeah, you've got the marks," said the white-haired bear, frowning expertly at the red marks on Howard's face from those plastic pads pressing in.

Then he carried Howard's glasses into the back of the store and Howard heard the sound of water flowing. Then he came out and handed them back. "I dipped both earpieces in a bath of hot salt water and bent them outward to lessen the pressure. And I widened the breach on the nose."

As soon as Howard put them back on, it felt better. He thanked the bear and walked through the sunlight to the next bus stop, laughing at himself for ever having thought it was a matter of developing calluses on his face or behind his ears.

It had been Frankie who'd suggested he get them adjusted in the first place. He hoped he hadn't upset anything delicate and important there with all his blubbering and blundering.

Over sushi with her in a small blue former laundromat, Howard owned up about his crush and told her it was making him nervous the last time he'd seen her. He could have gone into the whole difficulty-talking-to-people-since-the-accident thing, (which got worse whenever his heart was in play), but figured he'd try to outsmart himself instead. He felt happy and nervous. "How's work?" he asked next, then immediately realized he was always talking to her about her job writing grants, which she hated, and announced he'd try to work alchemy on that karmic role by finding her a better job.

"I haven't been able to find any jobs myself yet, though," he told her. "I don't want to be a teacher, 'cause I don't feel comfortable leading a group. I just want something like data entry, but so far every lead I get turns out to be a scam. So far I'm just a freelance writer."

He just kept talking, unable to hold back the naked, confessional guts of his personal truth, admitting he didn't have a realistic perspective on the economy and lapsing into into a clumsy confession of how his bookkeeping job for his mom paid way too much and made him too dependent on her for his age. "I'm very grateful for it, though, don't get me wrong. But I'm thinking D.I.Y.'s the way to go instead of working for some corporation. I might try hosting another writing group."

Frankie said she was halfway through paying off her credit card debt, which made Howard feel foolish and small for his own race against likelihood as a would-be freelance writer keeping books for his mother for rent and reliable spending cash late into his thirties like some desperate bum. They finished their dinner, paid the bill, and walked around the condemned high school building with the boarded-up windows then back to her car. The air was cool, the grass was green. her tall beautiful body was walking beside him. "You know what's up with all these pink ribbons?" she asked.

"I think it's a breast cancer thing. Maybe they're having a rally or something."

A woman was walking a dog down the sidewalk across the street. The dog turned its head and barked a friendly greeting as it passed them. "Awww," said Frankie. Then she pointed at another pink ribbon tied into the schoolyard fence. "You ever notice how we never really go after the root causes of things? We use problems as excuses for parties."

"I guess people think it's more effective fighting symptoms or something. So in a way they sort of celebrate the symptoms, to get people's attention. Maybe they're trying to raise awareness."

"Cancer must be a terrible way to die. Seems like that's how most people go anymore."

"So you wanna come back to my place and let me read you some writing?" Howard asked her.

"Okay."

"Good, because I think I really understand you now, and I think it comes out in this new piece I wrote."

"Inspired by my writing?"

"No, just . . . your selfhood."

"Okay, the 'hood." Her laughter jingled in the air between their heads. Was this another magic moment? When they got there, Howard showed Frankie into his living room, explaining how he'd rearranged it recently. She sat down on the square red piece of furniture that had been disjoint to the prior arrangement but fit the new one perfectly and Howard took out his writing. After reading a part about her prettiness making him blubber, he rushed into the next paragraph, trailing off, "So. Yeah. There. That last part's terrible, sorry."

"Can I use your facilities?"

"Sure, it's around there to the right."

When Frankie came back, he asked her, "Is it okay that I have a crush on you?" and she said it was okay. Then he asked if he could kiss her and she said, "I don't know if I'm ready for that yet."

After Frankie left, Howard looked around at all the stacks of books and papers in the room, all the shirts and sweaters and jackets and pants strewn over the crumby rug with its bright film of cat hair. It was a pretty small place, everything was sort of jammed in together. But the ceiling was high. He didn't have a vacuum cleaner either. Most of the clothes were clean, he knew—he'd done a big wash last week—but they were all mixed up with the other stuff now, and he couldn't really tell anymore which was which. Then he noticed the toilet was running and went into the bathroom to try to make it stop. He jiggled the handle, then lifted off the lid and set it down on the floor and looked in. The chain was broken. Howard got a paper clip from the jar on his desk, un-bent it, re-bent it, and rigged a new link. At last the toilet became silent.

"And now the toilet's broken," he muttered, putting the lid back on.

He threw his cigarette into the toilet. It hissed and was silent. He stood in the bathroom door and looked at the living room again. He looked at the bed. The sheets were dirty but still looked clean. There was some popcorn on the floor at the foot of the bed. He got the broom and dustpan from behind the bathroom door, went over and swept up the kernels, then dumped them in the wastebasket brimful of trash on the floor beside his desk and table.

THE PHONE RANG. IT WAS TRENT BOGCHAR. He refuted his former manager Chief Tobasco Sound's claims as nothing but blatant slander. "I'm about to start making the whole world do a double take," he continued in a steely, determined voice, "Few people know this, but there's an inter-dimensional chasm, at the very bottom of the Grand Canyon, and crazy shit is gonna happen in about 42 months when the bottom falls out. That's why I'm doing it now. So far, you know me as a ventriloquist, but that's not all I am. In the new act, *I'm* the dummy! Little Punchy speaks through *me!* Very soon I'll—"

"Wait a minute, are you talking about 2012?"

"More like mid-13. Lotta people gonna have their heads sticking out in a whole other world once it shifts. And their hearts."

Howard kept telling him he had no way of recording their conversation and asking if Trent would let him send a few questions by email, but Trent never answered that appeal.

"What about the moon mission?" Howard hazarded. "They're gonna crash two spaceships into the moon tomorrow—what's that all about?"

"It has to do with the earth's alignment. I'm just going by government files of what they're doing, you know. All that stuff Chief Tobasco's been saying about my father and I getting arrested, it's just bullshit he spreads around the internet to make himself feel powerful. He's the one who's going to jail. He might end up losing his life."

"Well, I'm glad you called, I want to get your side of the story, too. What do you have to say about Joline Larue, the Costa Rican dentist now living in Ontario who Peirson Pierson says is really Roberta Bogchar?"

"Joline Larue's a good woman."

"But is she Roberta Bogchar?"

"She can be anyone she wants to be."

"Is she your mother?"

"She's not my mother, but she can be anyone she wants to be. On planet earth, you can be anyone you want to be. Peirson Pierson just wants to make money. Tonight
will be a very interesting night,"

"Oh yeah, what's happening tonight?"

A pause. "Do you—not have internet capability where you are?"

"Sure I do, I'm just uh—not knowing what's happening tonight."

Trent informed him there was an invitation-only performance

of his Thinking Lobster ventriloquism group at the Trip Ship that night. "I've been holding a grudge for 36 years." He was referring to the fact The Maker and the Marvins were banned from the Trip Ship, formerly their home base, decades ago over the scatological nature of their improv classic, "Self-Digested."

"Oh—uh—break a leg."

"Chief Tobasco Sound is gonna burn," Trent swore darkly before hanging up. Howard decided to get one of those telephone recording devices from Radio Shack after all. That way I'll be ready when he calls. I guess I should have asked why he refused the DNA test. I'll know better next time.

That thing about the spaceships crashing into the moon on purpose was freaky. They said they were looking for water, but maybe they were doing it to knock the moon out of the path of Planet X when it swung by.

Or maybe there really was an interdimensional chasm at the bottom of the Grand Canyon, and it had to do with that somehow. Or it was some kind of weapons test.

That happens tomorrow, Howard realized, right here in the same solar system with me. Will I notice? Hope it doesn't knock the tides off course. As near as Howard could figure it, the giant shift ongoing involved individuals expecting their best and worst ideals into existence, a natural law so obvious now as to be undeniable: What you thought into being, you got.

Of course, what you surrounded yourself with, the books you read, music you heard or created, whatever you did in your life, affected your thoughts, and everyone had a different opinion about what was real, so you had to be selective. Howard knew the media eye was controlled by the fat cats, but he'd been able to use Doggerel to publish articles on DIY writing and Facebook to spread petition links supportive of fair elections and women's rights and the environment, which gave him a satisfying feeling of contending with the world of junk encroaching on his private solace rather than ignoring or denying it. Ancient monks had secluded themselves from the same encroaching junk in favor of God or the gut. Had they been wise or were they cowards?

Was Tewodros Magness really on a visit from the future? And Miranda's silent boyfriend Scott? What was he up to? Why do so many things appear solid if everything's moving? All these questions.

Science fiction prophet F.P. Deringer's widow Roulana commented on or "liked" Howard's every move on Facebook ever since he'd interviewed her, sometimes even leaving comments like, "purr." Howard wondered who was sreally peaking? Roulana or her Petland persona, "Scrappy"?

He hardly ever responded, since Roulana was connected to several right wing political groups, even one called "Patriots For Palin", which characteristic to Howard seemed obscenely contradictory of her late husband's thesis of awakening from the trance imposed by Empire, and directly contrary to Howard's own attempts at manifestation of the new.

One day she posted a clip of UB40's "Red Red Wine" wrongly credited to "UB40 With Bob Marley," and after some inner debate, Howard let her know about the error.

"Well I give up," began her flustered response. "I do know they recorded with him at one point."

Howard knew his Bob Marley from old, and really didn't think they had, but maybe so, and caring about it felt like being stuck to the past. "No blame," he responded. "A common mistake." The last thing he wanted was an argument about reggae music with F.P. Deringer's widow complicating his earnest attempt at dimensional shifting.

.

HOWARD MET FRANKIE AT CAFÉ GOLGOTHA AND raved about the new pair of shoes he'd just purchased at Goodwill. "Tonight I just wore Converse, but these new ones have these silver buckles on the sides, like I always wished I had in high school. It's funny, with all the talk of calluses lately, but they have these thin, hard backs, they're already starting to cut me. I've decided to break 'em in slowly. It always takes a few days."

"I've had some winter shoes misadventures of my own. Maybe I should go to Goodwill, too."

"I didn't look at the women's selection, but I learned that—you know, sometimes you just see one shoe—and today for the first time I took one up to a clerk and asked if the mate was in back—and I guess it always is. *Nondsmertenfwce!* Mm. Excuse me. "

He picked up a napkin from the table and wiped off the clear strings of snot hanging out of his nose. Frankie blinked and said, "Yeah, that could be a good headline for the Turnip: 'Local Man Learns Goodwill Carries Complete Pair of Shoes.'" They laughed about it.

After saying goodnight, Howard walked home very fast through sudden darkness and cold air over sidewalks and sidewalks of unseen symbolic cracks. He felt like he'd crossed an abyss. In the morning after rubbing lotion into the cuts on his face from the new pair of glasses—perhaps the best looking pair he'd ever had—he rubbed vitamin E oil into the cuts in the back of his heels from the new black shoes with silver buckles—perhaps the very best looking pair of shoes he'd ever owned. Assuming this new form took effort, top to bottom.

At Pay Mart, none of the sheets on sale said "deep pockets." He chose a green and black polka dot pattern that was on sale, only hoping it would be the right size. It wasn't, so he went to Goodwill the next day and tried finding the right kind of sheet and was again unsuccessful. Attempting to return it he got into a shouting match with the gay Hispanic clerk since he couldn't find his receipt.

When he got back to K ZIP, he found it in his pocket, but lacked the energy to go back to Goodwill and apologize for shouting "Fuck you!" at the clerk. Howard took to using a sheet with green and yellow stripes provided by his mother. This didn't exactly fit either, but he did the best he could.

His glasses needed adjusting again, so he went back.
This time it wasn't the same old white bear who came out but a younger, smaller version of the same form, like a terrier. Howard told him he'd had them adjusted once already but the right earpiece was pressing in too hard, and asked if he'd loosen them. The terrier

took his glasses into the back of the store as the original bear came out on a separate mission. "How are you doing today?"

"Well, and you?"

Howard worried the terrier wouldn't use water to bend back the earpieces as his superior had done, but he was already gone and maybe these opticians always used that method, so he didn't say anything.

"I hope that's good enough, then," he said when the terrier came back and gave him back his glasses. But by the time Howard got home, the earpieces were already hurting the backs of his ears again and he knew he'd have to go back there at least once more to solve the problem. On the bright side, he was slowly developing a resistance to the hard, stiff backs of those new black shoes with the silver buckles. But why was it taking so long to grow calluses?

Howard did a Google search on "breaking in new shoes," and all the advice had to do with bending out the leather, so he started pulling at it with his hands and trying to stretch it, with near-immediate results, which gave him a fleeting of having come that much closer to figuring out the big mistake he'd been making about reality all his life. On the anniversary of Frankie's dad's death, Howard sent her the poem he'd written about his own dad's death in an email headed "hope this helps." He wasn't trying to rub it in or anything, just show affinity. She'd shown up just in time to remind Howard of the day his own dad died, now he was honoring her anniversary.

●

Dim Jim Driscoll played it cool among the multitudes, wearing shades and a smooth hip suit, chewing bubblegum and glancing at his watch, bullshitting about the stock market, leaning back against a car, just jingling the change in his pocket. Unlike his fellows in the world of suits, he saw right through the true deadly grit of the whole dumb scene to the crazy bullshit of it all underneath. A whole tribe of wild kids made its home in the alley behind Dim Jim's office, with streetwise names like Rattlesnake and Superfreak, just playing cards and rolling dice, nine or ten years old, saying hardened, streetwise things like "Fuck a duck" and "Not 'til the fat lady sings."

He useta gamble with the urchins in the alley on his break, and before long that strange otherworld of feral kids back meant just as much as his job in high finance. He just kept going back and forth, wearing a necktie, complaining of boredom. He wanted to live with his ass in the street just like one of his movie star heroes, standing there in the rain-slick alley, motorcycle helmet cradled in black gloves, hand on hip dramatically pointing at some strange monster bearing down with gnashing teeth. Unfortunately everyone saw him as just some ridiculous businessman darting around in a brown tweed suit. "God DAMN it!" he screamed in private moments, preoccupied with this.

But mostly everything was cool.

THE NEXT MORNING HOWARD CAUGHT THE BUS back to the optical joint and that terrier came out again. "How can I help you?"

"These are really great glasses, but still way too tight, Whatever you did didn't—well, it really seemed to make them worse. I guess the other guy used hot water to bend back the—"

"Let me get Vernon."

The bear emerged, retrieved his new glasses and carried them into the back. I heard the sound of water flowing then he came out and returned them to me. "I didn't want to bend them back all the way, 'cause then what happens, you look down and they slide right off, so what I did is I just bent them back a twinge more on each side." Howard put them on and for the first time, felt no pain at all. "Thanks a lot!"

That afternoon, Howard and Frankie had coffee at Stella's. He asked what her plans for the next few years were (Kat Works had recommended that as a good question for a girl you really cared about, and Howard was starting to think in that style anyway). But Frankie said she didn't really know, and Howard only had his own life planned seven or eight months in advance, so that gambit didn't go anywhere. "Can I tell you something?"

"Sure."

"The other day when you said you could tell my passion was the environment and I said no, my passion was passion?"

"Right."

"Started me thinking. Ever since the last skull fracture, I've had trouble forming sentences, like never before in my life, and it's made me sort of a Humpty-Dumpty about language, where every word has to mean exactly what it describes, if you can understand that. I often wish I'd said things differently. What I should have said was my passion is God, which can mean anything in my book, but what it means to me includes all that: love, sex, the environment, music."

"I think I might like to move to Portland," Frankie told him.

"I have a lot of friends in Portland."

"People from Denver?"

"Mostly people I met at Power Mountain. But my friend Holger Donovan lives there, he's from Denver. I've thought about moving there myself."

Frankie told him she'd come up with three first drafts at the last session of her writing group, and Howard told her he was thinking of co-hosting one of those again in January. "Let's start going to poetry readings," he suggested. "You ever been to that place, Gypsy Hole? "

Frankie gave him a ride home, and driving up the streets past all the parked cars and apartments, Howard got excited and raised his voice. "All these people have unlimited power, they're just stunted and stalled by the effects of what they think they have to do and how little seems possible to them!" Getting out of her car, he added the coda, "Remember how powerful you are. You magic person," and Frankie thanked him. The new version of *Kiabonga!* arrived on his doormat a few minutes after he went inside. It could've been worse. Howard liked the new cover picture better, a cartoon he'd drawn of himself as a stubbly bespectacled boob, and this time it had a copyright page, and the text began on the right hand instead of the left, but all the writing on the back was unintelligible.

His printer was working again, so in the next few days he'd print some hard copies of Stomach number 12. He sent Wilson Bishop an email letting him know hard copies were coming out soon and received a jumbled message in return of different products and their prices incoherently assembled in a cluster. The next day Wilson sent this email: "People are sending me emails in response to emails that I DID NOT SEND.... a junk marketing scheme... I'm very sorry and do not endorse these products!!!' and Howard wrote back, "I thought it was just some weird postmodern gesture."

"I also feel that way," came Wilson's response. "but only love and art etc... really longing to talk to you...running thin lately...but will call soon.. I absolutely promise and look forward to hearing your part of a conversation... its been too long >>> OF COURSE". Howard decided to run that ad scam email in Stomach 12 with the words "love", "art" and "etc" superimposed.

He discovered a plastic rectangle marked "CARBON MONOXIDE monitoring unit" plugged into the wall above the washing machine in the K ZIP laundry room, emitting a high-pitched beep every thirty seconds. He lived with that intrusion to his headspace for a day, waiting for whoever put it there to come back and pick up whatever it was. No one came. At the end of his rope, Howard called old Rosie and explained the situation.

"Oh, I know what that is," she quavered grandmotherly. "Just set it on top of the storage lockers and I'll come see about it when I get back to town."

The device kept on beeping even after Howard unplugged it, so he took out the batteries, too. He saw something on YouTube that evening predicting the imminent announcement of extraterrestrial contact by Obama as step one in a project where benevolent aliens save mother earth from the people infecting it right on the brink of apocalypse. Howard told Frankie about it on Facebook chat and she replied: "That's silly. Gotta run. I'll give you a call about the Hooked on Cold Facts reading tomorrow, k? Bye."

Silly? he thought. It turned out that reading was canceled, so Frankie and Howard went to Golden Bowl, ate Japanese fast food and read their writing at each other in the corner until the place closed. Halloween was coming, so Howard read her his *Tale of Four Skulls*, and her laughter felt like magic in his ears. Then she read him a poem of hers about the US occupation of Iraq while he chewed his curried meal.

"I think if we create our own reality," Howard told Frankie. "we're creating all that kind of stuff too, but unconsciously somehow, all these suffering, warlike cultures piling up unintentionally. You know?"

"But you can't say it's just your illusion. There are people who've spent their whole lives studying those cultures. They really exist."

"Of course they exist. I'm just saying, their relevance in my reality tunnel. I mean, it has a different relevance for everyone, this situation. In human *reality*. You know?" Howard really felt himself to have stumbled upon some kind of magic realization without meaning to as he said that, and wasn't sure Frankie understood, although she nodded.

"I'm looking for a job too," he changed the subject.

"Oh yeah, what brought this on?"

Howard's mother had just formally retired, and the church would begin seeking a replacement pastor after New Year's. "Well, editing Doggerel doesn't pay anything . . . I'm just coming to my senses or something."

Here began another war between the parts of himself believing anything could happen and the ones thinking nothing seemed possible. He really did need another job, but what kind of job could he get? He went home and wrote something about Frankie's long treelike limbs and thought about showing it to her, then threw it away. Fluffy white flakes floated down outside his window, each one indescribably unique. His worst fear was his weakness of making things worse for himself every chance he got.

THAT NIGHT, HOWARD POSTED A LINK ON Facebook promoting the public health option, thinking that might liberate him from the shackles of who provided his seizure pills where. In the morning, after reading about Obama declaring the swine flu pandemic a national emergency, he posted another link, this one to an article he'd seen about the possibility of enforced vaccination for US citizens. Supposedly swine flu vaccine contained mercury and the contaminated fish and fruit he'd heard about, plus, some claimed, a living bit of H1N1, as part of a depopulation program by the global elitists.

Well, goddammit, Howard fumed, if I don't expect it into being, that won't happen to anyone else in the world I'm manifesting. Or will it? And did I expect it somehow without meaning to? Who's in charge of everything?! Which side am I on?!! More insoluble riddles.

He started thinking about Frankie Addams. She was one of his very favorite fictional characters, and so beautiful besides, but she still hadn't called him back. Well, he mused, I guess she's got the message by now and decided she doesn't really want to know a bum like me anyway. Then he reminded himself it had only been two days since he'd last seen her, and nothing had happened to give him that impression, certainly she never had, but he kept slipping right back into the same stupid funk anyway, thinking, Well, I've done it now. She's probably just trying to avoid me at this point. Then Frankie called and right after hanging up, Howard laughed and cried for a second and raised his hands to the sky in gratitude.

A girl with black hair and a squinty face sat in the passenger seat the next time she showed up outside the K ZIP in her white station wagon with softened corners. "This is my friend Plam," said Frankie.

"You know my X-girlfriend, Betty Bolt. She's mentioned you."

She squinted at him from behind her glasses. "You're Betty Bolt's X-boyfriend?"

"Yes."

"Don't think you've ever talked to me about Betty Bolt before, Howard," said Frankie, turning back to look at
him for a second as she started driving up the
street. "No, I haven't."

Thankfully, this time no one pursued it.

Howard had invited Frankie to the light museum since
he knew she was a dancer and would probably like it, but he didn't feel prepared for the experience. Mona hadn't called him since the night he'd flashed his forehead at her, but they'd exchanged a few

comments on Facebook, so everything was cool between them. "Obama declared the swine flu a national emergency and I'm kind of worried about it," he announced as they came to the intersection of Colfax and Washington, passing the Fillmore and the city-state of Argonaut liquors just opposite. "Sorry to be such a downer, it's just freaky."

"Did you know that the swine flu isn't even as harmful as the common cold?" said Plam.

"Yeah, I've just heard some scary stuff about the vaccine, what's in the vaccine, and they're talking about enforced vaccination, which is freaky. I feel like I should tell you guys."

"You know, we're lucky to live in Colorado," Plam sounded bored. "it's one of the best places for guerilla activity."

"Aw geez, I don't want that reality either."

Plam turned around and gave him a dubious look. "You have to be ready to fight for your freedom."

"You really think it's gonna get that bad?"

"I believe that anything is possible, but not everything is probable."

"I believe anything can be proven, but nothing is meant to be."

A song came on the radio—*If this ain't love, you better—let—me—go!*

"Did you know Huey Lewis and the News were the backing band on Elvis Costello's first album?" Howard ventured.

WHEN THEY GOT THERE, HOWARD SPOKE WITH Connie Trask for a few minutes about her inspiration and aims for the light museum, taking mental notes for a followup article. The music was loud, and Connie was only about five feet tall. If he leaned down it was easier to hear what she was saying. She made a point of telling him that she and her late husband had first been inspired to work with light in the sixties by members of the counterculture younger than themselves, "you know, stoned kids."

"Are there any works in progress I can look at?"

Trask led him into a hidden back chamber and showed him a striking blue cat silhouette called "Slim Cat" and a bristling, prickly, red bunch of flames. "I'm asking everyone to give that one a name."

"Blossom," Howard suggested.

"Blossom?"

"Yeah, 'cause it's fire, of course, but you don't need to come right out and say it like that."

A few minutes later, with Frankie standing there, the wizened little woman seemed to ask, "Do you like smoking bowls?"

Had she really said that? Howard leaned down. "What?"

"Smoking bowls."

He still couldn't be positive. "Okay."

"What about her?"

"I don't think she does."

"I do," said Frankie.

"You do?"

She nodded.

"Put that in your article." Connie smiled at him.

Howard looked at her. "I don't know if I should, people might not like that."

"Why not?"

"Well, you're trying to grow a business here, I probably shouldn't put that in the article. The cops might try to shut you down or something."

Connie shrugged and glided away to the music.

Frankie and Howard followed her back to the main room, where Frankie started dancing to the pulses and bleeps coming out of the mounted speakers spaced around the room. Plam looked up from a black couch where she sat sketching in a tablet. "I love electronica!" she raved. Howard sat down at her feet. "It's not really my kind of music."

Frankie Addams was exactly Howard's height, six feet four inches. He kept staring at her beautiful body swirling around and around in a blue dress like a ripple of jagged moonlight dancing, conscious of Plam sitting there and wondering whether she noticed his awe and if so, what she made of it. After Frankie finished dancing, the three of them sat there in the darkness underneath the glowing sculptures and shifting filmstrips. Howard told her, "I thought you never smoked pot."

"You shouldn't have answered for me. I can answer for myself."

"I didn't mean to answer for you, I just thought she said, 'smoking bowls,' so I said, 'I don't think she does'. 'Cause you told me you didn't."

"Next time I'll answer for myself."

On the way back, the wheels of Frankie's car started wobbling and making a loud knocking sound, and Plam said, "I'm gonna stick my nugget out here and see what the wheel's doing." She leaned halfway out the window and looked down, then back in and said, "Yeah, it's doing one of these," shimmying her hand. It was a long way back and the car kept knocking.

They pulled over on 11th and Washington before anything came loose, and Howard heard the happy shouting voice coming out of her phone when Frankie called her friend Steve for a ride the rest of the way home. They stood by the car waiting for him beside a square brown apartment building waiting for Steve to get there. A dry bush stuck out of the pavement.

"Does anyone here believe in predestination?" surveyed Plam.

"Astrology works," said Frankie.

Howard said he thought anything could be true for whoever believed it, "but not as like a curse or a commandment," and the same went for astrology. "But I believe in astrology."

"I'm an atheist," said Plam, "but I believe in spirituality."

Frankie said she believed in The Three Sisters. Howard tried to express that he believed God was a word that applied to what everything was made of, and that he
didn't want to give up words like that since he thought everything deserved that much respect.

"And nothing does," pointed out Plam.

Howard wasn't sure what she meant. "Yeah, everything including nothingness."

Plam was planning to give a letter she'd written to somebody she liked. "Is that how you're gonna make your move?" Howard asked her.

"My 'move?' It's not a chess game, you know."

"Well, this is someone you want to be with, right?"

"'Be with'? It's someone I care about."

"Right, someone you care about, someone you want to be with."

"When you care about someone, you want them to be happy. And if you care about someone, you want them to be with whoever makes them happy," she continued, seeming to gesture at Frankie, who was leaning down into her car to get something. Were they a couple? Was that it?

"Right, I agree with you," he told her. "I have trouble choosing the right words lately, since my second skull fracture. I was in a coma for a month and had to learn to walk and talk again and ever since, I have a hard time finding words I'm looking for. I use the wrong words. That's my excuse."

"Your 'excuse'?" Plam demanded. "Excuses are bullshit. That's a valid reason."

"What is the universe trying to tell me?" broke in Frankie. "Everything was fine until I got the oil changed."

"Do I know Steve?" Howard asked her.

"I don't think you do. I've only known him about two and a half weeks. So he and I have and don't have a history."

Steve arrived just then in a bulky black vehicle, climbed down and poked Frankie's belly. He was burly and tall with short black hair.

"So where'd you come from?" Frankie asked him. "Superior," he fluted in a high-pitched musical accent. That was a town halfway between Boulder and Denver. "You have a spare tire here?"

"It's not a flat," she told him. "Everything was fine until I took it to Meineke yesterday to get the oil changed, now the wheel is about to come off. I don't know what to do."

"What you need to do is come to this party with me."

"I don't know. What I need right now is a coke."

"Well, let's get you a coke."

"Can I leave it parked like this? I think I'm far enough away from the hydrant."

"Absolutely," fluted Steve. They got into his bulky black van and he started driving. Howard thought he heard Frankie call him Esteban so he started to also. "Esteban, I'm Howard." He leaned forward and offered his hand. "If you could drop me off at 1st and Ogden on the way, I'd very much appreciate it."

"You been drinking tonight, bro?" "No?"

"Guess it's just me, then, hahaa."

They pulled up outside a gas station convenience store, and Frankie told Steve or Esteban to open Plam's door, then hers, and he said, "Then open his too, right?" pointing at Howard with a snicker.

Frankie smiled at him then turned back to Howard. "Do you need anything from inside?"

Howard sat there stunned. "No." Esteban got out, went around the back, opening each woman's car door then holding open the convenience store door for both. Frankie came back first, explaining, "He has a thing about opening doors for women," just before Esteban and Plam returned to the car.

"What you need to do, baby, is buy a new car," said Esteban on the way to Howard's place.

"I'm trying to save money."

"So you're going to a party?" Howard asked from the backseat.

"Yes, we're going to a party," answered Steve or Esteban in a satisfied lilting tone.

"You had asked me," Frankie clarified, "but I hadn't decided yet."

Esteban pulled up outside Howard's apartment. When he opened the door and stepped down from the car, an empty fast food cup fell out right after Howard, and for some reason he picked it up and showed it to Steve or Esteban like an offering to his conqueror. "I'll throw this away for you."

The clock read eleven thirty when Howard came inside. He got right into bed and started reading *The Last Picture Show* by Larry McMurtry without paying any attention to the words, in a form of mild shock, mind reeling, something about Coach Puffer's wife. Then he turned off the light and lay flat on his back for about ten minutes before getting up, calling Frankie, and leaving this message: "Sorry to call so late, I just wanted to say, I hope you don't go to that party, because I know you have a lot to deal with tomorrow, but if you do go, I hope you have a good time. I just realized: I'm part of what the universe is telling you. And you're part of what the universe is telling me. I just want it to say something good, you know? Give me a call when you get a chance. Thanks. Bye."

He turned off the lights and got back into bed and lay there. It was yellow and blue behind his eyes. Howard kept wishing Frankie safety, and blessing her over and over, then blessing Steve or Esteban, even though he'd insulted his manhood, then hating him for it briefly, stupid fucking piece of shit, fuck you, then blessing him again, for giving him another chance to face himself, and unlearn hate, then blessing Plam and everyone else whose name came into his mind, then blessing Frankie's name again and lying there all night waiting to fall asleep.

CATERPILLAR MULLINAX LIVED WITH HER TWELVE YEAR old son in an apartment one block over from K ZIP. She was a tattoo artist who felt she didn't fit with local tattoo culture and was "over the hill" at thirty-five. Howard hadn't seen her since that moment on Lala's porch right after King Baker's wake at Post-Normal Café, when he'd been shadow dancing and she'd asked if he was tripping. Just after the biggest fall of snow so far that year, she sent Howard a message on Facebook saying she'd seen him walking around the neighborhood and they should get coffee. They made a plan to meet at Café Golgotha but there weren't any seats when Howard got there, so he stood outside waiting for Caterpillar, who walked up just as an unexpected gust showered white powder over him from a big pine tree in whose branches it had collected. They started heading for another coffee joint nearby down streets of piled of snow. "I thought I was gonna be late," she said as they rounded a corner. "I would've called you if I was, though."

"Well, I don't have a cell phone, so you wouldn't have gotten through."

"What happened to your cell phone?"

"I've just never gotten one."

"Man, how can you walk through a rain storm without getting wet?"

"I know they're common."

When they got to another coffee joint on Broadway called Mozart's, they ordered two cups and sat down. Howard told Caterpillar about Funk-Burn Willoughby's trip to Bali, and tried to explain AND Thinking, winding up, "so I'm trying to train my whole self into manifesting something great."

"You mean like God's Law not man's law?"

"No, 'cause that's another absolute. I'm trying to unlearn absolutes. Each of us is the God of a personal tunnel of Being. All possibilities coexist, is what I'm saying. I think that's what they're getting at when they talk about anomalies in quantum physics. That's where we are in history now."

"Well, I was raised Christian Science, so I know all about manifesting. But isn't that too mushy? Reality was a lot meaner to us before we had science."

"Aw nuts, I don't believe in that stuff." There he was again, no faith in science. Caterpillar reminded him she'd been working on a book about the difference between subjective and objective reality when they'd met years ago, and had been obsessed with that concept all her life.

"Well, okay," Howard said gratefully, "so you know what I

mean. I think science is—maybe not the best form of dealing with nature, you know."

Caterpillar showed Howard her apple. "See that? It looks like an outie bellybutton. Have you noticed that more and more lately the fruit you get is mutated?"

"I hadn't noticed."

"So if our fruit's mutated now, aren't our manifestations mutated too?"

"You're the one getting mutated fruit."

They walked up the snowy street back to Caterpillar's apartment a block away from Howard's to smoke some pot. "All my hotness is going away," she lamented, sitting at a desk by the window. "I'll just wither into a matronly wisp of thin air, I'll just fade." Howard was about to say something complimentary when Caterpillar's son Jake rushed into the living room and growled, "You must not fade!" at her in his best robot accent.

"What do you think about the state of the world, Jacob?" Caterpillar asked her son.

"Sucks."

"It sucks, and how do you feel about that?"

"Yeah, what about personal freedom?" Howard wanted to know.

Jake shrugged his shoulders. "Some things are just illegal. Not everything is legal." It seemed Jake thought he was talking about pot, since he and Jake's mom were smoking some, but Howard was thinking about the swine flu vaccine being poisoned again. "Sure," he said, rather than go into all that. Jake left the room.

Caterpillar looked at Howard. "Well, we've had relatively happy, peaceful lives up till now," she said. "That counts for something, right?"

A wave of self-consciousness rose in Howard's gorge. "Thanks for talking to me about this stuff. It's not the kind of thing you can talk about with—most people, uh . . . I'd better go."

FRANKIE ADDAMS LET HIM READ HER HIS record of their last evening together the next time he saw her, laughing in all the right places but never asking what's the deal with Betty Bolt as he'd hoped she might, or clarifying any of Howard's own assumptive speculations about her love life. "That guy Steve turned out to be sort of a bad guy," she sent. "I shouldn't have let him be so rude to you." That evening she removed the "it's complicated" from her Facebook profile, which Howard supposed meant she was single now.

He ran into an old friend named Rosetta Clark at Café Golgotha the next day. She'd just moved back to Denver after a few months in L.A. where she'd gotten involved with improvisational online jams from musicians all over the world. She'd also known King Baker, so Howard told her about his death. Then he told her his father had died.

"Everyone dies," she assured him. "That's something I'm learning." It wasn't a lesson he wanted to learn, but he was grateful to see her again. Maybe she could play keyboards behind he and Frankie Addams at the light museum sometime.

After Rosetta left, Yago Valdez showed up, very intense and slow talking and serious of manner, that gray beard sticking out of his chin, as he told Howard all about an industry big in Japan called *chindogu* based around pointless "unuseless" inventions, like rolls of toilet paper mounted on hats for all-day hay fever relief. Yago had to invent three things like this each day as a part of the deal with his publisher, who'd found some way to make it pay. "Now what I want to know is: the difference between a blog and an actual website."

"I don't know, man," Howard told him. "I've never been part of that whole blog world."

"Yes, you have. You moved the Stomach to Blogger."

"Well, that's true, but I never really saw it as a different kind of thing, just another place to run the Stomach."

"And Doggerel looks just like a blog."

"Yeah, that's true. I guess I don't know what the difference is, really. Just the way it's set up, I guess."

"And I notice you have some ads on there. How much does that pay?"

"Well, nothing yet. That's just the Google ads."

"My publisher's been talking about starting a new website, so I'm trying to figure out the best way."

Howard thought Yago might have been hoping to involve him in some new internet scheme, or hoping Howard would offer him one, but no. "You just have to do it and hope it works! We all have to! I don't know why I'm shouting at you, I'm trying to give you encouragement."

"All right, man, I'll stay in touch," said Yago, cutting out. Sam Dent showed up just then in a snap-brim cap and black coat, shrewd and businesslike as ever. "Yeah, Dlineator's getting a lot of hits compared to the Doggerel," he observed. "They need to share the wealth."

Sam and Howard walked back to his place. "Hey, you changed everything around," Sam said when he came in. "It looks more spacious."

"Yeah, it has better flow now."

"I knew it was time to leave Chicago when it started getting predictable. Denver's starting to feel the same way."

"Yeah, me too. I miss that feeling of being a foreigner somewhere and reaching for every next step with my mind." Howard had felt that kind of freedom in the nineties when he'd moved to San Francisco once and Austin, Texas twice. Each of these attempts had lasted about six months, and been foiled ultimately by the lack of dependable or tolerable jobs. "My friend Miranda says the longer a plant's in the same soil, it takes on the shape of the pot. These days anywhere I go in Denver, it reminds me of something else from the past."

"I'm sick of wasting time," agreed Sam, then went into a Velvet Underground lyric: "all the politicians makin' crazy sounds."

They talked about truth and fiction in autobiography and Sam Dent formerly Sam Kane (both pseudonyms) encouraged Howard to go ahead and change some of the names in the book he was writing rather than face the trial of getting everyone's permission and living up to all their self-concepts. "For example," Sam told Howard, "that novel of mine being serialized at Doggerel is the autobiography of another pseudonym I've since abandoned. So it's mine to fictionalize at will, if you see what I mean." Then Sam told Howard his real last name, something he'd always kept cryptic before. "Just don't use it in your book. My cousin's looking for me."

"Well, who are we really anyway."

"Good point," Sam allowed.

"So I guess Obama's not a good guy like we wanted."

"It's not his fault," Sam reminded Howard. "He didn't start any of it."

"That's true."

"I really want to go to Paris," said Sam. "I have a strong feeling that's the place where something's gonna happen."

Emma Browne sent Howard an email that evening letting him know she'd just received her copy of *Kiabonga!* "So far I've only read the first paragraph, but that's enough to let me know the whole thing's great."

Howard thought he'd removed all the copies and was surprised there were any available. "Here's hoping I still own the copyright," he typed back. A hard joke. The phone rang. Someone wanted to ask him a series of questions to see if he qualified for a week's paid vacation in Cancun, but he was one year too old.

ON FACEBOOK CHAT, FRANKIE TOLD HOWARD HER astrology showed communication as a challenge or hardship in her life that was potentially a great gift if overcome, and he told her he remembered someone reading his own chart years ago and telling him the same thing "and now I have a tracheotomy scar right on my throat chakra."

"Wow, what do you think that's all about?"

"I don't know, but ever since the accident, I've had trouble talking to people, so it's freaky."

"Sometimes I think I was a beheaded witch in a past life," she sent back.

"Oh yeah?"

"Gotta go. More later."

They met at Café Golgotha the next night around nine thirty and Howard proudly presented her with a copy of Stomach number 12 featuring her Wind poem illustrated by a couple of pics from her Facebook account to which he'd helped himself. "Pure anti-fame in black and white, starring you."

The place was being painted and Frankie attempted to reroute them to the Stingray but Howard had already ordered some tea, so they sat there a few minutes in the fumes, then stepped outside to smoke two cigarettes. It was dark, they tried standing in a few positions and couldn't look at each other without OPEN or EXIT signs of the café shining in their faces. Howard felt like talking about past lives and beheaded witches and their dead fathers, but the moment wasn't right. There was a dog leashed a few feet away jerking back and forth. They kept looking over and sympathizing, "Aww," each time it reached the end of its tether with a jingle clink. Frankie stubbed out her cigarette before finishing it, and Howard said, "Already losing their appeal," in an encouraging voice since he knew she was trying to quit smoking.

"Yeah, I have to say that tasted pretty gross."

Howard thought of throwing away the one she'd just bummed him in a gesture of support, but decided that would seem corny, and smoked it to the end while she stood beside him, unsure whether or not that seemed hypocritical or stupid after being so encouraging about her quitting. "Well, I'm gonna go home and take a bath," she said after he finished. "That's how I'm feeling. I don't think I can do it tomorrow, but we can get together Saturday and do a rehearsal."

☻

One winter evening Dim Jim Driscoll was sitting cross-legged on the floor of his tarpaper shack on the outskirts of town when he felt all these tight, fiery tingles beginning to rankle and sting below his knees and in his ankles. "Hm, I wonder what that feeling is," he twinkled, as the strange feeling kept getting stronger. Dim Jim figured he'd better keep feeling it this time instead of just running away like he always did, whatever this strange burning feeling was, these long, sharp tingles below his knobby knees. He might learn something new if he waited it out this time instead of quickly jumping back at lightning speed, his oversize pantaloons flapping—like the grand flash-daddy he'd always been and was. What the hell is really going on? he wondered. He enjoyed getting down to the nitty-gritty. "Hey there, Love Numbskull," Dim Jim uttered, "do you feel something funny?"

Dim Jim's roommate was lolling back in the cushions like a snail or locust relaxing back into its gossamer web. People thought Love Numbskull was stupid, but he watched dvds about the making of bricks—he knew what it took. "I think your foot's falling asleep," he pronounced, his yellow eyebrow wryly raised in one more sardonic quirk of his nature.

"I must be having a foot attack!" cried Dim Jim, and stood up quickly to let all the blood flow back down his legs into his feet. "Haw haw!" he added.

But it was too soon. He fell over into a chair.

"Oh, sorry!" he sparkled, organizing his neck with a loud, snapping pop like he always did nervously after he did something foolish. The two friends had a good chuckle.

TEWODROS MAGNESS HAD A HABIT OF THREE word Facebook headlines beginning with the same three letters, in homage to a graffiti crew he formerly belonged to. Frankie knew Tewodros too, and had recently left a comment under one of his updates: "How come every time you post another headline, it's exactly what I'm going through?" so on the way to pick up Howard's old friend from the deliberately unjoined Bat Sandwich events, keyboardist and sorceress Rosetta Clark, who'd recently moved back to Denver, Howard asked Frankie, "So you were Recently Totally Deceived?"

"Oh yeah, you saw that?"

"Yeah, what happened?"

"That guy Steve was born a woman!"

""Wow, I couldn't even tell."

"I'm pretty open-minded, I might have gone along with it if he wasn't such a control freak."

It was starting to snow by the time they got to the home of Denver punk-and-weirdness-rock legends Little Kafka and Amerika in the Highlands district, where Rosetta Clark was staying temporarily after returning to Denver from years in Santa Cruz, California, where she'd hosted collaborative online musical seminars. Howard and Frankie did a quick run-through of their set-list in Little K and A's basement, then loaded Rosetta's keyboard into Frankie's car and took the highway to the light museum. By the time they arrived, the snow had turned to rain. They went inside and milled around the rooms with the coterie of hippie regulars.

Connie Trask smoked a joint before they lit up the sculptures, and Howard tried explaining how that was ironic considering his argument with Frankie about what she'd said on their last visit. "You must have noticed! Perhaps you noticed?" Connie smiled and danced away with her stern, kind face and white hair. On his way around the gallery maniacally tidying, Raphael picked up and folded a chair just as Howard was about to sit down but he caught himself just in time. More people arrived and Connie turned off the lights.

The reading began.

Howard's could barely see the page, his vision focused to a pinpoint of blue light, standing in front of them all reading two selections from Tales of Dim Jim behind a black podium. Rather than create obvious illusions, Rosetta Clark used her illusion-projection effects to partially or completely block the viewers' senses, project an illusion of darkness(similar to that of Shadow Lass from DC's Legion of Superheroes), or disorient the audience by making it appear that their skin had vanished. The room was full of intricate acrylic sculptures blinking off and on, the walls scurrying with shifting shapes on film, all the spectators hunched and slumped on padded couches. Howard only read one piece before walking past Rosetta Clark offstage into the corner of darkness beside it.

Frankie stood there. "Aren't you gonna read the other piece?"

"Oh shit!" he hurried back onstage and read the other piece while Rosetta Clark kept playing keyboards and stringing shadows along the ceiling.

Frankie read next, her words rang strongly in the air. She didn't use the mic, just shouted and shook her arms. Inspired by her success, the next time Howard went up, he tried reading that bit about peace symbols seen in the cracks without using the microphone. It seemed to work. After the reading, Frankie was talking to a friend of hers named Samantha with friendly eyes and dark brown hair and Howard walked up to them. "Yeah, we were just taking about how it feels like our jobs are sucking the life out of us," Frankie joked, smiling at him with her loud blue eyes. "Hey," Howard butted in, "I thought about how you said you wanted to be part of the counterculture but you kept on expecting the nine to five syndrome, and that's why I said we should start a band, you know? Are you still into doing that?"

"Um, not at the moment. I think I want to get into graphic design now. Thessaly's gonna hook me up with photoshop, I need a new computer."

"Well, I'm gonna do it," Howard told her. He'd been practicing guitar the last few days and come up with two respectable runs so far.

"You're looking for a new printer, right? A lot of times that has to do with the compatibility of your computer. That's a problem I've had." The electronica got very loud as Howard was saying all this and he found himself shouting at Frankie: "Just do a GOOGLE search on YOUR TYPE of comPUTER, they'll PROBABLY have a LIST of what PRINTERS go WITH it, you KNOW?!!"

He walked away from the two women and sat down on one of the couches too low to the floor. Thessaly came up and handed him a tambourine, high fiving him with the other hand as she did it. Howard gave the thing a half-hearted shake. "You kinda phoned it in, though," she observed.

"Yeah, it's not really my kind of music."

"Yeah, me either."

"Maybe I should just say, 'Yeah!' every few seconds or

something."

"Or just go *huh!* That's pretty popular these
days." "Or just hoowAA!"

One of the hippie regulars turned his head when Howard
made that sound as if he'd taken offense, though the room was
pounding with electronic rhythm and Howard doubted he'd actually
heard him.

Raphael came up to Howard, earnest and bald behind black
frames, a black fringe of hair on the sides of his head. "Rosetta
Clark was just telling me about some events you put on once called
the Bat Sandwich?"

Howard pointed toward the other room, where it was quieter.
They went in there. "Yeah, Bat Sandwich."

"Wow, how stoned would you have to be to come up with
that!" Raphael condescended.

"Heh," Howard faked a tolerant chuckle. "You ever heard of
Situationism?"

"I'm sorry?"

"Never mind. There was no set list at Bat Sandwich, no
specified performers, and each event was like an experiment to see
what form the spontaneity would
take. We got musicians and artists and writers to donate
instruments, typewriters, paper and art supplies, and agree to let
strangers play with them, then we hung signs all over the place
reading YOU ARE THE SHOW."

Raphael had an excited look in his eyes. Howard realized
that if Billy had still been in Denver, he'd probably
have agreed to hold one there, but explained why that couldn't
happen again, with Billy in New York and Garza Garza in Boston,
"and it's been so many years."

"Well, these friends of yours, we could do an internet hookup
to Boston and New York."

"But that sort of defeats the purpose of no set
performer, if you see what I mean. Rosetta Clark does that kind of
thing, though. Talk to her."

The same guy he'd seemed to alarm a few minutes earlier
approached Howard, holding his crumpled gray jacket, which he'd
noticed lying on one of the couches—"Is this yours? May I make a
suggestion?"

"I'll take that." Howard went outside and stood with Frankie
smoking another cigarette and watching drifts of snow pile in the lot.
They both said they were glad to have read with each other and
talked about how some of the words in each of their pieces should

126

have been emphasized or downplayed for greater effect.

After finishing their cigarettes, they went inside and said goodbye to everyone. Little Kafka and Amerika had shown up, they were driving Rosetta Clark back to their house. The guy with the ponytail took time away from walking around in a circle beating a drum to come over and specially thank Howard for coming that night, like their conflict was something personal.

"So I think that beats anyone else's version of Recently Totally Deceived, don't you?" said Frankie, as they approached her snow-covered car. "The person I thought I was dating!"

"Yeah, that's actually never happened to me."

"I know, right?"

Howard kept wondering what Frankie's attraction to that ultimate control freak Esteban said about his own masculinity whenever he opened a door for her or tried to
do her any other favors that might be misconstrued as sexist. At one point, he got a brush out of her front seat and brushed half the snow off her car.

Frankie stood on the other side. "I can get this half."

HOWARD REMEMBERED HOW FRANKIE ADDAMS HAD WISHED people could "change back and forth from boys to girls" in that McCullers novel, how her cousin John Henry had wanted them to be "half boy and half girl," and how their housekeeper, Berenice had wished for a world where "all human beings would be light brown color with blue eyes and black hair." He kept hoping she'd ask him to show her all the peace symbols he'd found in the sidewalk cracks as they swung down the highway toward town, but maybe she thought that was only a metaphor, and it didn't seem like the right time to bring it up. "So that piece I read tonight—about Dim Jim always jumping back—do you see any connection between that and the swine flu thing I pulled the other night with you and Plam? I mean does it help you understand my take on that kind of thing a little better?"

"But why doesn't he just stand there and live his life?"

"Oh, he does! I just wrote a whole episode where he says, 'Jumping back had its place, but standing still was what really counted.' Or something like that. He doesn't see himself as afraid, more like smarter than fear—like he's avoiding it on purpose. I guess that isn't really bravery, though."

"Really?"

Fucking Dim Jim was so hard to explain, and Howard could feel his talking problem coming back the more excited he got trying to relate that uncommon perspective. Almost before he knew it, Frankie and he were deep in a conversation about the difference between surrender and defeat and whether or not Dim Jim's belief in unseen forces trying to program his behavior was realistic.

"You've heard that quote about how you don't have to control people, just control what they think," submitted Frankie. "It's just so much misery. That whole thing of having to starve to be an artist is miserable."

"You ever heard of a book called *Hunger*?"

"No."

"It's by a Norwegian author named Knut Hamsun. The main character won't eat anything unless it's paid for by money he makes from his writing, he's that dedicated."

There was a lot of ice and snow all over the road and the car kept drifting every few seconds.

"And maybe it just has to be that way, in this cancer culture," Howard continued, lifting a metaphor from one of her poems in an attempt to make a connection. "you have to be really dedicated to succeed as an artist. That's one of my favorite books."

"But you don't have to starve."

128

"Well, no, but—"

"Could you wipe off that side window for me?"

"Sure. But it's like seven years of the author's life compressed into a month or something, so it's exaggerated, and—" They slid into another bank. Frankie spun the wheel and they slid back onto the road. "I'm just trying to drive here!"

Frankie thought Howard was trying to argue with her and he thought she was trying to argue with him. Neither one of them wanted to argue. They turned left and started heading south on Broadway.

"I'm sorry, Frankie, you're one of my favorite people, you know." Howard was watching the side of her face and imagined he saw her eyes roll when he said that. "You really are one of my favorite people right now," he continued. "I know you don't want to love me, or be loved by me, but—I promise not to be freaked out about it or weird about it—I just—"

"I think we've already crossed that bridge," she laughed.

"Ah, shit—well, I hope not so far you can't forgive me."

"There's nothing to forgive. I feel like you put me on a pedestal, and I'm not ready for that right now."

"You know why that is? Why I think I make you feel that way? 'Cause I really barely know you—but what I see of your personhood is—"

The talking problem. Howard waved his hands in the air, out of words. "I do, I put you on a pedestal. You're right."

Frankie sighed. "I just feel—pulled a certain way I'm not ready to go. And I'm worried about the financial thing, it's only been one day since I stopped working at my job. Does this street go all the way through?"

"I think so."

They kept driving past hills of white flakes and rows of pointy houses.

"Maybe I was too hard on you about the starving artist thing," she said. "I just don't think it has to be that way at all."

"I'm totally not saying it has to be that way."

"Well, you brought up that book about starving, and you said maybe it has to be that way in this cancer culture."

He tried again. "*Hunger* is a comic novel anyway, it's like a burlesque of tragedy." Howard remembered that phrase from a paper he'd written. Maybe someday I'll show her Maria Giese's film, he thought, where the hero catches a ride with an eighteen wheeler at the ending instead of finding work on an ocean vessel as in the original. "No, I'm dedicated to making my living with art. That's what

129

the whole freelance journalism thing is about. That's why I like *Hunger* so much, since—"

"You have to understand," Frankie broke in, "I come from a family where—we never admit it if a person makes us feel strongly, or makes us angry or upset. The women are all artists, but there are a lot of shady dealings, like a lot of my aunt's paintings just showed up on EBay with jaw-droppingly low prices, so that whole starving artist thing is more than an abstract concept to me. It might even be the reason to explain my own existence, because my mom wanted to be an artist but my grandmother told her, 'You'll never be an artist. You lack dedication,' and talked her into marrying my dad and having kids instead."

Just his luck, now Howard had blundered across the central tragedy of her family history all unknowing. It made him think about all the habits and faults in his own constitution that had their roots in family conditioning. He'd never been without the family safety net financially, for one thing. Starving was an abstract concept to him, it was true. "That's another good thing about bands," he segued, "they make money."

"Bands make money?"

"Enough to get by, I think. Better than writers or artists."

They arrived at the K ZIP. "You're too serious," Frankie chided him.

"No, I'm a comedian!" Howard tried unlocking his door with the buttons embedded in the armrest which took a couple of seconds of windows rolling up and down as Frankie laughed before he found the right one, "Hyuk hyuk, anything for a laugh!" He got out and walked up the front steps.

When he saw her icon glowing green on Facebook chat a few minutes later, sent, "Thanks for talking to me tonight."

"Sure, thanks for listening. I'm not sure what happened, but it was cathartic."

EMMA BROWNE'S PUBLISHING CONTRACT WITH THE VAUNTED Simons & Co. a few years after graduating from Power Mountain came about through a combination of innate talent, practical ambition, and her fortuitous attendance of a literary conference in Georgia where she met the perfect agent. Her first novel made the New York Times bestseller list, and there was buzz about a movie coming soon. She was on a promotional tour, giving readings in bookstores all over the US. Every time she posted another video link on Facebook, Howard reposted it on the Doggerel fan-page. "I just had the opposite experience myself, pretty much," he let her know during their telephone interview. "I wish there was someone to talk to about it, but the whole thing's automated."

"I have a lot of distrust of the whole print on demand vanity press racket anyway," Emma replied, in her Appalachian twang. "My brother got mixed up with this shady agent a long time ago who had him pay to have his manuscript read. It puts less value on the writer, too. It's actually something special that we have, you know, it's something we are able to do that other people in the world are not able to do."

Howard remembered Emma had made herself a sparkly fairy suit with luminous green wings and cloudy glowing hair for Power Mountain graduation, and made a comment that night about how she felt like an unkempt hick from the backwoods among all the intellectuals on Power Mountain, or some other self-deprecation like that. Now here she was at the beginning of a promising life in the world of letters. She'd promised to give him a hand up to the next plane if she got there first, but he realized he had to have something to show for himself before he could ask for her help in good conscience, and *Strange Tales of Dim Jim* wasn't ready to show any publishers yet.

"I agree," he answered. "It's a magical, marvelous thing and I wish it was in greater demand. I'd love to get paid for what I see as my . . . um, magic talent." (Well, what else could he do? Be a dog catcher?)

"It is, it absolutely is magic. When I wrote about the 'magic eye' in my book? There are people in my family who are said to have it. I'm not one of those people, unless being a writer is a way of having the 'magic eye,' then I guess I do have it."

"You sound free."

"That's the way I feel," Emma confirmed. "And I don't want to live my life in any other way. You have to take steps to try to make it happen. And I really believe you can. If you keep putting one foot in front of the other basically and trying to make something happen, it will."

"Thanks for wishing me that, Emma."

"Anytime."

"Marvel Kelly's book on her escape from Prxxscorpismics just came out."

"I know. She's really brave. I think what I write is more emotional than political, about where I come from and the people I know, but I hope there's something universal at the heart of it that any reader could connect with. I usually don't write with any kind of agenda."

It was nice hearing Emma's voice again. After hanging up, Howard wondered what Emma would have thought about Dim Jim Driscoll, which character he'd begun thinking of as a sort of idealized postnormal sad sack he was writing into being in which to inhabit reality after the shift. Could it be?

☻

Dim Jim's first step upon arriving in the Mustard-Custard Culture laid his nose in the dirt, coming, as it did, after he stubbed his toe real hard on one of the frequent plates of sidewalk jutting up too high, as if from the earth's vital turmoil pushing them up from below (which really sent the poor fool sprawling).

"Ah, this land of many hills!" he moaned. "I must get used to this."

Dim Jim started to do the "Getting Used to It Slide," gently rocking back and forth in his tennis shoes and velvet flares, no matter what anyone said, or whatever they do. In no time, he was able to outmaneuver all the sinister bulging forces underground determined to make him trip and fall someday.

"But not anytime soon!" he palavered. "Ah ha ha, they can't trip me! I'm too light on my feet!" The sidewalk still didn't say anything.

Dim Jim felt so light on his feet he just went floating out into the garden over a field of lighted candles with little flames for faces. Ah, the flickering. He saw the world as being divided up among all these preset clubs and teams, different countries and organizations and parties and squads, and unless you joined one of these groups, you were a helpless individual, one lonely voice. That's the way it seemed to be. Then he floated back into his room. "Ha ha, politics!" he chided. "Ha ha, religion! You tried to make a fool out of me with your confidence games—well, it won't work!" Down here in Mustard-

Custard Culture, nicknamed M.C.C., they would all play Jumping Jacks every chance they got, leaving hardly any time for Spiderweb or Rubber Buggy Clusters, two of Dim Jim's favorites. "Soon enough they'll play my games!" he swore. Dim Jim was not a fickle guy; he loved those games.

Some kids were beating on an old trashcan lid and having a small jamboree around a pile of burning trash on Seventeenth Street when Dim Jim flew past. "Thanks, guys!" he shouted, thinking of them as his comrades in some unspecified conflict. "Gotta keep those feelings flowing!" He was on his way back to the Old Campground, where strange angels were said to pay visits, as recorded faithfully in native culture record and colonists' history, and finally get to the bottom of what those strange lights on the prairie stood for. There were bound to be developments.

That first night at the hotel, he lost himself falling right into the luggage-closet, unnoticed by the soft soap-talking salesman on the corner outside, whose cries of "Religion!" and "Politics!" came wafting through the shades pulled down to the sills. Falling asleep that night, Dim Jim went deeper and deeper down into a tree full of stars. Without any reason to run, he was taking it easy, considering what to do next, the painted sides of all the stagecoaches and covered wagons in the hot street outside glowing red in the campfire's reflected light. The colonists knew all along what was going to happen.

The natives didn't. Or maybe they did in a way.

Oh, it was all so strange to think of!

SO HE'D GONE TO A LASER MUSEUM with a character from a Carson McCullers novel barely known to modern readers. That was the problem of meaning for writers. All the impossible seeming characters were veiled representations of actual celebrities and conspiracies Howard came across in his adventures as a freelance writer at the end of time. He just changed the names, a few crucial particulars, and in one sense, the gender, to avoid being rubbed out by someone or other. That's why the critics carved it into thousands of little official classifications like "fiction" and "memoir" and "creative nonfiction". Everything felt very different. Howard hadn't been in a real relationship since the one with Betty Bolt, throughout which he felt like he'd been smiling with half his face in some way. Before which he'd played the foil for Marlene's troubled soul. Whenever she came back, the stars would change color again. But this time it felt different. He took a deep breath and called Frankie Addams, whoever she was or would be from now on. "Can we start over?" he began.

"Sure."

"I'll go first. We used to work together in the deli at Health Store. We never really got to know each other well, but we were friendly. I remember you always wearing a denim jacket. We had New Mexico in common but we never talked about it. I dated the coffee shop girl, Sn—"

"What are you doing?"

"I'm trying to start over, see."

"I don't think that's

necessary." "Okay, well uh—"

Howard told Frankie he'd written all about their reading at the light museum and convinced her to let him email her that chapter. "But I don't wanna do it unless you'd really like to read it. I mean I don't want to force myself on you or anything." Howard was smooth. Next he tried tying up all the loose ends in one deft spasm, winding up like so: "'Cause I could use a friend. I guess we've both got our love lives, but we can keep those sep—"

"Wait a minute, what?"

Howard was trying to lead up to some kind of conclusion there, but his approach was too indirect. "Well—I guess we're really not compatible as lovers, I mean—you have this love of going out to nightclubs and slam poetry uh so—"

"Yeah, I thought we resolved that."

Um uh, blubber glub duh . . . "Well, you may have resolved it right away, but I was still love-struck."

"Yeah, is that still the case?"

If Howard said he wasn't still love-struck, she might think he'd considered loving her a passing fancy. If he told her it was all he'd thought about or felt for weeks, she'd recognize him as delusional. There he was, sealed in a trap of his own devise, just like Dim Jim and his compulsive need to escape apparent reality over and over again. Could it be that Howard and all the other people in his life were actually playing out a crucial analog of human destiny, not merely bungling along as themselves? It seemed likely. "Aw, fuck, Frankie, I don't know."

After hanging up, he remembered Frankie telling him learning to listen was step one in learning to love yourself on that night at the light museum when she thought he'd been answering for her. She sent him an email the next day saying she was offended by the latest piece he'd written starring her, and felt attacked especially by the part about Howard thinking Plam and she might have been lovers. She said she belonged to no club and was a member of nothing in the world. Howard called her right away and would-be-cleverly thanked her for showing him Dim Jim's dark side. "I never knew he had one."

"Of course. Any three dimensional character would."

"But I want you to know, I never attack anyone in my writing, this is never my intention."

"Sometimes intentions are different from effects."

"Wasn't my effect either, no, what I was trying to express—" Frankie hung up. First Howard's problem was not enough words, now it was too many, or the wrong ones or the right ones. Frankie had become an unjoined person who hung around in doorways, and she was afraid. Well, maybe things were too mushy. Howard went back over the piece he'd shown her and everything seemed to be fine. He sent Thessaly a chat: "Frankie's mad at me."

"Yes, well . . ."

She let Howard know Frankie felt he'd ignored her when she told him she wasn't interested in him romantically, instead persisting in his delusional attitude, even sending her some writing about it—"and I'd call it lazy writing since it depicted actual conversations and events."

"But that's what I do," Howard sent back, "Write down my life. Self-deprecating humor."

Howard's unfortunate fetish for unrequited love really got in the way sometimes. Those pages he'd sent were intended to make a joke out of their evening together by emphasizing his love-struck discomfort. Howard was just making fun of *himself* for being so stuck on the mystery he'd made out of who Frankie might really be, just drawing a picture of *himself* cracking up, not trying to make any kind of pronouncement on who or what *she* was besides the object of his foolishness, couldn't she see? I'm the holy fool, baby, that's lazy? I make an ass out of myself again and again for the sake of a higher standard. For the common good. Like Inspector Clouseau or Arturo Bandini or *Hunger*'s nameless hero! That's not lazy! Is it? But he didn't say any of that out loud. "Are you planning to make the party at my place this evening, or would that seem disloyal in some way?"

Thessaly declined, "but keep in touch, Howard."

Just like before with Alina and Sadie, Howard found it easier to relate to Frankie's best friend than she herself. Or was Plam her best friend? Or was she Betty Bolt's? Rosetta Clark hadn't sent him an email or called since his formal rejection by Frankie, probably out of loyalty to her. They were friends now. Everyone else had friends. Unlike me, he thought. Howard went into the bathroom and looked at himself in the mirror. His misshapen forehead. The scar on his throat. Had Sad Comic said something wrong to deserve all these wounds? It seemed likely, considering all the bum kicks.

He remembered how intent his dad had been on telling him one last thing from his deathbed once unable to form words or make any sound. Was it something about his responsibility to his mother? Was he saying, "Get a job, you lazy bum"? Well then, what kind of job could he get? A library somewhere, perhaps? Data entry? He applied for a couple of writing positions on Craigslist, which filled him with a sense of hope and purpose, then he remembered having felt this way before via Craigslist without any ultimate benefit, which brought him right back down again, kerthump. In the morning on the way back with his donuts, he stepped over that board on the sidewalk again, this time heading in the other direction. He wanted back out of wherever he found himself suddenly.

Howard's friend from late in the Sad Comic period Julia Mathers came over and paid him a visit at K ZIP that afternoon with red hair and a pair of silver glasses shaped like oversized cat's eyes. Julia was back in Denver staying with her parents after the dissolution of her marriage to a guy named Fowler Howard hadn't met, with whom she had a year old son named Terry.

Howard remembered Lonnie Culot telling him about the "second sense" he'd developed since his son's birth, and Tom-Roy Peralca's declaration there were two types in the world, those with kids and those without. Along with all those powerful feelings of parenthood, now Julia was dealing with the unfinished bruise of a broken relationship too.

"But everything's okay," she said. "All you can do is love yourself and your kiddo and enjoy as much of it as possible and let the rest just blow away in the breeze or run down the drain with the shower water or whatever." He'd had a crush on her for years, but her son needed a new father now, and Howard was only beginning to father himself. "You ever read to Terry?"

"Sometimes."

"I'm writing this book for kids called *Tales of Dim Jim*. I guess he's still too young, though. I'm never sure where to draw that line."

In the next few days Howard was throwing a party at K ZIP for his old friend Gustav Harkness, who was about to move to Berlin for a few months and make a new movie with Howard's old friend Billy's younger brother Benjy Possibility. Julia said she'd try to make it, but might be too tired after her shift at Cafe Post-Normal.

He ran into his neighbor Gabe Kotter in the hallway cradling a purple plastic crate. The door to his apartment was open. "You moving out, Gabe?"

"I am," he said pleasantly. "Reminds me of the time my uncle Salvatore Kotter passed a gallstone, summer of '56."

Kotter lived right across the hall, and might have smelled him smoking pot from time to time, but was always friendly, and once Howard had overheard him chatting with someone in the hall about problems he'd had with the K ZIP heating, which Howard could relate to. The night before had been so cold in his own apartment he'd worn long underwear and a jacket and turned up the heat all the way, putting on shoes to warm his feet, and even considering putting on gloves, but no matter how many layers he added, he still felt that cold tingling deep in his bones. At the top of the stairs a curly-headed former student of Kotter's in a sleeveless denim jacket held the door open for Howard, who noticed there was an orange U-Haul truck in the sunlit parking lot full of more of the purple crates. "Nice knowing ya, Gabe."

SPACE DAVE, A HALCYON ZYLON RESEARCH EMPLOYEE, was first to arrive for Howard's party that evening. "Can I put this in here?" He leaned his bike against the bookshelves just inside the door. "I don't have a lock right now."

"Sure, that's cool."

"The air smells clean in here." Space Dave removed his glasses and started wiping them off with his shirt. "You're not smoking cigarettes, that's good."

"The landlady called me today asking if I'd been smoking cigars in here. I think it's the tenants upstairs. They have parties a lot, had the cops here once so far, and sometimes I hear 'em up there shouting, singing, laughing, stamping their feet . . . I guess they smoke cigars, too."

Kat Works came, and Howard's old roommate and fellow former Zylon research interviewer Gordon Callahan. Gus arrived in a padded aviator's helmet, carrying a portable dvd player. Howard's friends Bellamy and Caterpillar came by, and Lala, who he hadn't seen since King Baker's wake. Playing Scrabble online with her recently, he'd been pushing through words that couldn't be real, like "badhiuluwu" or "foex," but the game kept giving him credit, which he'd reveled in as a sign of reality's porous nature, like those peace symbols in the sidewalk cracks, but as it turned out, they'd unknowingly been playing a version of that game designed to let players make up words and bluff unless challenged—oops. But it sure had felt good while it lasted, to see something unlogical proven in virtual logic like that.

What was it Maria Reynolds had said at his other party? Sites like Google and Wikipedia were the external manifestation of our collective consciousness. Howard remembered Miranda telling him the internet already had him. Spiritual masters had been calling life a game all along, and recently Howard had started thinking of his own as a video game, where each move guaranteed success or failure according to your inner sense. This hypothesis seemed to accommodate AND Thinking, since it allowed for unlimited outcomes. At the same time, objective facts like dogs smelling fear seemed almost to bear it out. Howard felt perhaps he'd stumbled onto something crucial when this last occurred to him, but held his peace, as it didn't seem the proper venue. Gordon Callahan started talking about a trip to Buenos Aires he'd taken earlier this year to visit a cousin who worked there. He said there were prisons in Argentina where inmates convicted of drug offenses spent their prison terms packing and shipping drugs to pay for their imprisonment. "They've really turned the so called drug war into an industry."

"Do you have any water?" asked Caterpillar.

"I do," Howard told her. "It's even filtered water or, you know, spring water or something." He emptied another twelve bottles each couple of days, but Rosie didn't recycle, so he'd been dumping in the next door neighbors' cans, always hoping there'd be enough room. Sure was a lot of plastic.

"But does it still have the fluoride that hardens and encapsulates the pineal gland?"

"Haha, is that what it does?" Howard opened the refrigerator. There was a rubber magnet on the door of his freezer compartment emblazoned with a winking capped head, which he'd colored in with a green marker shortly after it came in the junk mail. HELP IS ON THE WAY!, the jovial green head shouted, giving Howard a knowing wink, that he might BUY THIS NOW! "I'm not sure, it isn't listed on the label anyway." Howard still thought about fluoride every time he brushed his teeth or took a shower.

That recording device he'd picked up after receiving the call from Trent Bogchar was still hooked to the phone underneath Howard's desk. Bellamy spotted it and frowned. "You record your phone calls?"

"Just interviews."

Like Caterpillar, Bellamy had fallen for Sad Comic In the years of all day cigarettes and coffee every day at Café Post-Normal. Years later she played cello in Ty Cropper's band PorchCore. She had a sympathetic nature. When Howard told her people had been pointing out the scar on his throat and it was making him self conscious, he remembered Bellamy had said, "Why can't they just think it's your birthmark?"

"So where's Bellamy tonight?" Howard asked her now. (She was engaged to a man also named Bellamy, her apparent ideal counterpart).

"Oh, he had to work tonight."

Everyone huddled around Gus's portable DVD player to watch his new film, *The Subhuman Love Song*. He'd brought a couple of sections, both concerning orphans pining for their parents, metaphorical and actual, in different strange ways, and intelligently satirizing the self-indulgent performance artists popular in super cities like Berlin and New York. There was a lot on Howard's mind, which made it hard to pay attention to the plot. Was he in love with Frankie Addams? Was it fucking he wanted or love? Was Dim Jim brave? Was Howard evil? Did he deserve to be destroyed? Wa he good? Did he deserve salvation? Was Dim Jim trying to escape?

Was he a coward? So now I'm trying to answer for Frankie's affection, meanwhile questioning her family's whole concept of art and dedication like the ultimate control freak, and throwing up my two-dimensional superhero of avoidance like a defensive hex on misfortune. That's how it must look to her, he realized. She didn't even seem to *notice* what *he* thought he was quite *obviously* doing in writing about her, namely lampooning *himself* for being so preoccupied with the unobtainable goal of her *love!*

Wait a minute, is that what I'm doing? That is. That's what I'm doing. And why am I doing *that?* Are the Dim Jim tales my subconscious mind's way of telling me something about myself? Well, shit. He always has these unjoined comrades like negative space to pit himself against: the armchair scientist Maxson; that acrobatic circus numbskull arching eyebrow quirks. Just like me and my friends, he saw clearly, far distant and distinct, but together somehow, but maybe only in my mind. Even Sam Dent had grown distant. The cellar apartment felt crowded and drowsy and warm. He was starting to drift by the time A segment of film featuring co-director Benjy Possibility came onscreen, which revived him temporarily. He looked forward to seeing the rest of it in a better mental frame.

●

Dim Jim's beard took a long time to fill out. At first it just looked like he needed a shave, and he considered buying some tar or molasses to darken the bristles, but no. "I have to be patient," he cautioned himself. "It's the same thing that happened before with those tight, fiery tingles just before my foot attack. Love Numbskull saw—I'm always jumping back too soon." Each day his bristles grew darker and darker, and after about a week or so, Dim Jim felt like a brand new man with his new bearded face reflected in all the shop windows and pools of melted snow all over the sidewalk. One day on the way to the bingo parlor to meet Love Numbskull for tea, Dim Jim passed a couple of gypsies sitting together on the sidewalk engaged in earnest conversation. He smiled at them.

The road was full of potholes and a couple of cars came bumbling down it, making clanking sounds. Dim Jim smiled at the drivers. When he got to the bingo parlor, he noticed another two gypsies perched high in the bleachers engaged in the same kind of earnest confab as the earlier pair he'd seen. He smiled at them.

Love Numbskull arrived and joined a game of bingo that was starting. Mrs. Harkington Marx of the town blacksmith's office

140

won three or four hands, and Love Numbskull won two. Dim Jim didn't play, just sat there supping a cup of peppermint tea, soaking up all the friendship and confidence. More gypsies showed up and entered quiet dialogues with one another in the rafters.

Jumping back had its place, but sometimes Dim Jim wondered what he might be missing out on. Standing still instead was a great temptation that always tormented him in all of his rustling and rousting about and bustling. Dim Jim was conflicted. He wanted to jump, but then again be here now. He knew about time and he knew about faith, but what about everything else?

EVERY DECEMBER SINCE HIS DAD'S DEATH, HOWARD'S mom requested his assistance with some aspect of the Christmas tree tradition. When he got to her house one week, near the same Ballardian commercial district as Sam Dent's current place, Howard stood beside the Christmas tree holding it up while she screwed its base into a green and red metal stand.

"What is it about you and Christmas trees?" he asked her. "It's a kind of punctuation mark to end the year for me." "Well, that makes sense."

His mom tried cooking chicken vindaloo for the first time on Christmas day. She seemed dissatisfied with the result and inordinately pleased when Howard requested a second helping. They started talking about Howard's last trip to the Caesar Forever approved doctor to find out what had gone wrong with his leg after that road trip to Culchack Corners and back with Betty Bolt. "He kept asking me whether or not it hurt—but it wasn't a pain, I could just tell it was loose. And you'd think he could tell, some doctor, getting paid thousands or millions to know about that kind of thing—"

"Well, he probably just wasn't a joint specialist."

"He said I could make an appointment with physical therapy, but isn't that just motions and exercises?"

"I think so."

They agreed the world was in a crazy time, politically and otherwise, and in a watershed moment, Howard seemingly won her over for the first time to the notion of a secret government. You'd think two illegal George Bush war-fests might have done the trick, but he thought it was the health care bill, which had looked so fair at first but now seemed flawed to everyone, plus the snazzy new president's failure thus far to effect any of the sweeping change he'd suggested was imminent. "But for all we know, he's not really in charge of anything anyway."

"I'm afraid that's right." Howard's mom shook her head.

"I'm not saying everyone should fear the government, but just dismissing every scary thing you hear as a 'conspiracy theory'— just because you hope it isn't true—that doesn't make any sense either."

"That's true."

Sensing his advantage, Howard showed her examples from all over the world he'd noticed recently on YouTube of an ongoing UFO flap everywhere but in the US, plus a couple of dramatic examples in-country, including one sighting in the town her parents had lived in. According to several of the videos recommended for him by YouTube based on his viewing preferences, a big public

Disclosure of the U.S. government's longstanding connection with one or several extraterrestrial races was expected to occur very soon in conjunction with earth's passage through some huge strange galactic cloud, which allegedly caused the Haiti earthquake and the one in Northridge, CA.

"Have you ever heard of Carl Gustav Jung?" his mom asked.

"Of course."

"And you know what he said UFOS were?"

"Oh, projections of the subconscious mind or the unconscious mind or something."

"Right."

"And I think that's true in a way," Howard admitted. "But it's an earth-bound truth. I mean maybe that's not *all* they are. Whatever they are. For instance everything in material reality is really a bunch of atoms in motion, right, and we only think it's real—or stable? Right?"

"Well, yes, quantum science proves that."

"So maybe the same thing is happening here, only on a more elaborate level. I mean, it's pretty elaborate imagining a whole other person, right? But we do that all the time, we're doing it *right now,* for instance, and maybe the same thing is at work when we imagine UFOS or a ghost, or whatever it is we make ourselves see. They're just as *real* as we are."

Howard had the feeling everything was about to catch up with him suddenly. He'd read a lot of books over the years about the ancient astronauts who founded humanity in ancient Sumer in their desire for "intelligent slaves," and never doubted that thesis since, but had allowed his faith to lapse, since it didn't seem pertinent to his progress as a freelance writer.

"I believe that humans have an innate myth-making ability," his mom proposed when Howard brought that one up.

"Well, of course they do, but this isn't even presented as fiction or anything, this is their history, the Sumerians."

"Well, you don't think, for instance, that Greek mythology is based on actual historical events, do you?" she asked.

"Well—but they have so much in common with so many other myths—you know how myths have things in common, representing the same figures, or concepts, right? Like a sun god or whatever."

"Go on."

"Well—I think since they have so much in common, they're probably based on some prehistoric happening really, wherever they first began."

"What are you saying they have in common, and who with?" He'd just seen a documentary on YouTube citing the commonality in different cultures' hieroglyphic representation of three or four different gods, and how all the ancient pantheons on both sides of the Atlantic Ocean paralleled the one set forth by the Sumerians. "Well, Gilgamesh, the Bible. The whole Noah's Ark story is in the Sumerian myths but he has a different name. Utnapishtim, I think. And Moses is Musa. Supposedly they're all the same, but they have different names because of all the languages there are—but even those have a similar sound . . . I don't know."

"So how do you feel about this?" His mom asked. "Mostly positive or mostly negative, excited, confused or what?"

In the last several days he'd seen sites proclaiming an official cover up so extreme that Earth's immediate atmosphere, just beyond the naked eye, was infested with warring spacecraft. There'd been postings on YouTube that morning of a seven mile long ship above the South Pole, but when he clicked on the link to show her, it was gone. "So that was either a bluff or it's been removed. But there's a guy who can summon them using ancient invocations from the Torah. He just holds his hands up like this and says, 'Oh, hallelu Yahweh' like that, and little silver orbs appear. It's on YouTube, and other people are doing it now too, reading the same verses, holding their hands up the same way, and making these little silver orbs appear."

With all her years of study, Howard's mom would understand the metaphysical lesson of being confronted with the seemingly impossible and bravely following through. That was the very essence of TAOUBT, not to mention AND Thinking, but it was such a giant feeling that he couldn't boil it down to simple words.

There he was trying to prove the existence of extraterrestrial life to his own mother, seemingly contradicting himself with a very definite point of opinion. A position he felt pressed into by his feelings.

Like telling Alina he didn't like life.

Telling Lonnie he hated scientists.

Like a kid at the wheel of a hot rod, a monkey stuffed into a clown suit. Was he making a mistake? Mere language, with all its built-in delays of finding the right words and explaining and not understanding and misinterpreting seemed inadequate to telling this gigantic feeling. Was there really anything to understand?

"I gotta agree with you that a significant buzz is sounding about extraterrestrial activity," sent Lamar Cobson that evening. "Even mainstream sources. Maybe something really is about to come out. For some reason though, that possibility does not engage my imagination on the same level as supernatural activity right here on Earth does. But perhaps they are the same thing. I remain open to the idea of extraterrestrial activity nonetheless."

Sent Funk-Burn Willoughby, "the most important thing to me is that *I* know ETs are real and are here, and *I* am doing everything in my power to share that information in a fun and exciting way with the world :) :) I sure hope disclosure does happen... it's time for reality to completely crack!" His most recent mass-mailing included an invitation to their latest spoon bending party. This ability, to make spoons bend using telepathic force, seemed like another perfect metaphor for transition from this dimension to another where will is undeniably the shaper. "Physics is showing us in greater and greater detail each day that the world that seemed so solid is a projection of our minds," Funk-Burn wrote. "The outer changes we look for are NOTHING BUT inner changes."

Miranda seemed listless when Howard stopped in for a bag, wearily resigned to the current proliferation of medical marijuana dispensaries driving black market dealers like herself out of business. "It's so obvious what they're trying to do, it's just some novelty for people, they think, *'Ooohh, purple weed,'* and it's really not even that good."

He told her about all the symbols he'd seen in the sidewalk cracks. "The first one I saw looked too symmetrical not to be man made. It was probably man-made. Just over there." He pointed in the direction where it was, half a block away outside. "But I kept walking and came across all these others that were definitely natural. Like the earth saying something. You know?"

"Okay." She looked at him.

"So how's Scott?"

"Oh. We broke up."

Scott's black acoustic guitar remained in its stand beside Miranda's couch. "I've always had a crush on that guitar," ventured Howard. "Would you ever consider selling it?"

"Well, it's not mine, really."

"Okay. Um. So have you seen that footage on YouTube that's supposed to be of a few mysterious spacecraft circling the sun?"

"How could they be circling the *sun*," she started, Virgil to his Dante, "the sun is billions of degrees—"

"Well, but maybe we don't know everything, about what's really going on, what's possible with science or anything else like that. Because the information's so tightly controlled, or that there's so much disinformation now, we can't tell which parts are true, so we have to read between the lines."

Miranda frowned. "Yeah."

"And if they're aliens, they may have a whole different . . . concept, you know?"

"Right."

"Maybe nothing is true, but maybe there's some hidden *truth* to it all somehow, right?"

"Well, let's hope so."

After a few days went by and nothing further appeared in the sky or on YouTube, Howard slipped back into his usual state of false complacency.

Miranda posted something about "getting the fuck out of dodge" on Facebook, and the next time he called, her line had been disconnected. Howard walked over to her place and looked in the windows. The apartment was completely cleaned out. He contacted Clipper, who got him a bag from a dispensary. Miranda had been Howard's de-facto confessor through some hard times, and he romanticized her sudden absence as more proof of the great change ongoing, as if she'd been too pure and fair to remain in this hell-realm. Howard was glad she'd broken up with Scott before burning away, whatever his unspoken mission in Central and South America was, having always idealized the beautiful Miranda.

According to some of the theories Howard had read, humanity was really one giant person manifesting into infinite subjective selves, so Howard Plumber thought of his weekly visits to his mom's house as visits to the part of himself she represented as an old woman living alone there with the ghost of his dad in the house where he'd grown up. His conversations with this part of himself were exacting. One day she talked about starting a bookstore after retiring from the church. "And I thought I might include you in that undertaking."

Howard didn't say anything for a minute. "Yeah, all right, that could be good, but—" then he told her he wanted to leave town, even leave the country, "get out of the empire," he kept saying, and they ended up having this whole rocky conversation about the empire.

"Well, we could go to Canada."

"No, that's just the empire's backyard, I mean *out* of the empire."

Howard's mom seemed to think it was inescapable no matter where you went in the world, and maybe she was right.

"But there are places—I mean, Gustav just went to New

York for another screening of his film, and Wilson Bishop makes a living as a freelance production assistant, also in New York—"

"But in New York, your insurance—"

"I'm not saying I want to live *there* necessarily, just—there are places where it's easier to make a living as a creative type, is what I'm trying to say, better places than Denver. And all my connections are everywhere else anymore, not just New York City—San Francisco, Boston, Los Angeles, Vermont, Portland—everywhere else."

"Where would you rather be?"

"I don't know, I haven't—I mean, I've been here since Dad died, I haven't looked around. There's nowhere calling me. My friend Holger Donovan lives in Portland, maybe I'll go there. Or Boston. I have a lot of connections in Boston."

"I think they have state sponsored insurance, too, come to think of it. I'll have to ask your cousin."

"Fucking insurance, shit. Sorry."

A BABY BLUE TRUCK WITH TINTED WINDOWS and the nose of a car asserted itself as Howard started to cross Alameda on his way to the bank that evening. The WALK signal was on and he shrugged exaggeratedly at whoever it was behind the tinted windshield a couple of times before stepping in front of its hood. The driver's voice shouted something unintelligible from the cab as it turned down Alameda behind him, and Howard flipped the bird over his shoulder on pure assumption. For all he knew, they were apologizing. Howard remembered that woman at the post office telling him the only way to find what you needed was to ask someone who knew, and after he left the bank, he walked across the parking lot to Pay Mart, where he asked the check out girl where to find "deep pocket sheets" and with her help, was able to find a royal blue set that fit his new fat mattress perfectly. His favorite color. Of course he wondered what it all meant, the dentist's discovery of "deep pockets" in his gums, his own discovery of a mattress requiring a sheet purposely fitted with "deep pockets," two apparently contradictory but undeniably complimentary appearances of the same mysterious phrase in his personal affairs with no apparent order.

Which came first? What was the message?

There didn't seem to be an answer.

This might mean something about me and women, maybe, he thought, since after all, it might have meant that. Maybe it means I'm building a nest. It seemed a rite of passage, getting those sheets that actually *fit* the new magic blue mattress he'd found, like crossing a mystical threshold of sorts. Howard knew he'd sleep tight, and have good dreams, sealed in that royal blue berth.

He talked the Scrutinizer into giving him another two columns and started talking to a local comic book company that was supposedly negotiating with big shits Marvel and DC.

He considered republishing *Kiabonga!* but wasn't sure whether or not he still owned the rights. That auto-publisher had sent him an ISBN no. at one point and he didn't know whether those had an expiration date or not. It had never occurred to him to figure out how to get paid through that publisher either, though he doubted he'd sold more than three or four copies by now.

Howard drifted into a bank of unremembered dreams dwelling on all this, and was awakened very early the next morning by shouting and laughter in his upstairs neighbor Ray from Something Wild's apartment, 3 AM. Normally someone who kept to himself, it bothered Howard to the degree he dragged himself upstairs and pounded on the door.

Ray appeared, slicking his hair back in a white wife-beater and a silver skull shaped belt buckle. "Charlie!" he beamed with fake camaraderie, as in Demme's 1986 classic.

Howard couldn't see all the way into his apartment, but it didn't seem like many other people were in there. "The name's Howard. I live downstairs. It's three o'clock in the fucking morning. I'm trying to sleep. You can have friends over, that's fine. Just stop shouting. Why shouting? Come on."

"Okay, man, sure." Ray seemed agreeable.

"It's 3 o'clock in the morning," Howard repeated, then went back downstairs and got back into bed and lay there for about five minutes before he was again disturbed by more laughter and unrestrained shouting, presumably from the same location. This time, when he got up and climbed up the stairs to the lobby to investigate, he discovered the party had relocated to a house across the street from K ZIP.

"Have a heart, quiet down!" he shouted, to no effect, standing there on the cement walk to his apartment building. "Quiet the FUCK down!" he tried again more barkingly before realizing he was doing more harm than good, going back inside and finding his way into sleep.

That bad luck board he'd seen across the sidewalk remained in the verge of grass where he'd thrown it for weeks until Howard picked it up—it turned out to be a piece of cardboard—and threw it into a dumpster a few blocks away, along with a black hair ribbon he'd noticed for some weeks on the way back and forth from 7-11 after his morning donuts.

Howard felt charmed by delicate whispers after every exchange of money and goods with a beautiful brown-skinned woman in hoop earrings, and soothed by rustling wings after every commercial transaction with a gentle old soul in oval lenses with long black hair parted in the center flowing over her shoulders. There was also a dapper clerk who he thought of as "the owner" for his well-behaved mustache and efficiency of manner. Interacting with this colorful family of characters felt better than going to Safeway, more human somehow. Maybe he'd write an article about it, the role of assumptive familiarity in commerce, something like that.

☻

Dim Jim Driscoll kept racing along the highway in his Volvo, with slicked-back blue-black hair, whistling through his teeth in the blown-out shell bottom of a ruined, crowded world. It kept getting darker and darker. Was he looking for love or the graveyard? Every ten or fifteen miles another roadside billboard heralded the world's largest prairie dog. In a way he wanted to see that. He set a course for the next big town, thinking what will I do when I get there? What will the new town be like? Maybe he should get some seeds. He probably already had them—the backseat was loaded with indoor planters and spades and rakes and sprinkler-heads and stacks of plastic tubs.

He decided to become a gardener as a statement against today's defeatist mindset. Rows and rows of shooting stalks would announce his return to the old neighborhood as a gardener in service to growth everlasting. He wanted to liven up the joint. He figured it needed some livening up.

That'll teach those motherfuckers! thought Dim Jim, when suddenly—*POW!*—a huge fissure of blue light bloomed into the black air above the cornfield he was rocketing past in his car. He threw up his pale hands in shock as his car skidded crazily toward the cornfield, then grabbed the wheel again and hit the brakes.

The blue Volvo lurched to a halt at an angle across the black road. There were no other cars on the road. It was late and the air was hot. The blue light had vanished entirely. For a long time nothing happened, and Dim Jim laughed off what he'd seen as just a trick of his complicated mind and got ready to drive on, clearing his throat and inserting the key in its socket.

"That never was," he muttered. But the words rang hollow and false in his skull. Something new had grown at last and he couldn't deny it. All his enemies would say he was a liar for pretending there was nothing all these years. That lunatic I saw today with two black eyes, or that prune-faced man at the Better Than Better Than O-Kay Corral! Dim Jim sat there in the cooling, ticking Volvo thinking hard, his life flashing before him, the good and the bad, staring into the cornfield and waiting for another big blast of blue light. For a long time nothing happened, and he laughed off what he'd witnessed as one more passing trick of such a complicated mind, clearing his throat and inserting the key in its socket, then proceeding along the dark highway again like a silver moonlight teardrop on its way back to the source.

150

AFTER FINDING OUT HE DIDN'T HAVE THE 3-way calling feature on his line after all, Howard decided to excerpt parts of Z. Zippo's Stomach interview where he'd talked about founding the Pore and intersperse those with quotes from Dalton Perkinson about his experience as the Pore's first photographer. When Howard got him on the line, he noticed the wheels of his tape recorder weren't turning. Maybe the tape just needed rewinding. Either that or he'd stepped on the recording mechanism; the phone was under his desk, and he had big shoes. "Ah well, we'll just have to use my memory—so—how'd you meet Z. Zippo?"

"What you need is the new Apple iPad!" sold Perkinson.

"Yeah, I don't keep up with that kind of stuff. Just have this tape recorder, thought it would work."

Howard told Dalton Perkinson he thought DIY endeavors like Perkinson's Photography Workshop, Z. Zippo's Stubborn Stain Books and the Stomach and Doggerel were the sanest response to the recent Supreme Court ruling legalized unlimited corporate boosting or smearing of political candidates, effectively sacrificing everything to greed in a giant public ritual. "And if that's gonna be the new medium of exchange, I think we should all incorporate ourselves." Was it crazy to think he could outsmart them somehow by playing right into their hands? Well, he'd give it a try.

"I agree with you," said Dalton Perkinson. "Once people realize they're capable of doing it themselves, they won't settle for anything less."

After hanging up, Howard sent Wilson Bishop an email letting him know he was almost done writing the new book, and after telling him all the pseudonyms he'd used for everyone, told him he'd caught wind of a buzz on YouTube about imminent disclosure of the government's contact with aliens and had a feeling it might be true, then set out for the P.O. with his package.

When he was halfway there, Caterpillar Mullinax pulled up behind him with her son Jake in the car and honked. "Oh, hey, Clipper."

Howard wasn't in the mood to be rerouted, so after a moment of small talk, they parted. When he got to the P.O., sweat was running down his face and stinging his eyes and he couldn't figure out which one was the right envelope to use. A sweet-natured gray haired lady emerged from the back room in a tie dyed shirt and tried to help, telling him, "It's just like when you take guys shopping. The only way to find out anything is to ask."

Howard thanked her for helping him while at the same time trying to let her know she shouldn't judge him by what most people are like in a prescribed situation, since individuals are rarely properly represented by the stereotypes used to scapegoat them. Some ass-backward construction like that, and she didn't understand. "Well, if you want to be a scapegoat—"

"No, no, that's not what I'm saying," he touched her gently on the shoulder. "You said something about taking *most guys* shopping."

"Well, I'm not like most girls, either."

"Of course not, no one ever is. That's what I'm trying to make you admit. But not in a bad way." He smiled at her.

"Let's just say this conversation is over," she told him.

"Well, we could finish talking about it."

"Let's just decide that this conversation is over.

That poor woman was trying to help me, Howard realized.

"My last four dollars," he told the bearded clerk behind the desk with turquoise rings on his hairy fat fingers as he handed over Wilson's package, containing two copies of Stomach number 12 with sticky notes attached to the pictures of Frankie requesting he change those before reprinting, and both volumes of Ed Sanders' collected poetry. Wilson had met Sanders in Woodstock a few years ago, and nearly interviewed him for the Stomach.

Howard hadn't heard anything from the Coccaluccios in months, despite Johnny C's mention of quarterly payments a long time past. As far as Howard knew someone else was taking care of the advertising receipts, if there were any, and he'd never asked, just kept on refreshing the content as frequently as possible. The most recent update was a story from him about dancing with a one-legged woman and throwing cow's brains at a punk rock prom night audience, plus the latest chapter of Yago Valdez's uncle's autobiography, detailing Johnny Goo Goo Eyes' resistance of his relatives' attempts to tend to his bloody head wound in the previous scene ends up saving his life, since part of his brain had been exposed at the time. "The medic pushed it back in . . ."

He sent Maria Reynolds an email asking how she was and letting her know he was almost done writing the latest book about himself, and Johnny C wrote back a couple of minutes later thanking him for introducing them to each other. "We're still so happy together."

It had been a few months. Howard sent Frankie Addams an email letting her know he wanted to return a book she'd leant him, "no weird pretext I promise." When she arrived, he told her he was sorry their spirits had clashed, and assured her their encounter had gotten a much more sensitive and thoughtful treatment in its current form than what she'd seen so far.

"Well, hopefully we can move past it."

"Sure we can. I have an unfortunate habit of showing people stuff before it's anywhere near ready."

Frankie stood up in her long dark dress. "I'd better go. Here. I'll give you a hug." She still had the copy of *Kiabonga!* Howard had lent her. He'd been hoping she'd return it, but decided not to mention it.

Everything was catching up to him.

That evening, Sam Dent formerly Sam Kane posted this benediction on Facebook: "Alright Denver, after 12 years of continuous bloody battle of wits, I give up, you win; yr skull is too damn thick. I'm leaving and I'm taking what's left of my soul, liver, lungs, and sanity with me! . . . Now I have to find a new state that'll take a shady character like myself . . . anyone have a spare ticket to Interzone?" Howard hoped Sam would make it to Paris someday.

He checked Doggerel's email and found this from Roberta Bogchar's cousin "Wrinkled" Pete Plucnakern, who'd been accused by Chief Tobasco Sound in his article of setting up the Trip Ship and possibly murdering a few celebrities: "Young Howard, did you not think it wise to consult me before going to print with such statements, allegedly from my own mouth?"

Quick thinking was required. The appropriate response. Who was it said the best ideas come while walking? Nietzche? Ben Franklin? On his way to the store, Howard noticed a brand new peace symbol in the sidewalk cracks just past one of the looming apartment buildings, just past where that bird had hopped backwards at him as a message from the planet months before. Either that or it had been there all along. Sometimes Howard thought about spray painting all the peace symbols in the sidewalk cracks with glow in the dark blue spray paint, then photographing them all. In the end he decided not to, since they weren't all peace symbols, because they were hidden in plain sight, as it were, and pointing them out would destroy their oracular power.

Left to his own devices, Howard likely never would have taken out an insurance policy. Now that Obama had signed health care reform into effect, when the one his mom paid for ran out, he'd have to buy a new one or be fined, but supposedly this process would be easier and more affordable. That's what he'd narrowed it down to in terms of personal relevance, though even Michael Moore was up in arms about the mandatory insurance and noninclusion of abortion coverage.

Howard never saw these kinds of shortfalls as defeats, just

inspiration to improve. And despite all the bum kicks so far, he didn't see his health as relative to societal laws or codes, more a property determined by his or soul or his will, so wasn't very realistic about the effects of these sorts of societal clauses. He realized he was extremely lucky to have that overpaid job keeping books for his mom, which allowed him to live with his mind in the clouds as an artist, the way he desired. Oh thank GOD for my overpaid job, he affirmed. But what am I doing with all that freedom? Well, I'm trying to make the impossible happen. We'll see what happens with this tragedy. Or is it a comedy?

AFTER WALKING BACK HOME WITH HIS GROCERIES, Howard placed a call to "Wrinkled" Pete Plucnakern at the number he sent to the Doggerel email address. "I'm afraid my device to record phone calls isn't working right now, but I'm happy to get your side of the story, too. Thanks for getting in touch."

"Ah no, nothing of the sort," Pete deflected in a crisp, intelligent voice like buttered liquor, "that's not why I contacted you. I just wanted to know, who's this Dim Jim Driscoll character?"

"Ah, well," said Howard, taken aback, "Dim Jim is like—a cartoon version—of myself, in a way."

"Well, whatever caused you to lower your standards to the kind of *tabloid* trash in that article you wrote about Chief Tobasco Sound and Trent? I'll need you to make a few changes."

"Of course."

"Wrinkled" Pete emailed Howard several clippings about himself as bygone comedy great Roberta Bogchar's staunch defender and his time as Mister Hoopley's Funny Crunchy Happy Family Hour host Barry Hondo's spokesperson. Howard told him he'd get back to him "within about a week" and spent the next couple of days writing a strong seven pages based around all the clippings he'd sent, then posted that on Doggerel after three drafts and a spell-check. He went upstairs and checked his mailbox. The post office had sent a form saying the address he'd used to send Wilson and Hannah Gut 12 and those Ed Sanders books for his birthday was "insufficient" in some way, and the contents of his package were "loose in the mail." Howard decided it was his own fault because of his mood when attempting to mail it, especially since the postal service had never lost anything else of his. Wilson called that evening and filled him in on several "real world" problems he was undergoing when Howard mentioned aliens, which was sobering.

"I'm not saying it's true," Howard waffled, "There's just all this evidence."

The last time he'd seen Wilson and forgotten he owed him some money. This time he felt like he'd forgotten something else entirely different but every bit as obvious.

The next time he went over to her house to do the church accounting, Howard's mom remarked how the whole country seemed be wobbling between right-wing conservatism lately and other more hearty and positive trends. He told her he thought all the political and economic tumult lately represented the last gasp of a dying power structure. This attitude came partly from a website he'd seen which seemed to imply the current shakeup was necessary before the new form would arise, and partly from his own reconsideration of AND Thinking, which seemed to imply that transformation required our acceptance.

"Well, I hope so," answered his good strong Mom.

When Howard got to Safeway that evening, he walked to the gardening section and told the pillowy clerk he was looking for a plant that didn't need much light. "The window's frosted, and faces south."

The clerk told Howard his best bet for something like that would be a philodendron, three of which hung from plastic hooks above him with many dark green shiny leaves in dark green plastic baskets. Crossing Cherry Creek, he became aware of that old black man or neighborhood angel just a few feet ahead, looking over the bridge into Cherry Creek, sloppily dressed and looking strangely uncoordinated.

"Hi," Howard said, walking past with his new plant.

The being turned and smiled, saying, "Well, hello," in its usual silvery, cultured voice, looking at him with an open, expectant face, but Howard didn't say anything. That devil or angel or old man fell in behind him as Howard headed down the sidewalk toward Safeway after crossing Speer, and Howard kept hearing a slow deep sound behind him like, "Hooorooolooooorooom," but didn't turn around, thinking: Is that him making that sound? Why's he doing that? What is that? Well, what's the rational excuse, and, What else might be making that noise? When he finally turned around, no one was there and the noise had stopped completely. When Howard got home, the phone rang. It was Caterpillar Mullinax inviting him to go swimming at the Congress Park pool. She arrived with son Jake in the backseat and the three of them drove there and paid three of four dollars access through male and female showers respectively, where they changed into their bathing suits and showered as ordered by the health code, to a crowded pool bright with blue light where people took turns sliding down a curved ramp into giant splashes and Caterpillar sprayed him with lotion and called him, "my poor pale boyfriend," but he couldn't tell if she meant it in a romantic sense.

All three of them went down the water slide a few times, Howard felt nice to be swimming again, then he and Caterpillar spread their towels and lay tanning beside each other on the banks of the pool while Jake kept splashing. Howard looked over and saw her eyes were closed. Caterpillar sure looks great, he thought, the sweet curve of her belly and legs ooh ah, but felt unsure of her motive and conflicted about his own. Can I even have sex with this woman in good conscience, he asked himself, without filling her in on my whole crazy trip about the malleability of circumstance? Well, of course, I can, he shortly realized, that's exactly the kind of crazy trip it is. Then he remembered Caterpillar was the one who'd tried writing a book on the difference between subjective and objective reality, and for a fleeting second, it seemed all signs were go. But a heavy conversation like that might take sex off the table, he realized. He tried to think of an opening line, lying there beside her beautiful body. In the end, her son Jake being there made that whole side of his own motivation seem comedic and false, so he kept his mouth shut, since he was genuinely grateful for her friendship, and didn't want to foul it with any wrong moves.

When he returned from this adventure in temptation and unfulfillment, Howard checked the Yahoo news alerts. Science had learned how to synthesize life. NPR reported that an atom's ability to be in more than one place at once, as demonstrated by quantum mechanics, had been verified in the visible spectrum for the first time, researchers reporting, "there appears to be no upper ceiling" or limit, to this, from micro to macro-.

There'd been an earthquake in Chile, with aftershocks that may have shifted the earth's axis and shortened the length of our days. Then another in Turkey, then one in Japan. Then Sumatra. Then China.

The Pope and his brother had been implicated in a child sex scandal. Barack Obama had expanded offshore drilling. Minor damage was reported in Mexico's northern Baja California after a magnitude 7.2 earthquake that was felt in Southern California, Arizona and Nevada.

All the oceans losing oxygen.

Spring in the air.

This was everyone's fault.

The human body would transmute to its very most aerodynamic rendition in the new paradigm, resembling a lightweight transparent glider. Howard had lost three belt notches himself in the last several weeks. How's your waistline?

157

THE DAY BEFORE THAT BIG LIT FEST hit Denver, Howard's mom picked him up outside the K ZIP and made a couple of wrong turns on the way to the Little Greek Café on 12th and Clayton Streets. He'd planned their lunch appointment without knowing there was a limited window of time to get downtown and secure his free pass to the fest coming up the next day. After they got themselves straightened out the second time and were again heading toward the Café, Howard asked, "Is there a way to get there without going through Cheesman Park?"

"Yes."

"Good, 'cause that's where it always seems to go wrong." He tried to minimize the lack of patience in his tone.

Lunch was tense, but amiable. After his mom dropped him off at K ZIP, Howard had just enough time to catch the bus downtown and pick up his free pass to the Lit Fest beginning the following day. In the morning, he cleaned and vacuumed his apartment and mopped the bathroom and kitchen floors in case any important publishers came over, then caught the bus back to that giant glass building downtown full of carpeted ramps, stairwells, elevators, escalators, walkways and lounges with the sculpture of a giant blue bear attempting to force its way inside.

The book fair took place in a giant room upstairs filled with thirty or forty long rows of display tables stacked with merchandise from thousands of small presses and magazines and graduate creative writing programs. The Power Mountain table, in row E, became a sort of base in Howard's otherwise aimless wandering around in search of familiar faces throughout the three day fest.

He ran into a workshop leader from grad school named Miss Michael Kellerman, and told her he was almost finished writing a book that was half a kind of tribute to his time at Power Mountain, and half a journal of his attempts to break into the freelance writing market. "And your book's been a great inspiration," he concluded. Miss Michael had recently published a treatise on memoir Howard had reviewed for the Scrutinizer.

She told him she looked forward to reading the book he was writing when he finished it. Howard knew from her Facebook headlines Miss Michael was a big fan of the Maker and the Marvins, and told her he'd recently lucked into a connection with an intimate of the Bogchar family he was unable to name ("Wrinkled" Pete had sworn him to a confidentiality agreement). Did she know any publishers who might be interested in something like that?

"I'm sorry," she demurred. "I have to limit that part of myself to my five advisees. I just don't have the time, I'd really like to. Finding an agent will be no problem at all for him or her, I assure you."

"I understand. Power Mountain is known for that, advisors' devotion to their students. Thanks very much. Just thought I'd ask."

It was the first time Howard had ever tried selling a prospect to a potential benefactor like that, and he was eager to get it over with, despite having hoped for a lucky break. He wandered around and around the book fair, staring at all the people and realizing they were all writers or publishers of some kind until his legs became tired, then caught two buses home.

The next morning, he spilled a glass of orange juice all over his newly mopped floor and mopped it again before heading back to the fest. On the bus there, he saw a piece of plastic hopping across the ground and briefly mistook it for a bird. He was standing right under the giant blue bear statue outside the tall glass building shortly after arriving when Lamar Cobson walked up, beard grown into a little bun under his chin, a tall girl at his side with friendly eyes and high cheekbones. Cordelia taught at the same high school in Santa Fe as Lamar and had been seeing him for several months.

"There's Howard!" Lamar yelled. They hugged and clapped each other on the back.

"Cordelia asked me, 'What does Howard look like?', we were looking for you in the crowd, and I told her, 'Howard looks like no one else. You'll know him when you see him.'"

"And I did!" Cordelia chimed.

They walked across the Light Rail tracks and around a few corners to a Peruvian restaurant full of downtown lunch rush diners serving spicy dishes heavy with potatoes from a buffet of round covered pots.

"Look, a fly." said Lamar, swiping his hand in the air. "Wrong time of year, though."

"Maybe it was a bee," cracked Howard, "remember the bees in Vermont?"

At one of the grad school residencies one afternoon a few years ago Several people had been standing around the picnic table outside Greystoke dorms when a cloud of curious bees bumbled past, nosing in to smell all the colorful clothing. The other students ran away clutching their study outlines, screaming and hissing over their shoulders. Howard and Lamar just stood there.

"They don't mean any harm," said Lamar. "They see colors and think it's a flower."

"Right," said Howard. They'd both known it.

The restaurant was full of talking diners. Cordelia and

Howard began spontaneously flashing imaginary symbols at each other with their fingers in mutual acknowledgment of the din of talking that made real conversation such a task. It gave Howard a sense of her as a very good person and he felt glad to see her with his friend.

Lamar had been to Peru and he and Cordelia were going back together this summer. "Machu Picchu is this whole complex built on top of these steep hills in a remote and inaccessible valley," he told Howard. "The whole place had a mystic sense of focus on learning."

"Sorta like Power Mountain."

"I learned a lot about the Inca empire too. I think it was one of the most impressive social organizations in history, not about subduing other tribes so much as encouraging them to join an alliance."

"Like America."

"No, that's just how they hypnotize their citizens."

"Good point."

Just then an old man wearing steel-rimmed glasses seated beside Lamar added a vial of purple liquid to his water with a flourish, causing noises of approval in the immediate vicinity.

"What's that?" Cordelia leaned over and asked him.

"Just my super-supplement!"

Co owners of a nutritional supplement company, this man and his wife were also in town for a convention and seemed uncannily devoted to promoting their cause, distributing organic energy pills and pamphlets to all their onlookers.

"We're in the top 99 per cent!" qualified the man's wheat faced mate from her form fitting faux velvet jumpsuit. "I'm sixty years old! Do you think I look sixty years old!"

"Well, you know," responded Howard, "I'm a writer, and everyone thinks the ostriches are hiding their heads in the sand, but who can say? That's the problem with meaning for writers. Sometimes it's like planting your garden too close to the street." Even he didn't know what he was trying to imply with that one, but it seemed to go over like gangbusters; the woman erupted into an uproarious sustained titter, her steel jawed mate smiling grimly. On the back to the convention center, Howard noticed a decorative column on one corner reading ALLTOGETHERNOW in different colored letters. Reading it from the bottom, Howard briefly took it for a foreign word or the name of a bank or a company.

Crossing the Light Rail tracks, Cordelia said, "I don't know if I could ever be so into my job as those people were."

160

"Maybe that's just something they've 'mastered,' though," Howard told her.

"Yeah," commented Lamar. "Once I saw the Amway tag, I sort of didn't trust them anymore."

That evening the three attended the Power Mountain social in a crowded basement bar on Market Street bisected by a staircase. They established an outpost in a corner, from which Howard made periodic reconnaissance missions, circling around the small dark room full of groups holding drinks and talking.

No Heidi Luger, but that place was so crowded, she may well have been there somewhere. He ran into a few other people he knew from Power Mountain, including a friend from grad school named Danny Cluck leaning against one side of the staircase, drinking a beer. Howard knew from their conversations around the picnic table outside Greystoke that Cluck had been subjected to shock treatments as a teen by his procrustean Mormon parents. "So Danny, did you join MENSA before or after getting the shock treatments?"

Danny's stubbly mug split in a broad smile. "You know, I wanted to see what effect they'd had, so I took the test again and still qualified."

"Hey, where'dja get those frames?" someone asked him when he was getting another drink.

"Oh, uh, this optician on Colorado Boulevard, I can't remember the name. He looks like a bear."

Cordelia, Lamar and Howard got dinner in the crowded Thai restaurant next door with four others from the party after it broke up. An elderly couple sat across from Lamar and Cordelia, the wife a poet and Power Mountain graduate, and the husband a mathematician like Lamar. Howard sat between this man and a woman with a sharp nose and long black hair named Jessica, right across from a middle aged woman named Becky with a child's round face and thick glasses.

At one point he was impassionedly trying to summarize the book I'd been writing for Jessica—"So this is my nutshell: anything can be proven—but nothing is meant to be! You can take anything—any point of opinion, and come up with evidence proving it on the internet, right? So the point is, to have any integrity, you can't have right and wrong! It's a matter of—"

The restaurant was crowded and loud enough that Howard couldn't be sure how much of their exchange was audible at the other end of the table where Lamar and Cordelia were. After paying his part of the check, Howard left with them, crossing the outdoor

161

mall at 16th just as one of the free shuttle buses rang its bell, closed its doors and set sail for the next block, closely followed by an unmarked white squad car. The mall was glowing brightly with neon graffiti from all the marquees thronged with beggars and buskers and shoppers. "It's a living metaphor," Howard thought aloud.

"We walked past these singing grates the other day," said Lamar. "Is that real or prerecorded sound?"

Howard remembered coming across a grate somewhere in that area years ago that emitted twittering sounds. "Prerecorded, I think," he replied. They came to a series of grates from which the sound of gurgling splashing flowing water could be heard. "See, here's one," said Lamar. They heard a deep fat splash as something plummeted into the flow. It didn't sound prerecorded.

After setting up the internet for Cordelia in their room, Lamar and Howard took three elevators down to the underground parking garage and smoked a couple of bowls inside their car, one benevolent cell in the body politic, symbolizing something, like those cracks in the sidewalk. Lamar looked around behind his shoulders then handed Howard the pipe. "So I guess you guys have medical marijuana here now," he said.

"Yeah, it's being marketed as this new cure all." Howard struck the lighter and inhaled from the pipe, then handed it back.

"I don't like marijuana being associated with sickness like that." said Lamar. "My friends and I used to have a campaign of smoking it openly to plant a subliminal message that it was normal and okay, seems like now it's being marginalized in a way."

"I never thought of it like that," Howard answered, blowing out his hit as Lamar took a draw. "Anyway I'm glad it's not as stigmatized."

"Not for the same reasons anyway," croaked Lamar.

After finishing the pipe, they rode three elevators back upstairs and walked through a little hallway glowing with pink and blue GIRLS and BOYS bathrooms to the lobby, where they said goodbye. Howard walked up the mall for a couple of blocks in the wrong direction before turning around and walking back past the same dreadlocked xylophonist outside Walgreen's and boarding a shuttle bus packed with drunks bound for Market Street, where he disembarked and caught a number zero headed south down Broadway. When he got home and looked in the mailbox, he found a package from "Wrinkled" Pete, twenty seven press clippings on a disc to help with composing a synopsis for his book, and an email from Heidi Luger saying there'd been some unexpected trouble with her family causing her to leave early.

THE NEXT DAY, HOWARD WORKED THE POWER Mountain book fair table for a couple of hours, referring questions to one of the administrators or litmag editors whenever possible, then went back to the Peruvian place for lunch with a college teacher and screenwriter named Lorna Mays who'd befriended him on Facebook as a fellow Denver writer attending the lit fest. She arched her thin sharp eyebrows at him from across the wooden table, complaining about one of the authors making a blatant pass at her. "I was like, have I done anything to give you that impression? Did I come here for that? What the hell?" She seemed really worn out and disappointed.

Howard touched her hand impulsively—"I'm sorry to hear about that."—then drew back lest she think he was hitting on her, too. Had he been fast enough? He wondered about it. She knew. Neither of them mentioned it. "Well, this big lit fest is sort of like the kingdom of being a writer," he continued, "and a lot of writers sort of have a false sense of entitlement when they come here, you know."

"So you've written a book?"

Lorna told him her boyfriend Dirk had a press in Patagonia called Silver Spit. "They're always looking for new authors." Howard agreed to send a copy.

There was no buffet, so he studied the menu. The waiter appeared and Howard tried describing the dish he'd liked most the day before—"It had a lot of potatoes, and peas—and beef, but not a lot of beef." He ended up ordering something else that sounded very good but turned out to be a kind of frozen spicy cake that was just okay.

"So you never learned to drive?" she asked him. "How old are you?"

"I'm waiting for a non-polluting car."

"You'll be waiting a long time, then."

Lorna offered to give him a ride home, and on the way to her car, she told Howard she'd had a bad year, first a divorce, then the death of her father, then becoming seriously ill. "I know I never expected any of that. I'm still sick." She told him there was a twenty per cent chance she would die of whatever it was, and Howard tried to think of what to say in response as they passed her old office just off 9th Street Park on the Auraria campus.

"I know enough to know I don't know anything," she told him. "Well, sometimes—you don't know—what you're expecting," said Howard, flashing back to his wild insight in that conversation with Frankie about the warlike cultures persisting indefinitely through unconsciously expecting war with each other forever, and their wars appearing on the outskirts of Howard's own trip for the same unlikely reason or another even stranger. "In a way it's not really about knowing anything. I mean it *is*, but it's not really based on the facts, so it can't be known. Hey, look at that."

There was a perfect peace symbol on the sidewalk right next to her car. For a second both of their shadows were touching it.

"Wrinkled" Pete liked Howard's article. "Let me get your address. We'll start our tour of gypsy villages, the true circus life, I was trained as a young sprat to drink dirty slop from a bucket, I—"

"Wait a minute, Pete—all I need is two more weeks to finish a novel I've been writing all year, then I'm at your service."

If Howard was honest with himself, this whole thing could be a plot by the forces of MK ULTRA or even the Cult of Cold Hands to undo him somehow for his existential heresy, but he couldn't seem to muster any panic. All this evil built up in the world—maybe all anyone really had to do was overcome his or her own resistance to perfection, and all that seeming opposition and likelihood of defeat would atomize and disappear, irrelevant to the new program. Maybe all it took was faith.

Lorna Mays' boyfriend was an absurdist or "bizarro" writer, so Howard sent him some diary excerpts with a few of the minor characters changed into superheroes or pop culture icons, which, to his pleased surprise, lent those bits a sort of manic dreamlike flair. It was only a matter of time.

The world was getting excited. Thoughts were turning into miracles and crimes all over the place. A volcano erupted in Iceland, shutting down air travel indefinitely and costing the aviation industry billions and billions. Admitted racists accused Obama of being a racist for no apparent reason. Arizona legalized racial profiling in a war against illegal immigrants. Next an oil well blew in the Gulf of Mexico, displaced crude spreading farther each day, making everyone fierce and sad and angry. Next Greece went bankrupt, then Portugal.

Howard found a website alleging all the earthquakes and eruptions were part of a "weather war" initiated by the dying power structure as Obama overhauled their finances and prepared for full ET disclosure, and his interest was piqued by another theory postulating Obama was the Pharaoh Akhenaton cloned to push through imposition of the Pharaohnic system of infallible ruler and dronelike subjects in the United States. But the same group opposed immigration since it weakened cultural distinctions and made us more susceptible to one world government, which seemed far too fear-based and determinist for any aspiring AND Thinker to take seriously.

"Make no mistake, Obama's the butcher of Afghanistan," Eddie Flavius pronounced in an email.

Howard remembered his father's lament on the eve of Bush II's reelection, "I'm so tired of being in the minority."

"Well, you're a writer," Howard had tried to reassure him, "you're an artist. That's just how it is around here."

The apparent C.I.A. coup made it seem like the fix was in long since.

Conditioned by decades of reflexive competition in the wasteland playland, neither the "liberal" nor "conservative" party stood for anything but opposition of each other.

Everyone racing to overconsume more and more puffy treats and stuff them down everyone else's throats—for cash! But cracking down on Wall Street, solar panels on the White House, more PTSD help for veterans—how could those be bad ideas? Assuming he was really just a figurehead, to Howard it looked more like the current president had taken office just in time for a no-holds-barred hate crusade against himself as token other, just in time for all the reservoirs to burst and all the oil pipelines to blow, in a manner of speaking. Like the butt of some ultimate practical joke. Or maybe that was just the way they wanted it to look. Whoever "they" were.

Had Obama known what he was in for all along? Maybe so. Maybe not. Such was the disconnect between rulers and ruled in Howard's funhouse mirror of a country, where shared control was based on advertising, and there was no sure way of knowing anything and certainty was a trap. He preferred to remain unaffiliated, to effect a greater future than the many on sale.

Roulana Deringer responded to something he posted on Facebook about Obama's failure thus far to repeal Bush II's unlawful arrest and imprisonment policies with a comment saying George Orwell had seen the future, just gotten the date wrong.

Whenever Howard thought about how centuries-entrenched the self-destructive streak in American government was, he felt inclined to give Obama as long as he needed to change everything.

Or maybe it's all a big setup for conservative siege in November, he thought, after realizing what a checkmate blind faith put on his own sense of urgency, and he's leaving it unchanged on purpose, so they can tighten the screws once he's elected. Or something else is happening. He kept realizing he wasn't even a little bit worried, then questioning his lack of worry or excitement and realizing he was completely terrified, then laughing about it all over again.

Very well then, he quoted Walt Whitman, I contradict myself. In the 21st century. However many lives I've lived so far and everything I've learned or failed to learn or ever will or won't. He responded to Roulana's comment: "I think Barack Obama is at least as good as any other fat cat from the past, and possibly even much better, given a chance to change things. There's my faith."

The latest phone call with Hal Blare posted by Jordan Sections on YouTube featured him ranting about the current state of the economy. According to Blare, everyone in the American continents, North and South, should trade in one kind of dollar, just like the Europeans began doing comparatively recently with the Euro. "And ultimately, we'll have one kind of dollar for the whole world!" Blare enthused.

This seemed more like something a government official might say, which made the whole money-concept seem even more arbitrary and ridiculous than usual to Howard, reminding him at the same time of the rumors that the murders committed by Blare's Cult of Cold Hands were the spillover of a deliberate experiment in the creation of mind controlled assassins by the MK ULTRA program. Up was down, in was out.

Howard remembered Funk-Burn Willoughby's words about the rabbit hole, giving thanks for all that was, blessing everyone else for their part in his perception, even the government agents, and felt a warm glow in his breast as he did that.

His mom offered to give him a ride home the last time he went over there to keep the books, and he accepted. "Life is always opening up new vistas like that," she said on the way down Speer toward K ZIP after Howard told her about "Wrinkled" Pete's ghost writing proposal.

"Yeah, that's its *holographic* nature," he agreed. "So AND Thinking was a very helpful model for me, since it *actualized* things like um . . . the mutability of life, malleability of reality, by giving them a kind of scientific platform in a way."

"But if there is no right or wrong—well, how would you ever know what you should do, from moment to moment."

"Well—intuition, you know, everyone has to choose their own way, it's all *your* hologram."

"Well, now that you've added the word 'intuition,'" said Howard's mom as the car pulled up to the curb outside K ZIP, "I think I finally understand AND Thinking."

"Hhhhahhh," Howard's weary sigh—blame it on his talking problem, or their inbuilt conversational difficulties as mother and son, but her use of the word "added" there made him realize he'd failed again to describe AND Thinking exactly for his mother, and perhaps irretrievably. But she'd spent most of her life understanding indescribable things like this one. He wasn't worried about her. "Thanks for the ride. I'll see you next week."

He came home to a series of argumentative comments by Eddie Flavius on the Doggerel Facebook page jumping to all these conclusions about his political stance, and erroneously attacking him as a fervent Obama supporter: "You feel accused, perhaps, because your heart knows it's true. Have whatever kind of day your denial allows you to."

Flavius' rant had apparently been provoked by one of the posts having to do with processed meat being declared unsafe for human consumption. Wonder if he'll write a song about it, thought Howard, who wanted to understand every perspective without committing to any.

He likened this form of selective omniscience to a drift through cyberspace a la psychogeography.

This made it hard for him to relate to other people with more specific viewpoints, and hard for them to understand his lack of one.

He was already in a bad mood and fired off a hotheaded email in response, telling Flavius he didn't feel like an "exploited bloodbag," thanks, and honestly wished him a much better feeling or discipline himself, ending, "Get off my case, sorehead."

Then he caught the bus to 30th and Larimer to pick up unsold copies of the Stomach from a gallery that was moving, and while standing at a bus stop on that long hot green strip, thought he saw Tewodros Magness disappearing into a warehouse with Harvey Zylon, founder of Zylon Research. Tewodros had always joked about Harvey being the pontiff of some kind of underground empire. Howard crossed the street and walked into the warehouse he'd seen them enter. He looked around inside the empty tiled lobby, stood still for a second and thought he heard an elevator door open deep in the basement, then went back outside and crossed the street just as the bus heading home pulled up.

•

That's what jumping back was all about! Jumping off the time-track! Staying in charge! Dim Jim Driscoll knew all that. Likewise he never watched the news broadcasts or read the paper, despite an inner curiosity he couldn't deny about what it said inside. Sometimes he wore a raincoat on the days it ended up raining, as if prompted by some irresistible force and he'd think, "Ha! Lucky!" But was it really luck, or some strange science? He knew instinctively to keep on jumping back. As long as he kept jumping back, his life was unpredictable. According to Gurdjieff's *Beelzebub's Tales To His Grandson*, the Archangel Looisos, Arch-Chemist-Physician of the Universe, had implanted an organ Kundabuffer at the base of every human's spine to keep them away from their heart's desire. Dim Jim socked a fist into his palm. "Well, he won't get away with it this time!"

"HELLO THERE, MR. PLUMBER!" BOOMED THE JOWLY cashier scanning Howard's groceries at Safeway. The previous week, he'd overheard the same clerk tell a woman in line before him buying wine how he'd been sober twelve months and didn't miss it one bit. "Still got that drinking problem beat?" Howard might have asked him now. But no. He respected his boundaries. "Yeah, what's YOUR last name?"

The man lowered his voice. "My *last* name? Uh . . . Pobbleton. But you probably don't wanna—"

"Mister Pobbleton."

"But you can just call me Bucky!"

"No, if you're gonna call me Mister Plumber, I'm gonna call you Mister Pobbleton."

"Oh—well, okay, that can work also."

Howard plugged his cart into a row of identical others before walking out with his water and food in the black Safeway bag. When he got home, YouTube was full of doomful posts about speculation about the hurricane picking up all that oil and raining it all over the world, beginning with the East Coast US.

At the bank, Howard's teller, a pale curvy girl with freckles, said, "It's been so hot lately."

"Yeah."

"A week ago," she twittered, "it was chilly, then it warmed up for a couple more days, then it rained all day, now it's hot again, such crazy weather, ha ha."

"Yeah, then there's global warming." Howard's mouth felt tight. "And that geyser of oil shooting into the Gulf of Mexico for a month now so far with no sign of stopping, I guess you've heard. Sorry to bring you down, have a nice day!"

Walking home, every car that drove past looked just like a cumbersome manifestation of reckless gluttony. Going through the motions felt more unnatural than ever. He even choked up during his next phone call with "Wrinkled" Pete, alarming him into nixing their ghost writing project entirely. "I don't think you're the man for this job."

"Maybe not," Howard took the easy way out. To tell the truth, he was relieved, considering the rumors about "Wrinkled" Pete's connections to MK ULTRA and the Cult of Cold Hands, though he realized those allegations might well have been groundless. Plucnakern needn't have worried; the Bogchar secret was safe with Howard; it was an explosive story, sure to reframe everyone's conception of the last thirty years, but no one would ever learn of Roberta's connections to the secret government from him. After hanging up. he noticed there was a Distant Energy Healing Session coming up in the next few days, and "liked" it.

They finally managed to cap that blown well in the Gulf, after which a series of procedures on the order of whether or not to leave it capped and raising the damaged blowout preventer and what about the hydrate crystals we'd better be careful began starting and stopping in media limbo. Howard had given up trying to second guess the future or perceive the hidden order since any decision he came to was as likely as any other reality tunnel, lately turning his attention to the most obvious opponent, corporate personhood and all its evil implications, and started posting links to petitions against it on the Doggerel Facebook fanpage and pushing DIY words art and music instead of the Pay Mart or Mark Twain Dinette grade confetti. He was negotiating with a comic book company about his idea of a script starring Dim Jim as a lover and hater of science, foiling unsolvable crimes by unerringly blundering into the perfect solution using spit, faith, and a band aid.

Rosie stopped him in the parking lot as he was on his way to Ray Bradbury Books one afternoon to get some comic books to study. "We had to let that boy upstairs go," she confided. "That Ray."

"Well, good riddance to bad rubbish, then."

"Ha ha, yes." Gentle old Rosie. "He was supposed to be dead! The police never even believed he was still *alive,* after a knife fight with his X wife's new boyfriend, Charles Diggs!"

"Yeah, that used to be my favorite movie."

"Not only that," Rosie quavered, leaning forward in the full-length flowered dress she always wore. "His apartment was trashed. I mean, *filthy.* I'm ashamed to let the handyman up there to remodel. Just *filthy.*"

Images of this tall old woman, who lived in an immaculate blue shingled house a few blocks away from K ZIP, or some agent of the mafia owners breaking into his own cluttered apartment, deciding it was filthy and evicting him appeared unnervingly in Howard's inner eye. I'll have to do the dishes tonight, he reminded himself.

A solar flare erupted, inaugurating a contagion of uprisings from Tunisia through Wisconsin, building over a few weeks to fear of a partial government shutdown in the United States, where people wondered if all the Middle Eastern uprisings were genuine or simply made to look that way by the C.I.A. After dumping the latest batch of empty water bottles, Howard started heading down the alley toward Safeway, that black bag swinging at his side. When he got there, he walked up and down the aisles under beeping noises and coded messages on the intercom, like "Floral Department—two zero one," collecting what he wanted, then went to the front with his cart. "MISTER PLUMBER!" hailed the undeterred Pobbleton from a neighboring lane.

"That's *Mayor* Plumber."

"I'm sorry?"

Howard turned to face his accuser, squaring his shoulders, all the other cashiers and customers looking at him. "Mayor Plumber, if you don't mind."

Walking home with twelve more plastic bottles full of water and a few other things in his bag, Howard felt he'd won an abstract contest with that jowly clerk by refusing to comply with his would-be folksy gesture of assumptive buddyhood.

Next time I'll tell him to call me Com*miss*ioner Plumber. No, *General* Plumber.

He saw something on Facebook about the celebrity "bottled water scandal" defaming bottled water as a profit-based scam to rope in the paranoid. That made sense in a way, but it took more trust to drink the tap water than Howard possessed presently. He kept taking the anti-seizure pills for the very same reason. He felt slightly guilty about trespassing in the neighbors' purple recycling cans, but it seemed he was getting away with it so far. The first of three or four beside the dumpster was empty the next afternoon when he looked in, so Howard dumped in the latest batch of empty plastic bottles and set off down the alley toward Safeway, where his cashier was a middle aged woman with blonde hair and a pleasant expression, one arm in a green cast. "I'm sorry you hurt your wrist," Howard told her.

"Oh, I didn't really, it's for support. Carpal tunnel."

"Oh, okay."

"But thanks."

They smiled at each other.

Howard broke his fast the next morning and went back to 7-11 for a couple of donuts, where the owner seemed pleased and surprised to see him again. "Hey, man! Haven't seen you in a while!"

"Yes, it's been a little while."

"Good to see you again."

The owner added Howard's bills to the register and handed back his change in a single swift move, his mustache a short, straight line over his lips. "Have a good day."

"You too, thanks."

Howard knew it was more than just him in the world, but he

spent so much time in his own thought cloud it was hard being present for others sometimes. That 7-11 clerk had recognized him without using his name, and the effect had seemed less intrusive than the bungler at Safeway yelling out, "Mr. Plumber!" Same thing with that woman in the green support glove, their exchange had felt very smooth and natural.

Kat Works was on the guest list plus one for the PorchCore CD release party at Café Post-Normal, and got Howard in free. The only lights in the long wide room were hundreds of multicolored Xmas bulbs hung from the ceiling. It was beautiful and crowded. "Remember when we had the Bat Sandwich event up here?" Kat said after they got their beers and took two of the plastic chairs in a row of additional seating.

"King Baker's wake, too," Howard contributed, temporarily forgetting all about the Bellamys' wedding, which had happened in the same room a few weeks prior.

"Look, there's Ty," Kat pointed out.

Ty Cropper was standing up near the merchandise table. Once they'd run in the same pack but over the years their lives in Denver had diverged. Howard went over and purchased a copy of PorchCore's new CD, then Ty autographed it: "Thanx for being my longtime Denver friend."

In the middle of PorchCore's set, Howard saw her silver glasses glinting in the darkness and worked his way through the crowd to where Julia Mathers was sitting up a small flight of stairs in the back of the room with her mountainous, bearded new boyfriend, Sean, and a woman named Carly who Howard hadn't seen since just after the second skull fracture. They all shook hands and Howard lost track of Kat for a while, sitting there amidst mass swaying and clapping of hands, digesting PorchCore's ever-changing, eclectic mix of instruments and talents. He sure looked forward to the new disc, "Sunslap Hapflapp Happap Dap Vol. I" (its title extracted from gibberish scrawled on a scrap of notebook paper Ty had found on Colfax Avenue), which Ty had told him months before would amount to as studied a description of life's dark side as had the previous soul-stirring volume of its radiance. The next act, a bearded man with an accordion took the stage and began an interactive production, "This half of the room, you're the violins. This half, you're the trombones!" Kat Works and Howard got another couple of beers from the raised bar in the corner, and right after finishing his, Howard caught the bus back down Broadway to the waiting arms of K ZIP.

172

HOWARD MET JOHNNY C AND MARIA FOR lunch and drinks at a Mexican place on 8th Ave., and tried like usual to get down to brass tacks about how to make money with that website, but Johnny C remained amiable and equivocal, sipping his beer and saying he was planning a big upgrade for Doggerel. Howard had heard that song before, but maybe this time it would happen. Good moods all around, but the conversation wasn't going anywhere. The webzine had become infested with spam comments, and Howard needed Cuco's expertise to delete them. Under every piece of writing, art or photography, a phalanx of sales pitches disguised as comments accrued within days, stuff like this: "Thank you for sharing this information, which I learned a lot, but also know a lot of knowledge. I promise you the cheapest and hottest wholesales jewelrys are selling now like hot cakes in our new website at" and so on. Howard had learned to live with this cosmetic dysfunction as a mark of the site's living grace, like the auto parts ads cropping up on the Stomach blog, which turned out to have been the right choice, as Cuco and his wife Daria had recently adopted a child and he was hard to get in touch with. "Guess I'll try sending him an email."

"I want you to see our new house," Maria redirected.

"I've been meaning to come by. It's just so far away. Is that in the Highlands?"

"Sort of. I think it's technically in RiNo."

"All these districts get hard to keep track of. Well, there's probably a bus."

"How's your book coming?" asked Johnny.

"Supposedly a publisher is looking at it now in Timbuktu or somewhere."

"Well, let me know if you get to the end of your rope with that press. I know a few people."

"Well, I just realized I have to rewrite the conclusion, so it's not quite ready yet. But I'll do that this week."

After finishing his crispy relleno, Howard bid our happy couple fond farewell and bumbled home in zigs and zags to K ZIP. Only rarely did he find himself without the word he needed these days, and when it happened, the pauses were brief enough not to hamper the general ease of conversation. But whoever had reset Howard's skull after the second big fracture created a full-on depression in the center of his forehead, where before it had been just a gentle dent. One morning he awoke with a dark red dot of acne right in the center of this well, and experienced a more visceral dissatisfaction with this cardinal flaw in his appearance than ever before, all day long. He realized the latest Distant Energy Healing session had coincided with the above self-image attack, and began considering that bullseye zit's appearance as having been a mini healing crisis pinpointing the root of his social discomfort.

Selina Kyle rang unexpectedly and offered to bring Howard something called a triple layer cream coconut avocado dizzy-whip she'd made. "Carrrying it overrr to you will make me strrrongerrrr, much leanerrr and fasterrr." It was a very long walk, and at first he thought to talk her out of it, but she told him was toning her body for a new crime spree, and her sure, patented purr was extremely persuasive.

"Well, okay," he assented. "Then we'll go to Harajuku Sushi." Selina arrived in no time, lean muscles popping in her arms, bearing a plastic tub containing the aforenamed gigantic monstrosity of a delicacy, which Howard stowed in his refrigerator for later disposal, the green head smiling at him from the door of his freezer compartment:, reminding him to BUY THIS NOW!, then the two of them walked to the Japanese restaurant on Broadway. Over sake and sushi, she let him know that her father had just passed away. "I will neverrr forrrget him."

Howard lifted his cup. "Let's drink a toast to our late fathers."

"To ourrr fatherrrs," Selina Kyle averred, lifting one hand to the catlike mask she always wore in some private salute.

"Yes I," agreed Howard in Rasta slang and swallowed another hot mouthful of wine. Selina caught the bus back to her place after they split the tab and paid it, and Howard walked home and checked Facebook again.

Like always, the internet kept him everywhere. The latest headline from his former Power Mountain classmate Jesuit/Goth/Occultist/aspiring Yogi Dario Zazzarino stated that he'd always known that a Yoga teacher was the role model for his students, but was lately really learning how TRUE it was. The day before, he'd been complaining bitterly about a remark made by his Yoga teacher that Yoga was not serious at all, and people taking it seriously were going about it the wrong way.

"I've never come so close to picking up my mat and walking out of a class." It was always back and forth with that guy. Zazzarino's headlines recorded his mind's manifestation of an ongoing series of ups and downs to live and learn by, which bruising program Howard could relate to, though striving harder than ever before to overcome his tendency to same.

Just below Dario's headline, the latest from transgender womanizer Elvis Sunshine stated her "love and awe for this place, space, and reality."

Which place? America? Facebook? The fabric? Howard didn't know where she was posting from, with her jet set lifestyle. Earth, the Universe, Life. But he wanted to feel that way too.

Despite its seeming roots in vanity, Howard saw that forehead reshaping operation as potentially the very best way of liberating himself from body obsession after years of enslavement to that ugly spirit, and started looking into having it done.

It was considered elective surgery, so Caesar Forever Insurance wouldn't be getting involved, and Health Care Reform wouldn't have an effect.

He'd offered to pay it himself, but his mother was footing the bill, which made sense, as she'd been the one driving the car in their accident all those years ago. Howard punched in the numbers and hung there quietly a second, shadow blooming on the wall as it rang, the circuit uncompleted.

Am I spoiled? he grilled himself, running the tips of his fingers over the dip and lump above his eyebrows. "Reno-vention Clinic, Sandy speaking!"

"I'd like to make an appointment," said Howard, relaxing into the decision.

AND HE FOLLOWED THAT FEELING AS FAR as he could, losing his temper at no less than three doctor's appointments. He was sure he remembered his mother having told him something about one of the doctors saying it was time to get the levels of meds in his blood system checked, and he clearly remembered the quacks testing his "Dilantin levels" years previously, but when he pressed her about it, his mom didn't remember anything about it. One of the visits was to the latest "personal surgeon" assigned to his case by the faceless, omniscient Caesar Forever, an attractive blonde woman in her middle to late forties with silver glasses sitting on top of her head, from whom he learned he was taking the proper dosage for someone of his height and weight, and the only known side effect was the potential for a short temper.

Howard's poor bedraggled mother sat there at his side through all these visits, captive of his whole ugly forehead dilemma or drama. At the last preoperative appointment, another quack with a bushy brown mustache that made him look like an old prospector told him he'd have black eyes for at least two weeks after the surgery and Howard's heart turned blue and sank into the pit of his stomach with a long deep squeaking sound only he could hear. He hadn't counted on that, and it made the whole thing seem like a vanity trap at both ends. The decision to reshape his own forehead out of some fear of others was no less than the choice between the facts and the unknowable, the proven and the meant to be, the mystery he'd flown after all these years. Deciding to do it was also a kind of surrender to the material world, still . . . he thought perhaps he was a special case, exempt from rules of thumb like that. But why? He was walking around in his apartment going over all this in his mind, and he came to the question: "Am I just a coward who wants a disguise?" and just as he asked himself that, in those words, in his mind, he unthinkingly picked up a book called "Damned Right" from the bookcase he was walking past.

Well, I knew that book was there. Maybe I'm just sabotaging myself.

But in the morning Howard realized he couldn't possibly get his forehead reshaped and called his mom and told her, then rang the mustached quack to cancel his appointment. Logging into Facebook after hanging up, he discovered there had been another Qi Gong Distant Energy Healing Session the previous night, coinciding with his own hot moment of doubt, as if instructing him to refine his focus.

He took pictures of all the peace symbols and skeletons and bullseyes and mosaics in the sidewalk cracks and talked a friend who owned a tattoo joint slash gallery on Santa Fe into letting him show some there in a few weeks. In the same spirit of creative regeneration, he started a band called the Drain Pipes with Nelson Habercorn, rediscovering part of himself that thought and felt in musical notes. Nelson had built a soundproof studio in the backyard of his house where they rehearsed. They got a gig at a coffee house right across the street from the gallery and made the planks shake. It was all coming true.

One afternoon Howard was photographing the cracks outside a house when the woman who lived there drove up. She thought he'd come to survey the damage since they were about to have it repaired. "No, I'm having an art show soon. See, it looks like a double-headed peace symbol."

"Hmm, well good for you." The woman went inside her house, leaving Howard uncertain what kind of impression he'd made. He had a feeling maybe he was really on to something with this sidewalk cracks motif; no one seemed to see the perfect shots he noticed.

Gus came back from his trip to Germany on a fundraising tour for Subhuman Love Songs, and Howard went over to Lala's house in Five Points for a screening of the final cut. He couldn't read the subtitles from the yellow couch where he was sitting, but he could tell it was a very strong effort. Gus seemed wiser and saddened somehow, said Benjy Possibility had "shot his wad" filming this movie and sending him back to promote it, and encouraged everyone to let Benjy know how much they liked it with posts on his Facebook profile at the soonest opportunity.

A friend of Gus's named Beth Murphy, with perfectly round eyebrows over round blue eyes and long dark red brown hair was among the guests. Howard had met her somewhere years ago in the Sad Comic era, but couldn't remember the circumstance. They introduced each other again and a few days later Beth contacted him on Facebook and invited him to join her on what became
a tour of all the bars along Broadway. At one point they visited a giant crowded dark joint called MEPHISTO'S newly established on the corner across the street from Jack Jorkensen's bookstore, Anarchy Now!, and Howard quipped, "Maybe this place is owned by actual hardcore Luciferians, or Satanists."

"The perfect cover," Beth rejoined without a pause.

She wore a tacky plastic heart around her neck with impeccable thrift store charm.

Howard had come a long way from Marlene. He hadn't talked to Frankie Addams in a long time. He felt very drawn to Beth.

Their impromptu adventure that night concluded at a small dark wine bar around the corner from MEPHISTO'S owned by the same mysterious investors, where they talked about mutual friends and tried again unsuccessfully to pinpoint the occasion of their meeting years ago, after which Howard invited her back to K ZIP to smoke a bowl with him.

She fell asleep on the green and white couch and Howard turned the light off on the shelf above her head.

As he reached to do this, Beth extended a hand to him without speaking or changing her position. As though asking him to take care of her. Or letting him know he was being given some kind of a chance. He didn't know if she was asleep or not. He held her hand for a couple of minutes then kissed it and put it back. He took it seriously because she was a person. But she was so tough.

A few days later she invited him into her apartment a few blocks from K ZIP, he saw the stacks and piles of paper and books and trash, her kitchen counter stacked with unwashed dishes and glasses. "I don't usually let people come up here and see this."

"I'm flattered," Howard told her. "It looks nice."

They sat down on a long white couch at one end of the cluttered room. Beth picked up a white envelope from the stack on the coffee table in front of them and handed it to Howard. "Here."

"What's that?"

"Your valentine," she told him. Valentine's Day was coming up. He tore it open and inside was a smiling rocket shooting out hearts. YOU REALLY SEND ME! It cheered. "Thanks." Howard tucked it into his inner pocket.

Before they went back to the bar, he stood in her hallway waiting, looking at all the rows of framed photos there. One autographed black and white shot showed a genial old man posed beside someone in an oversized rabbit costume. "Who's Uncle Funny?"

"Uncle *Finny*," came Beth's voice from the bathroom down the hall. "He was my great-uncle. His name was Finnegan."

"Oh, all right," Howard called back, feeling foolish. "Is that Harvey?" The character Harvey was a pooka, or creature from Celtic folklore, taking the form of a human-sized rabbit, but invisible to all but his charge, Elwood P. Dowd, in the Mary Chase play by that name.

"Yeah. Uncle Finny played Elwood Dowd. He was my dentist, too. As a little kid, it always sort of weirded me out thinking of him as this character with the imaginary rabbit friend. Being my dentist."

"Well, this is the year of the rabbit, you know. Robert Anton Wilson writes about that character a lot, too, Harvey the pooka." Howard had noticed they both liked books by that author on Facebook.

They went to the Indian restaurant and he gave her this tin bangle he'd received in the mail as an enticement from some religious group years ago.

He told her all about his forehead, what he'd almost decided to do, then decided against, and she told him, "You could just wear hats. You look good in hats."

After drinks at the Skylark, he walked her back to her car. "I'm not that short," she giggled as Howard stooped to kiss her the first of three times. Walking home as Beth drove away behind him, he thought, wow, this is going to happen.

It had something to do with dog energy, too. All these dog-related symbols kept popping up. Howard wrote a new Drain Pipes song that had a line about a dog without meaning to, then an old friend of his late father's sent him a poem about how guilty his dad had felt about putting the family dog to sleep (which bleak event, surely unknown to the poem's author, was associated, in Howard's mind, with years of neglect on his own part). Then he noticed another off the cuff dog reference out of nowhere in another song he'd written. Then Beth was dog sitting and the dog died.

She came to his art opening a few days afterwards, circled the room looking at the pictures, holding a jacket to her chest, and he asked her, "So are we dating?"

It was early, there were five or six people in the room. Shots of sidewalk cracks hung all around them. No one seemed to be paying attention to them. Beth looked at him, her beautiful eyebrows and steady, sure face. "I don't know," she admitted.

"So you're going to that 80's dance night on Thursday?" He'd been invited to an event and noticed her name on the list of attendees on Facebook.

"What? Yeah, I don't think you should tag along with us." Her voice had an edge. "Gotta go. Bye."

Nelson Habercorn broke both heels in a skiing accident, delaying the Drain Pipes' future, and Howard's art show closed without any sales. His mom gave him a ride to the tattoo joint slash gallery and he picked up all the frames but the man-made-looking peace sign shot had disappeared by the time he unloaded at K ZIP.

Beth Murphy called him very late one night. "Bad timing," she began, "life is full of bad timing. I didn't mean to be a bitch, wasn't trying to be a bitch, I just—"

179

All her reasons made sense. Some of them might have been wrong. Every time he went to the refrigerator, that smiling rocket told him "YOU SEND ME!" from under the winking, green-faced "BUY THIS NOW!" junk mail magnet. He didn't really understand.

The clerk who'd accosted him on his last trip shopping was bringing in carts from the lot and pushing them into their rows just inside the entrance when Howard went back to Safeway for another twelve bottles of water. "Bucky Pobbleton," Howard addressed him, walking up. "My name is Howard Plumber. I just took offense when you called me by name since you've never talked to me before, so it felt like a telemarketer was talking when you did it."

"I just remember the faces is all," smiled Pobbleton.

"No hard feelings."

When Howard headed out of the store after paying, Bucky Pobbleton attempted pushing one of the yellow carts into the long row of more yellow carts from a few yards away as a gesture of frivolity, shouting, "Kablam!" The cart hit a bump in the rug and fell on its side. Howard moved to pick it up, but Bucky, who seemed drunk with happiness after his informal pardon, said, "I've got it," before righting the cart himself and adding it to one of the rows. *"Whooopsie-daisy!"*

Howard walked away through the parking lot across the street, and started heading toward Speer down a sidewalk lined with square brown houses, sprinklers on in the yards.

About a hundred yards ahead of him, a woman in a straw hat with dark hair knelt planting a garden in the patch of dirt between the sidewalk and the street. Sort of late in the year to be planting, and at first that seemed like a strange place for a garden to Howard, all the cars rushing past right beside it, then he remembered his dad's white flag dream poem, and using every available piece of the earth for more flowers and plants seemed like the perfect experiment in this age of last minute miracles or bust. He tried catching her eye as he passed behind her but she didn't look up.

☻

First Dim Jim smelled something over by the fence. Then he caught sight of a guy in a black turtleneck on the other side of the fence kind of scrunching his body up over and over again as if trying to make himself very small that way and pull himself over the fence with his arms, but it wasn't working. Then he smelled some burning toast, and realized a whole gang of diners was eating it way over there by the fence. They had set up a table with a red and white checked tablecloth as if sitting in a park. Ha ha, the bumblebees. Everyone laughed and sang and danced around, making everyone sit on our knee and telling our stories of the woodland folk. There we were on the docks, near an old coil of rope and a can of gasoline. Maybe someone had been there starting fires. It was our turn to investigate. As soon as Dim Jim came close the turtleneck body shrank out of existence and maybe it had never even been there. The same with the gang of strange diners, their mad table cloth. Strange things happen in the darkness near that fence. Time has tested us with a coil of rope this time.

NOW AND THEN HOWARD WOULD GET LONG, high pitched bleeps in one of his ears, which made him feel perhaps he was being monitored by some unknown agency, be it human, divine, or extraterrestrial. It had been happening to him all his life. As a little kid he'd asked his mom about it and she'd told him the condition he described was known to ancients as a sign of divine reassurance, she must have read that somewhere.

Was it a blessing of sorts? Mind control rays from the government, maybe, like the kind making all the newscasters twitter off into gibberish lately: "dairson . . . blurubb . . . vertation"? Or an earnest attempt by benevolent extra-dimensional beings to patch through from the other side of the veil? It kept him guessing.

One day the skin around his left eye swelled up and Howard caught sense of an expanding mosaic of mazelike patterns just beyond the edge of sight on that side. He put on shades and walked to the organic market a few blocks away, where he bought two little bottles of lemon oil and a blue glass spray bottle. After walking back home, he mixed the lemon oil with water and a dash of dish soap for homemade spider repellent according to a holistic health website, then shook it up in the bottle and sprayed it all over his mattress and pillows and the air conditioning vent behind his bed.

The same website had also recommended alternating hot and cold compresses to make the swelling go down. Howard put some water on to boil. According to another site he drifted across, spider bites on the eyelid in dreams were supposed to suggest your outlook had been poisoned in some way.

Lamar Cobson was getting married that weekend in Santa Fe, New Mexico and Howard had purchased Greyhound tickets there and back from Denver online the day before. After the water finished heating, he stuck a wadded T-shirt in and pressed it to his eye for about five minutes, then put his shades back on and caught the bus through crowded, hot streets to the station downtown to pick up the tickets. The girl behind the desk told him that route hadn't gone out the last few days due to effects of the Arizona wildfire at the stop in Raton, and he'd have to call back early the morning of departure to see if it would be leaving. When he got home, he checked the news from Raton, which was all about the health hazards of inhaling particulate matter and soot of unknown composition, and Howard decided to get a refund. The tickets could be exchanged for a year, he could reschedule his trip to Santa Fe. He sort of liked the idea of a post apocalyptic Greyhound trip through burnt cinder towns, but he didn't want to breathe that toxic smoke. Besides which, his eye was swollen and he had a pain in the small of his back from a few months sleeping on an extra-soft mattress he'd found in the alley behind his apartment.

The Drainpipes had experimented with a couple of other musicians, both female, but prior commitments to school, and in one case, Howard's breakdown at PostNormal Café's open stage, had dissuaded them from continued participation, and the band was on hold since Nelson's skiing accident. Have I misunderstood women in some final, tragic way? Howard mooned soundlessly into his mirror. Is that what's wrong with my eye?

Howard knew he was a handsome man, that if he ventured out with the right degree of confidence and grace, he'd meet someone who would find him attractive and intelligent in no time at all at one of the bars along Broadway, but he felt like such an outsider from the celebrity-minded, sportscar-souled mainstream anymore he stayed home watching YouTube and being a freelance writer instead. He'd been waiting a long time to network his way into something really juicy through dumb luck or sheer tenacity, which always might or might not finally have happened. One local company called SeaMonster had purchased some comic book scripts from him several months ago, then switched to distributing MP3s instead and would soon be publishing the short fiction submitted by Howard and others in 32-page "booklets" to be marketed on Amazon. The time felt ripe for this kind of grass roots action, the recession having made everything equally likely. Howard sure had wanted to make Lamar and Cordelia's special occasion in Santa Fe. But his not going meant the Drainpipes could practice again sooner, and once they had recordings, SeaMonster could market those too.

Nelson's wife and three kids went to a swap meet one day, and he and Howard had their first practice session in a few weeks. Nelson met him at the door on crutches, and Howard was especially conscious of his own eyelid drooping comically while debuting his latest song, about cellular memory coming unblocked, which was supposedly one of the effects of the three eclipses that month. Nelson seemed abstracted, showed him the before and after X rays of his shattered heels, the first featuring floating smashed chunks of bone, the second starring the same shattered chunks held together with screws and bolts. "I've never really thought about the inside of my foot before," said Nelson, "but knowing all that metal's in there now feels so unreal."

"Our emotional bodies and our bodies," commented Howard. He ordered a new bed from the mattress place. A couple of workmen dropped it off at his apartment and Howard discarded one dead plant from the row on his window sill and rearranged all his bedroom furniture to suit the new palate, which rose up from a box spring unlike its predecessor. Lying on it in the darkness at the end of the day, with the mazelike spider patterns expanding to his left, Howard felt a faint, strange wobble like he was going somewhere on a spaceship.

Wilson Bishop, who he'd met in the Power Mountain undergraduate program, and his wife, Hannah, had given birth to a daughter in New York a few months before, naming her Amanda, which meant "one who ought to be loved." Funk-Burn Willoughby, and his wife, BB, now called Jenny Funk-Burn, were renewing their vows in Los Angeles mid-July. And Howard's friend from teen years, Josh Lawlor, was getting married the following week in Denver. All his friends were getting married, having babies. Howard felt stuck in time, single forever.

More online investigation led him to another eyelid complaints website with identical pictures suggesting his affliction was probably something called a "stye", or clogged eyelid gland, which are often mistaken for spider bites. The idea of tiny unnoticed glands all over the human body that might become clogged and swell made Howard think about Nelson's X rays and how barely we know ourselves. He used a safety pin to pick open the clogged gland and got everything out except a tiny central ball of hardened oil that made him wish he had some tweasers. In the end he decided that letting it heal on its own was perhaps the wiser course. He had some rubbing alcohol and Q-tips inside his medicine cabinet and decided to swab the area a few times daily, which stung him a little. Just something he had to go through.

Howard got an email that night from Steve, the comic book publisher turned MP3 distributor slash publisher of booklets, who he'd never met in person. Steve told Howard he had a scanner in storage he'd like to give him. "I thought you might be able to put it to a better use." Who was this character, Steve? Was he gay, for instance, and waging an elaborate pass at Howard by way of publishing his writing? Or a member of some social or religious order or another, out to convert him? No signs of trouble yet, but Howard was given to imagining all manner of intrepid plots against him.

The droopy lid was barely noticeable by Josh Lawlor's wedding in an Anglican church in Westminster. Howard got a ride there from the sleek Dale Prescott, an old friend recently resurfaced on Facebook, perhaps his strongest early model of female beauty, and sat beside her wearing his new string tie through the Anglican service and following reception at the Knights of Columbus hall on Grant. He stepped outside of the long yellowish room at one point to smoke a cigarette with Penny Shattucker, an acquaintance from the days of Howard's patronage of the Denver open mic spoken word scene. She knew about the webzine he edited. "I've always liked your writing," said Penny, ashing her cigarette, red eyebrows flashing. "So it makes sense you're a writer now."

"Thanks, Penny." Howard didn't mention the Drainpipes, who hadn't done anything for a couple of months. It was true he was a writer of some kind.

Dale Prescott gave him a ride home through the hot afternoon. "June's the wedding month," she told him on the way.

"Oh yeah, is that the tradition?"

After Dale dropped him off, Howard walked down the street to the grocery store, where he ran into Miranda. "So how are you?" he asked her.

"Oh, not so good," she sighed.

"Well, hopefully you don't have to work tonight."
Besides being an artist and freelance Yoga instructor, Miranda worked nights tending bar at one of the dives on Broadway called Killer's Korner, which he knew she hated.

"I do," she said, steering her cart out of the path of an oncoming wheelchair piloted by a bird faced woman. "And it's panties behind the bar night."

He'd seen her use that phrase on Facebook. "Is that actually the name of the job designation?"

"They make me wear panties behind the bar."

Because of her body. "Well, shit. That's totally lame and sexist and awful. You should-" To Howard's right, an overweight man in a green shirt heaved a sigh as he bent to address the row of cans on a lower shelf.

"I should get a new job," she completed his sentence. "Right now I'm just accepting all this."

On Facebook that evening, Howard saw shots of a towering red sky and smoke behind ridges of trees looming over that lab where the Bomb was born, which terrified him in a cinematic way. Was it the mainstream media that was poisoning his outlook?

When that tsunami knocked a nuclear plant offline in Japan, Howard had briefly seen it as the beginning of a chain of short circuits, every concentration of misguided energy about to backfire, which hadn't ended up happening. Or was it happening now? Before the southwestern wildfires, there'd been a panic on in the media about a flooded nuclear plant near Omaha and another upriver from it.

Lamar Cobson sent him an email after returning from his honeymoon in Belize. "Los Alamos is out of danger now. The fires still look pretty bad, but our monsoons have started, so your wish of rain is already coming through. Keep wishing as we need a lot more. "

It rained very hard the next day in Denver, flooding parts of downtown, like a fire hose had been turned on. Climate change. Howard hadn't heard anything about those flooded plants in Nebraska for a few weeks. The mainstream media poisoning his outlook?

Steve the publisher came by the next afternoon, slight, twentyish, friendly seeming, wearing all black, having ridden his bike through the recent solar flares and their aftermath with the scanner sticking out of his black backpack. The skin of his forehead and around his eyes was bright red except for a pale patch in the shape of his sunglasses when he removed them. He dropped off the scanner, and showed Howard how to use it. There was a lull in the small talk at one point and Howard told him, "Yeah, I got bit by a spider last week, right on my eyelid. Or it could be a stye. That's what's on my mind."

Steve made a face of polite disgust. "I got bit by a bedbug last week. You ever seen one of those? They look like little roaches."

"Ugh, don't even bring that thought in here. Those are epidemic lately in Denver, you know. Last week you say?"

Steve seemed embarrassed. "Well, it wasn't my place. It was just a place I was uh staying."

Howard thanked Steve for the scanner and gave him some lotion for his burnt face before he rode away, telling him once the Drainpipes had recordings, he'd send those along too. He reminded himself not to look a gift horse in the mouth. Something very like this had happened to Bukowski-John Martin had appeared from nowhere and promised him $100 a month for life in exchange for first publishing rights. That evening Howard posted a blurb promoting SeaMonster on Facebook and sent Steve an email asking if he'd be interested in publishing longer works: "I just finished a novel and have several target areas of interest in mind." Steve wrote back and said he was very interested, so Howard emailed him the latest PDF and a synopsis.

☻

The strangest thing about the new toothpaste Dim Jim was using lately was that a little slit had opened in the side of the tube below the cap and a greenish bulb of product had begun to seep out whenever he squeezed it. A few weeks later the same kind of strange mouth opened up on the side of Dim Jim's thumbnail. The flesh there was tender and sensitive, a line of pink blood shining in the crease. His last name was Driscoll. He was Bad Thumb Driscoll, and his brown eyes helped him to see all the brown things in town. The brown bushes, the brown railroad tracks. All the citizens in the town saloon would raise their glasses in a hearty cheer anytime old Bad Thumb Driscoll came sauntering in off the street.

"Whatever makes your harness jingle!" he cried.
"You're either in play or at bay!" He acted as if he would shoot up the whole room if anyone tried anything. A real tough customer, raised on the salt flats, no respect for mining companies. That new toothpaste would keep his teeth clean. Little mouths would keep opening up in his flesh wanting more.

Gratitude makes everything a gift.

EVERYTHING LOOKED ANCIENT AND WILD AND DRY when Howard ended up taking the trip to Santa Fe a month so later. Never smelled any smoke. The bus to Albuquerque took all day, including a long stretch at high altitude where it seemed to drive right through a big bank of clouds, something he'd never experienced before except on airplanes.

He caught the train to Santa Fe from the bus station downtown. On the overhead speaker a voice announced, "Right now we're passing through a couple of native communities, and we ask that you not take any pictures by agreement with them."

When the train reached his stop, he crossed the highway on a red trestle to a huge parking lot where Lamar picked him up around sunset.

He stayed four days with Lamar and Cordelia in their home full of newlywed pictures and albums, one unit in a faux-adobe housing development outside Santa Fe. One day Lamar suggested they drive to Corrales, outside Albuquerque, and tour the landmarks of Howard's childhood.

Walking down a long street called Meadowlark Lane that led to the three ditches separating the town from the Rio Grande, Lamar and Howard were confronted by a series of unleashed dogs guarding driveways with growling and jaws. They passed respectfully without incident, Howard making an effort to witness the scene from above while being consciously bigger than self-vs.-dog conflicts and doing his best to love those barking guardians for honoring the only jobs they knew. This wish seemed to work; excepting one with a long black tail who hadn't shown up the first time, the guardians seemed more reserved on the way back down the same street from the blue-gray eldritch BOSQUE, just trotting up, barking once like punching a clock, then trotting back.

The trip to New Mexico was a strangely emotionalized experience for Howard. There was a powerful culture of cooperation with native roots in the southwest which seemed nearly beaten out of existence in his hometown. He broke down crying reading John Fante's "The First Time I Saw Paris" to Lamar and Cordelia after dinner one night, caught up in the swirl of all this, thinking about all of it and none of it.

After breakfast one morning he and Lamar took a walk down the long cement path through the bright field of live and dead trees and wild cactus behind the brown housing development where the Cobsons lived. In Australia, some pet cockatoos had escaped and taught much of the wild population to say things like "Polly want a cracker," driving residents into a panic until they found out why.

Howard told this story, thern hypothesized that what we know today as birdcalls might in fact be imitation of the language of some bygone human race. "It's possible," he insisted. Lamar seemed to agree.

That afternoon Howard and the Cobsons had lunch in downtown Santa Fe in the indoor patio attachment of the Mexican restaurant full of chattering diners that was Lamar's favorite. Two little girls were sitting at a booth behind Howard against the opposing wall, one of them interestedly relating a series of recent adventures to the other in a satisfied, instructive tone: "Then we went to the swimming pool, then we went to the zoo, where we saw the prairie dog mound, then we went to the circus. And THEN—"

Cordelia had to chair a department meeting in the morning and started worrying out loud about doing a terrible job, then apologizing for worrying out loud. "I always blow things out of proportion."

"I'm a worrier too," Howard told her. "For instance right now I have a stye in one eyelid. I don't think you can see it." Could she see it? "But I'm afraid you can. And I've been waiting for these sales copies to come in the mail."

"That happened to me once," she told him. "Woke up one morning and my whole head was swollen up."

"That's it! Did you know it's a gland in your eyelid? Our eyelids have these tiny glands."

"It's like we're all in a big school of fish!" the little girl sitting behind him instructed her friend at that moment, adding, "I like to have a lot of different explanations for God."

Howard, Lamar and Cordelia all thought that sounded like a good idea.

The next day, they took a tour of Santa Fe's art district, stopping off at a couple of used bookstores and walking around on those old streets past the Governor's Palace preserved from some time in the 1600s—1500s?—very old.

"It's been refurbished of course," Lamar told him. As they walked a little further, he pointed to a house on their left. "I bet those bricks are about 400 years old."

Passing a row of cacti planted outside the old house, Howard realized that every plant was grown from a cycle of seeds which began before time and every human body grown from ancient cells and genes. All of life was as old as life.

Lamar's friend was DJ-ing at a reggae sound system on board a train car in the railyards that evening, and before the show started, Lamar, Howard and Cordelia walked through the closed farmer's market there. Howard and Lamar climbed down into a ditch to smoke a joint while Cordelia stood watch at a nearby picnic table. They were halfway through it when an old lady passed with a couple of dogs on leashes and certainly saw them, but nobody said anything.

They finished the joint and rejoined Cordelia at the concrete picnic table on the ditch's bank. "I just feel sorry for that old lady," she told them.

Just then Howard caught sight of a stocky figure all in black with a badge left center approaching the three of them at an angle from the right. "Excuse me, guys," the figure said, as Howard's heart flew into his throat.

"Yes," answered Lamar in a confident tone.

"You guys seen my dad around here? He's got gray hair, green jacket, sunglasses, he's probably drunk."

The sun was going down and Howard's eyes were bad in the darkness, but as they came closer he noticed the sides of their inquisitor's head were shaved high, the top shag tied into a ponytail. That wasn't a badge on his chest either, just a badge-shaped white insignia of some sort. Just somebody trying to find his dad. Which made Howard think about his own dead dad, who had lived here in New Mexico with him and his mother years ago in the primordial dream of childhood. The universe saying something to the universe in the form of a riddle. Something about dads, and drunkenness, and getting high, and fear of cops.

"Where was he?" said Lamar, and talked to the stranger about his drunk, lost dad for a minute as Howard and Cordelia stood stunned, both having mistaken him for a cop because of his outfit. Lamar had 20/20 vision and had never lost his cool. "I saw the haircut," he said later.

On the morning Howard left, Cordelia dropped him off at the parking lot and he walked back across the red trestle to the train stop. About one hour into his homeward trip, there was a rest stop at a seedy general store where he tried to use the upstairs restroom but couldn't relax enough for a proper shit and an old drunk woman with long black hair sat at the picnic table outside smoking cigarettes, faking tears, and asking everyone "Are you the driver? I have ten dollars! I just wanna go home, wah!" Howard wished her luck. He got back on the bus and it zoomed along through the blackness, pulling into the downtown Denver Greyhound station very late that night. Howard carried his bag up the tiled, gray 16 [th] St mall from the station on 19th and Arapahoe to Broadway and the O bus home, where he smoked a joint Lamar had rolled for him and stayed up watching YouTube.

☻

Behind every face, another piece of corn. Behind every piece of corn, another face. Soon everything became a cornball in Dim Jim's mind. If he saw someone stupid, he'd think, "Oh, you corn face." Corn had become the wadded archetype of all he scorned. Even the word scorn had corn in it, which he felt was fitting. "You piece of corn," he said half laughingly half jokingly to the woman with the fake tattoo standing right in the door of Kirby's Saloon hoping to pick up some customers and give them a Tarot reading or school them in her other ways.

"I am not a piece of corn," she set him straight. "My name is Lulinda Cecile Harkinson, and I am here only as a favor to people like you. Otherwise, you would languish without me, for this is my penance."

Lulinda got so sad she started crying, which reminded him of all those plaster icons who start crying tears of blood all the time for no good reason. "Well, cheer up, Virgin Mary," Dim Jim reminded her. She laughed and the two of them went off together down into the town, just laughing and sighing, passing a bag of popcorn. There followed some interaction with the customer service agent, over there near where the old warehouse is, out near the dump, squatting there in a thicket of high weeds, looking like a mean old one-eyed encroacher on the land (being as how it sat out there amidst all the wild growth with two big windows in front and one was all busted and blacked out looking from vandals spray painting all over it). Many passing wayfarers had set up their camps in the corners and under the eaves, even now there was a smell of burnt chicken from somebody's breakfast, and the black smudge of ashes from the tramp's cook-stove.

Each former tenant had removed a long thread of torn cloth from his or her bundle of rags and tied it up near the door as a tribute to mark the presence of this or that gentlemen or young lady, person, or traveler. Many had even used shoelaces. There was a whole row of them tied up next to the door. Or maybe Dim Jim was imagining it. He kept on walking through the desert and staring up into the hot blank sky until he saw a long stream of faces coming out of the sun in a royal procession.

THE EAST COAST PRINT SHOP STEVE HAD been using had suffered minor structural damage due to Hurricane Irene, and thanked its customers in advance for their patience. Howard tacked another couple of weeks onto the sales copies' estimated time of arrival and reserved a couple of hours at a local bookstore and the record store next door for a booklet release party preceded by a Drainpipes set. The band had acquired a drummer, which had delayed the process for a couple of months, but recording was next on the list.

"Remember when the Arab Spring happened, and we said how great that would be if it caught on here?" asked Nelson, the bassist. Thousands of people were occupying Wall Street in New York City and the movement was beginning to spread all over the world. "It turned out to be contagious after all."

"I think it's beautiful," affirmed the new drummer, Shelby, the mole on her cheek only adding to her authority in these unknowable matters, according to old wives' wisdom. "We have to open the heart chakra, that's all it is. Then we can see a whole new way."

"It's like a video game," agreed Howard. That was the title of one of their latest songs about how there was always a way out.

"It's just survival of the fittest," offered Jenny-lee, the bird-boned background vocalist, gritting her small white teeth. Interesting outfit, the Drainpipes. Bound for great things.

When Howard got home, he checked his email to find another couple of significant figures from his Denver past, Billy Possibility and his wife, Olive, had given birth to a son named Ezekiel at their home in New York City. There was another message from publisher Steve. "They said that the production staff emailed me with a question regarding book size, but I never received it. That's what the hold up was. No big whoop. In a way, it's a good thing that this happened. It gave me a chance to fix some layout problems."

Howard remained conscious of a slight heaviness in his left eyelid, and he could find it in the mirror, though any irregularity in size was probably impossible for others to notice by now unless they knew what they were looking for. Or was that just more wishful thinking? It appeared the placebo effect worked both ways, perhaps the central paradox in the science of sickness and medicine. Howard was grateful for all his body's unnoticed processes, for all those of his emotional body too, and for those of all the zillion other bodies in this universe, hive minds and all the other kinds of minds. Good thing that lemon spray hadn't been poison. Shortly after moving in to his apartment several years ago, he'd seen a brown

brown spider spinning its web among the leaves of a plant on his windowsill while watering it and decided he wanted those beings to be his roommates in this world. They hunted flies and bedbugs. Breaking one of their webs with your nose meant good luck.

The next morning in the shower Howard discovered a pimple-sized growth between his anus and his scrotum, much closer to scrotum. Was it cancer? A pimple? A bug-bite? A tic?

A few days later, when it hadn't disappeared or seemed to shrink, he tore it off, it bled a little, then the wound seemed to disappear entirely, leaving him with the hot terror phantom of WHAT THE HELL WAS THAT and the terrible feeling of something invisible growing right there in his groin, pretending to be painless. A hot pinkish point of pure terror right there at the center of him.

More time passed. Holding onto his balls made the pain go away for some reason. Howard walked around and around in his apartment, reduced to that: a poor fool holding his balls. In the morning, the pain was gone. After thinking about it all day, Howard felt it coming on again by evening. But was it pain, or was it fear? He called and made an appointment with the "personal surgeon" assigned by Caesar Forever, his insurance provider.

☻

Dim Jim barely made it, hopping on just as the little train rumbled away from the curb, plunking in two dollars in quarters before slumping into the half foot of space between some weird old man and a young girl named Ernestine Matthews who'd just started working around the old Cob-Nob dispensary. Ernestine had a couple degrees and considered herself a healer and light worker. She sure was very pretty and Dim Jim respected her very much. If she was some kind of metaphysical light worker type, well he sure didn't want to upset anything with his trademark bumbling buffoonery, but at the same time he felt she might appreciate this forward approach. So that's what Dim Jim did, just pointed his ass at the half foot of space between Ernestine Matthews and some weird old man and they moved slightly farther apart by the time his momentum had come to a stop. A wry gleam in his eye, Dim Jim turned to Ernestine and smiled. "Hey baby. I've been—oh, you're not Ernestine!" Horrified, Dim Jim stumbled away from the too-crowded seat and took refuge in another on the other side of the train. "And stay out!" The weird old man shook his cane.

WALKING DOWN THE SUNNY STREET TOWARD THE Caesar
Forever Medical Castle to get tested for cancer, Howard felt so
swallowed by the terror of it all. A hollow, stunned, amazed, deep
feeling.

His personal surgeon was a slim, attractive blonde. He got
semi-hard when she handled his balls and told him, "You're well
outside the age range for testicular cancer. I believe it was probably
a skin-tag, because those do show up near the anus, sometimes
people pull those off and they do bleed. I can't find any signs of
anything here, well maybe this tiny place here with some raw skin.
Hopefully that provides you with some reassurance." Her smile so
sweet.

He had created all that fear, then, with his mind, and all
those tiny, evil feelings in his balls. "It really does, Thank you."

Rosie hadn't been by to change the smoke detector batteries
in July like she usually did. She usually came once every six months
to do that—"January and July, the only two months that start with J
and end with Y, that's how you remember," she'd told him once, and
it seemed to be true. Twice a year she showed up in her long
flowered dress with a younger assistant wearing white overalls and
a cap, and the two ladies went back into his bedroom where the
thing was and changed it. It was getting to be November in the tenth
year of his tenancy, and she still hadn't come by. Well, Rosie's
getting old, figured Howard. Probably just forgot.

This spring's wave of uprisings from Libya was catching up
with the U.S.. Increased solar activity seemed a likely cause of all
the uproar, but most people didn't seem to care. Howard wasn't
worried. Everything was going fine and he was sitting on his ass
beneath seven layers of dreamlike near-sleep, a sort of
consciousness huddled beneath checkered blanket atop picnic
basket. Until the day he found a note on his apartment door from the
building's new owners.

Rosie had passed away and a company called Warlock had
bought all the properties she represented. Their logo had a big W
just like Walgreens's. Tin signs embossed with that evil red "W"
sprang up all through the neighborhood as they occupied it.
Meanwhile legions of protestors were being evicted from New
York's Zuccotti Park near the financial district by trigger happy tear
gas cops.

Howard's mom lent him more money and with the help of his
old friends Benjy Possibility, in town from Berlin for a visit in the nick
of time, and Gustav Harkness, Howard moved the contents of his K
ZIP apartment to the Robert Frost Building on 10th and Sherman.

194

His new place was on the ground floor, but the window facing west was elevated about ten feet above the alley separating his building from the parking lot between two other apartment buildings back there. His old place had been in the basement, no view, but more light from larger windows better placed, and more space for his mind roam in.

Now his psyche had been elevated somewhat according to the laws of *feng shui* (or some Western pseudo-Jungian approximation of it). He could see all the way out far deep into town if he opened the shades. He saw darting fishlike headlights through the chinks when they were closed and it was dark. All night long he heard the yips and yelps of college age drunkards bumbling home through the parking lots, sometimes even sirens and coordinated yelling from the Occupied capitol a few blocks away, but there was hardly any space, and sometimes staring into the void beyond his computer screen Howard felt like he was still in the old place, until those parking lots came into view.

At first his phone cord wouldn't fit the jack. It was the latest in a string of unfortunate glitches in the wake of the Warlock coup. Howard had to wait for someone from maintenance to install a new jack before he could plug the phone in.

He tried making friends with the guy who showed up. "What's your name?"

"Travis," the man said, but Howard misheard it. "Trappist?"

The man gave him a funny look. "Yeah," he said, deciding not to hassle it. leaving behind a service receipt with his name correctly spelled.

No one knew for certain what was happening next with the Occupy movement. Howard tried not having any opinions and just letting the turmoil unfold as it wanted, but sometimes he panicked along with the rest of the frightened. The police crackdown in Oakland seemed hypocritical after the U.S. championed the Arab Spring of revolts in the Middle East, but there were rumors the whole uprising was all coordinated by the secret elite, with the Occupiers as unknowing pawns of some unpleasant "order from chaos" solution the Illuminati had in mind.

When President Obama signed the NDAA act permitting indefinite detention of citizens without due process, it seemed to fit the Worst Case Scenario perfectly. Howard's new place in the Robert Frost building was smaller than the last one he'd lived in, but certain things were much better. A coffee maker which had always leaked at the old place no longer did. And it had that parking lot view. Some telephone lines to look at. There was a big change on.

All over the world, even maybe in everyone's life if they went along with it. According to a majority of metaphysically themed Facebook pages, it had something to do with the solar flares. Solar activity impacted the electric and magnetic fields surrounding every person, the sunlight interacted directly with human DNA and stimulated changes in biosynthesis in cells. It was a cluster buster. What's it gonna do to our emotions? Howard wondered.

"GUSTAV HAS PASSED AWAY TODAY"
THAT WAS

the first Howard heard of it, anonymously posted on Gus's Facebook newsfeed as his latest status update. No way, thought Howard. I just saw Gus. He helped me move into this briefcase.

Since Howard met him twenty years ago at the bygone Gasoline Alley poetry reading, Gus had been one of the pillars of his own self-concept as a writer in Denver, and by extension, his very existence. They often quibbled over trifles, but Gustav Harkness was a part of Howard's makeup. Now he was dead.

And the posts kept coming. Local promoter Dario Saver and Kat Works booked a room at the Mercury Café for the memorial. Punk rocker Lucy Danzig said it turned out they were having a "special guest" in one of her Facebook posts a couple of days later, and Howard wondered again: is this some kind of gag? Then Gus's brother Tim called Howard and asked if a pastor might speak at the memorial, "By request of our mom."

"Sure, that's fine." He gave Tim Dario Saver's number.

People came from all over the country and world, many friends of long standing who hadn't spoken in years and some who'd never met before. Benjy Possibility flew back from Berlin to attend, as did his older brother Billy and wife Laura, in their case from New York, having left their newborn in the keeping of Laura's mother. It felt great seeing them again. Jimmy LaPeste was there. Howard hadn't seen him since King Baker's wake, which had also been held at the Mercy. That combined reunion and introduction of kindred spirits felt very powerful and fertile.

The pastor read some hymns, then Gus's friends who felt so move moved took turns remembering him.

Howard read one of Gustav's pieces called "Poem for a reunion" about "conducting the music/Of someone else's catastrophe."

A short haired woman with clear eyes named Olivia June, whose first lover Howard had been a million years previously while sharing a shotgun shack on Clarkson and 18th with a book collector and former burglar by the name of Clyde Sloan said she'd always loved Gus for his "amazingly fecund mind."

Jordan Clarkwell, a member of Gus's old band, Crop Dust, from The Woodlands, Texas, told of Gus's having spotted him reading a Steinbeck book in their community college and putting the bite on him for a ride home and some cigarettes courtesy of his parents' credit card, mimicking exactly Gus's nervous characteristic of fluttering his fingers while talking, "Come on, man they'll never notice."

The audience laughed.

Beth Murphy was there and Howard lashed out nervously and spilled her glass of water. He apologized and she was very gracious about it.

Tewodros Magness took the stand in baggy clothes and related the day he first met Gus at Zylon Research: "Now I'd been warned that this guy would be difficult, but we just started making up rapper names between calls. I remember Gus said, 'I think I'll call myself Womb-Scraper!'" Another wave of joy broke in the room when he said that.

After the memorial broke up, there was a wake proper at Olivia's house. Jordan Clarkwell and Jim Grape from Crop Dust started singing and playing a song by the Violent Femmes on their guitars with Lenny Zen, another figure from the spoken word past, on vocals: "*Guess it's got somethin' to do with luck, but – lift your pants and – I need a kiss. Why can't I get just one screw—♪*

Howard was sitting on the living room floor watching this impromptu jam when Olivia June came up and handed him a book. "Remember this book? It's still my favorite."

"What's this? Wow."

"You gave that to me a long time ago. Don't you remember?"

Howard had been this woman's first lover, and both of them were still marked by it but they never talked about it. That was probably his fault.

"Well—"he said, opening the book she handed him to an inscription in his own handwriting. He remembered having written it. As he recalled, he had given it to her to make up for something or cover up his cowardice or something of that nature, but he couldn't exactly pinpoint
it. "Almost."

Tewodros showed up at the wake with his new girlfriend Melanie, large bodied, with straight blonde hair. The two of them went upstairs to smoke a bowl with Kat Works and Howard and Jimmy LaPeste, who said it would relieve his sore back. Howard came back down the staircase into the kitchen from that adventure and a short woman with long black hair named Claudia was sitting cross-legged in front of the door to Lala and Olivia's living room taking photographs of guests collected there.

According to a conversation Howard had once had with Gus,

a friend of his from Houston named Claudia had once dated outlaw comic Bill Hicks. Is that her? he wondered. "Excuse me," he said, stepping by.

"Oh, sorry."

Collections of people kept watch on Olivia and Lala's porch throughout the night, smoking cigarettes and talking. Howard kept going out there and bumming cigarettes. At one point he and Billy Possibility made each other laugh guiltily realizing Gustav's death was nothing if not an inspiring advisement in valuing friends that was making them glad.

"He helped me move into my apartment," Howard told him. "That was the last time I saw him."

"It's a lesson," said Billy.

"I'm gonna stop taking my friends for granted," vowed Howard.

He went back inside just as a nodded out guy named Joseph in a black trench coat fell out of his chair, at length clambering back up with a groan and reseating himself.

"Are you okay?" asked Lenny Zen, touching his shoulder. "I think you've had too much to drink."

"Nah, nuh," slurred Joseph in response. "Just fell outta muh chair."

Howard went to the kitchen and got himself another beer before returning to the porch, where Jim Grape and Olivia June were standing on opposing eaves.

"My nose is cold," said Jim Grape. Olivia leaned over quickly and kissed Jim on the nose.

"Hey, thanks."

"I used to have a pen name too," said Howard, leaning toward him. "Jim Grape is your pen name, right? Your name is Morley? I used to call myself the Sad—"

"That's who I am," grinned Grape/Morley, swaying backward exaggeratedly. "I liked your poem, by the way. Everybody liked it. People said, 'Yeah, that Howard, he sure can read that poem good, good.' But now you're getting a little too close." He held up a finger in warning.

"Um, well you know that was Gus's poem, that wasn't my poem."

"'Well now, that Sad Comic,'" said Grape, imitating the audience's supposedly impressed reaction again. But he wasn't being serious. Or was he?

Howard felt slightly unsettled. "Well uh—"

Lala spoke from behind him just then, saying she would

email Howard King Baker's autobiography so he could try to get it published.

"Okay," he said, turning to see her. "I'll do my best, I'll get it done."

"What's that?" asked a man with long black sideburns named Presley Talbot who'd worked at Zylon Research with them all, leaning in from the side.

"King Baker's book," said Howard. "It could be the total work of art." Howard had written a poem by that name inspired by a conversation he'd had with King Baker many years in the past in which King had spoken of wanting to write a book every chapter of which contained the book's entire potential—"like a Biblical verse," King had said at the time, "or a microchip."

"Huh?" said Talbot.

"Never mind."

Jim Grape and Olivia went back into the house holding hands.

Gus's friend and filmic collaborator Cleo Exley, a short, fine featured woman with short, dark brown hair, late of Denver but now living in New York, said, "So you know how in Wishbone featured one scene with each of its characters singing in the shower, Howard?"

Wishbone was the title of another recent film co-directed by Gus and Benjy Possibility. The motif Cleo was describing was a nice way of tying all the characters together with a humble common thread despite wildly divergent private grandiosities.

"Sure."

"That was done at Gus's insistence," said Cleo. "Some of the actors didn't want to do it at first. That black guy with the crew cut didn't want to."

Howard told Cleo the story of the "freak-out party" thrown by Gustav years before, while his then roommate Holger Donovan was out of town, where everyone had to come nude or "at least wear a bathrobe, to show compliance."

Cleo laughed and said she'd thought it might be nice to be "haunted" by Gus, then realized how awful that might really be. "It could get wearing."

"You know?"

Tewodros and Melinda came out of the house just then, said their goodbyes to everybody on the porch and drove away.

"Later, Womb-

Sucker." "Scraper!"

"Sorry, Scraper."

Jimmy LaPeste started talking about the Temple of Psychic Youth or TOPY, the magickal fan cult of Genesis P-Orridge's punk band Psychic TV, which group had used Denver as one of its US bases for years. "Tom Headbanger's very fucking powerful," Jimmy swore at the conclusion of his anecdote.

"Don't think I've ever never known any TOPY members personally," said Howard.

"You've seen 'em, though." said Jimmy. He had connections to that scene through his sister Vondie, who'd once aggressively jumped the Sad Comic's bones and now lived in Australia. "

"I bet I have." When Howard had been a teenager, it seemed like every aspiring Denver punk's formative experience involved a visit to Wax Trax and an encounter with some aspect of TOPY. "You remember that Yugoslavian guy, Andros?"

"Who read your mind."

"And once he offered to take me down into the train yards and show me where the aliens came out."

"Andros, sure. Yeah, I need a glass of water."

Jimmy went back inside, leaving Howard on the porch with Presley Talbot and the short, sweet Claudia.

"So I'm a confirmed bachelor now," Presley said, with a sidelong grimace for them both. "I haven't had a date in almost two years."

"Well, you know," Howard said, "I don't want it confirmed in my case, but I've been single for a long time too."

"Why are men so afraid of commitment?" asked Claudia.

"Well, commitment," Howard's answer.

"All I ask is company for breakfast."

"I'd have breakfast with you."

She smiled. "I have a breakfast partner at the moment. Thank you, though."

Benjy Possibility drove Howard back to the Robert Frost building in his parents' blue van at the end of the night, the same van in which he and the now dead Gus had moved Howard into that building a week or two previous, and the two old friends talked about what would happen to them next as artists. Benjy was making a name for himself in the German film crowd. The film he and Gus had directed was making the rounds of the European film festivals and getting lots of good reviews. Howard told Benjy about the Strange Tales of Dim Jim, and he seemed to approve.

"Yeah, maybe you'll even do a film of this someday or something, Right?"

Benjy laughed. "Well, who knows?" "Right?"

☻

All the sidewalks between his new place and the grocery store were full of a hundred new symbols, which Howard found reassuring and inspiring.

After returning to The Woodlands, Jim Grape posted this on the Facebook page Howard had set up for Gustav's memorial: "Keeping the ball rolling! Gustav Harkness tribute disc. Record a cover of a Crop Dust song or an original piece about Gus or read a poem of his or something that is a tribute to our dear friend."

Howard had just purchased a new pair of gray felt skate shoes that maybe looked like surfer shoes of some variety, and had noticed an old man apparently sneering down at them while walking past, which had inspired him to the writing of a song for Gus called "Shoes of a Beachcomber," which he was anxious to record and send to Jim Grape. The way things had been going, it made sense in a way that later the same afternoon, Nelson declared an indefinite hiatus from the Drainpipes due to an increasingly demanding schedule and family demands. Howard knew he had to forge ahead no less.

The day after he wrote that song, a little dark spot of spilled oil or something like that showed up front right shoe. He figured he must have spilled something while cooking and did the first of several Google searches on how to remove oil from felt. Here began a lengthy humorous process of swabbing the area with dishwashing liquid or alcohol and periodically sanding that blemish out of visibility with a nail file only to witness its reappearance, doubled in size, in the same zone hours later. Well, at least he could laugh at himself.

He felt grateful when Shelby's boyfriend Erick, another old friend from the Sad Comic days, who'd never seemed interested before, took over for Nelson Habercorn on lead guitar. As with most instances of good fortune, this also slightly intimidated Howard, Erick the extremely skilled multi instrumental vessel of musical creation who sometimes flew off into gales of incredible improvised licks and riffs and rumbles, joining forces with Howard the fumbler and Shelby the novice drummer. But Erick was honestly willing and able to conform to any level of ability and add to its musical worth with his own master stroke, and after five or six sessions, it was all about effortlessness.

That aforementioned blemish on Howard's gray shoe kept going away and coming back over the next couple of weeks, and

Howard considered it haunted by Gustav'sghost as a gesture of disapproval toward the song he'd written. But since that song was all about his undying critical instinct as heart of his charm, he didn't change the lyrics any.

One night The Drainpipes were practicing Shoes of a Beachcomber at Erick and Shelby's house when she received a phone call letting them know Howard's old shotgun shack roommate Clyde Sloan, former teen burglar and ex-co-owner of the bygone Black Pearl coffee house where the Sad Comic put his poetic career to bed, had passed away. Howard had known Clyde was in town, and felt funny about not having called him, especially after going around saying Gus's death had taught him to value life more. He remembered Benjy telling him how William S. Burroughs had told him "things come in streaks" when he, Olivia June and Presley Talbot had gone to visit that author in Lawrence, Kansas some months before his death in 1994. Howard got an email from Benjy that night: "I have reoccurring dreams of Gus showing up and claiming that he faked his death. Sometimes I buy it and sometimes I don't, then I end up having to convince him he's dead."

Had it been foolish or noble of Gus to see flaws everywhere? Did he mean to revile or improve what he saw? More questions for the philosophers.

One day Howard went into the bathroom and unscrewed one of the giant round bulbs two of which hung each side of the mirror and discovered the sockets were standard gauge. Christmas lights would be the perfect size, all white, with maybe one blue to give his reflection a twinge of the freaky, sure why not. Standing there, he found himself remembering the Hopi (or was it Mayan?) prophecy about the future you agreed with taking form, and smiled to himself, looking into the perfectly lit future mirror he expected. It gave him a sense of editing his own microcosm in a positive direction, despite all the tumult and distraction and disturbance in the macro. No word from Steve about the new books being published yet. The new season was coming together. Maybe.

☻

A billboard whipped past Dim Jim's left ear announcing THE WORLD'S SMALLEST OSTRICH with a picture of that bird planting its head in the soil out of fear or embarrassment, and he decided he wanted to see a few roadside attractions after all. "A guy like me deserves a break." He swung off the highway at a sign reading OSTRICH and followed a narrow brown road to the top of a low, grassy hill where a small farmhouse grassy squatted in darkness, all its windows unlit. Dim Jim got out and stood beside the blue car.

"Hey!" he shouted. "I'm here for the world's smallest ostrich! How small is it! Hey! How small is it!"

He reached into his window and honked the horn several times, but the house stayed dark. It was very loud and the night was deep, but no one came out. He took a packet of seeds from the junk in back. "Wonder if that bird'll eat these." Then he jimmied a window, slipped in, and walked around looking for the world's smallest ostrich. He found what must have been the enclosure, shook the door, and heard shuffling and labored breathing in there, but couldn't see through.

Dim Jim left the packet of seeds on a shelf near the door, then thinking of fingerprints, went back and slipped them into his pocket. "However big you are, goodnight," he growled, one of his long skinny legs already back out the window into the darkness and smell of wild corn. Driving away he remembered the cartoon ostrich he'd seen on the billboard, sticking its head in the sand out of fear or embarrassment. That was only a sign, he reminded himself. It never was. For all we know, those great shaggy birds have been spitting out crystals and diamonds down there all along.

Colored lights of the next town sparkled into view far down the long black road ahead like a handful of glittering jewels flung down on the cold, lonely prairie.

Zack Kopp is founding editor of a webzine called *Doggerel* (formerly *MightyMercury*) specializing in short fiction, verse, art, photography and commentary from the anti-famous (from V. Vale to Rennie Sparks to Paul Krassner to Jenny Abel and beyond), before which he spent years co-editing an irregular journal of quantum thought called THE GUT *WITH PREISMATICS DISCOVER ANDREW WIBLE*. Kopp has been a creative artist or one kind or another from ever since. *HIS VISION I*s a vital blend of social and political themes with raw, wild soul from the bottom of the can. *HE* received an MFA in Writing (fiction) from Vermont College of Fine Arts in January of 2008, that magic year. Says he's not sure what form it's gonna take, this big shift we're undergoing now, but there are fools who would deny it.